CHR
ARA   Arana, Nikki
        As I have loved you

DATE DUE			
DE 0 6 '1 JUN 2 8 2013			
JA 0 3 '1			
MR 3 1 '1			

As I Have Loved You

Nikki Arana

Revell

Grand Rapids, Michigan

© 2007 by Nikki Arana

Published by Fleming H. Revell
a division of Baker Publishing Group
P.O. Box 6287, Grand Rapids, MI 49516-6287
www.revellbooks.com

Printed in the United States of America

Library of Congress Cataloging-in-Publication Data
Arana, Nikki, 1949–
    As I have loved you / Nikki Arana.
        p.   cm.
    ISBN 10: 0-8007-3167-0 (pbk.)
    ISBN 978-0-8007-3167-0 (pbk.)
    1. Mothers and sons—Fiction. 2. Attention-deficit-disordered
    children—Fiction. I. Title
    PS3601.R35A9 2007
    813'.6—dc22   2007001856

Scripture is taken from the New King James Version. Copyright © 1982 by Thomas Nelson, Inc. Used by permission. All rights reserved.

A Scripture marked KJV is taken from the King James Version of the Bible.

This book is a work of fiction. Names, characters, places, and incidents are the product of the author's imagination or are used fictitiously. Any resemblance to actual events, locales, or persons, living or dead, is coincidental.

For E. P. Arana

These things I have spoken to you,
that in Me you may have peace.
In the world you will have tribulation;
but be of good cheer,
I have overcome the world.
—John 16:33 NKJV

Man looketh on the outward appearance,
but the LORD looketh on the heart.

1 Samuel 16:7 KJV

Prologue

"Umm."

Jeff held his breath. *Pick me. Pick me.*

"I pick Timmy."

With the last spot filled, the two teams of ten-year-olds ran onto the field for a game of football.

"Sit with me." Mr. Campbell put his arm around Jeff's shoulder. "It'll be time to substitute before you know it."

"That's okay. I'm going to get something to eat." Jeff forced himself to smile at his Sunday school teacher. "I'll come back soon." He took off at a run toward the picnic tables.

"I'm over here."

Jeff turned at the sound of his mother's voice.

"Aren't you going to play football?"

He searched for something to say that would meet the expectation on her face. "Uh-huh. Mr. Campbell said my turn is coming up."

Not wanting his mother to know that no one had

picked him to be on a team, he snatched a cookie from a tray on the table and headed back to the game before she could ask any more questions.

Jeff heard his mother's voice behind him. "I'll come and watch as soon as it's your turn."

As he neared the field, he saw that many of the parents had gathered around the sidelines, cheering as Sam Kirby scored a touchdown. Jeff stopped and watched as Sam's dad gave a high five to the man standing next to him. Jeff swallowed the last of his cookie. Mr. Kirby tousled Sam's hair as Sam strode off the field. Jeff looked down at his feet. He was glad *his* dad didn't like to come to church.

He watched as the boys lined up for the kickoff, then turned on his heel and wandered into the grove of trees that bordered the field behind the church. Soon the sounds of the football game were muted, and Jeff began to kick a pinecone through the open spaces between the trees, following the bouncing cone into a meadow. His heart was heavy. He always seemed to disappoint his father . . . his teachers . . . his teammates. His mother said it wasn't his fault. It was that he couldn't pay attention to things like other kids.

He frowned. In Sunday school Mr. Campbell had said God was his heavenly Father. Jeff wondered if he was a disappointment to Him too. He blinked rapidly.

The sound of snapping twigs interrupted his thoughts, stopping him mid-stride.

Just to his right was a huge buck. Its broad rack of antlers brushed through the tree branches as the animal emerged from the woods. It stopped, gazing at him. Its dark eyes strangely calm. Peaceful.

8

A breeze rustled through the grasses as a lone cloud drifted overhead . . . casting a shadow across Jeff and the buck.

The big animal lifted its head as if surveying the open field, then turned and started walking. Jeff quietly followed at a distance. Before long the animal stopped and lowered his head, drinking from a small stream. As Jeff silently moved closer to the water, the buck seemed to take no notice of him.

Crouching on the bank, Jeff watched. Then he turned to the stream and cupped water in his hands and began drinking, imagining that he was an explorer and the big animal was a wild stallion he had tamed. They were on their way to places no man had ever been. He stole a glance at the animal . . . only to find it was wandering away.

He sank cross-legged onto the bank and dropped his chin to his chest. It wasn't a stallion and he wasn't an explorer. He was stupid. That's what he was. Just like everyone said . . . he wasn't good for anything.

Suddenly, the sound of the trickling water caught his ear. The sound of the water became music, and his eyelids became heavy. He rubbed his eyes and shook his head, but the desire to sleep was stronger than he was. He lay down next to the stream.

The warm afternoon breeze covered him like a blanket. As his eyes drifted closed, he caught a hazy glimpse of the buck. The animal's body became a silvery mist, and its antlers looked like upraised hands. Jeff struggled to raise his head, but sleep overtook him.

There beside the stream, unseen by the eyes of man, an

angel bowed in worship. Creating a portal in space and time, allowing the light of heaven to fall upon the ground around the boy. Making it holy ground. All darkness fled as the Spirit of God touched the child, imputing Christ's love to his innocent and pliant heart. Overcoming love that would see with the eyes of Christ and endure the reproach of the world. A love that could be used by God . . . to change the heart of man.

1

Leigh Scott rose from her bed and looked out the window at the moonlit driveway. Jeff wasn't home yet. Her son never came home past midnight on a school night unless he didn't have classes the next day. At least not until he'd started seeing this girl he'd met at Starbucks. Jessica.

Leigh tilted her head, broadening her view from the second-story window, hoping to see headlights. She looked at her watch again. 12:45.

He was twenty-one years old and a junior in college. Her friends said she shouldn't be keeping tabs on him at all. But they didn't know what she knew. They hadn't invested the years she had in bringing him to the point that he could function independently as a college student. They didn't know the subtleties of attention deficit disorder and how it stole the hopes and dreams of those it was visited upon . . . and of those who loved them. How treatment managed but didn't eliminate the fragmented thoughts and chaotic complexities that diminished her son's quality of life.

Sometimes she felt she'd worked as hard as Jeff had to

realize his dream of becoming a computer technician. He was only one year away from his degree and the promise of a job with E-Solutions, which was headquartered only twenty miles north of Cedar Ridge in River Falls, Idaho. They'd come too far to let anything interfere now.

Leigh climbed back into bed, turning on her side so she faced the window, watching for telltale lights to flash across her bedroom wall.

What if he'd started home earlier in the evening and something had happened? She sat up. Maybe she should try his cell phone again. She looked at her alarm clock. 12:49 a.m. She huffed a sigh. It had been hard raising her son alone, and times like this were the worst.

Blake. A faint sense of yearning passed through her. The remnants of grief . . . nothing more. She switched on the lamp above the nightstand and pulled her Bible into her lap. God was her partner now. And life was easier.

Turning to First Corinthians, she found the passage she'd been studying about the gifts of the Spirit: ". . . the manifestation of the Spirit is given to each one for the profit of all: . . . gifts of healings . . . to another prophecy . . . to another different kinds of tongues . . ." She lifted her gaze from the page. Signs and wonders, available to every believer. This was the awesome power of God. The Gift. Something *she* wanted, something she prayed for. She closed her eyes a moment. She deeply desired to work for God.

Her thoughts returned to Jeff. There was so much at stake. It wasn't just Jeff's degree and job, but her parents' home hung in the balance. The unintended consequences of carefully laid plans.

Rising, she set the Bible on the bedside table, then walked to her desk and sat down, ready to work on her book, *Second Chance*.

With her day job as a real estate assistant, her writing time was restricted to nights and weekends. But she was willing to do whatever it took to respond to God's call on her life. Settling in her chair, she clicked on the bar at the bottom of her computer screen and page sixty-eight appeared. She began reading the last paragraphs she'd written. Before she got to the end of the page her eyes darted to the little clock in the bottom right-hand corner of the screen. 1:03.

He was over an hour late. Maybe she should call the police.

What would she say? "My son went on a date and he's over an hour late." That didn't sound like an emergency even to her. Unless you knew Jeff. He was considerate, reliable, sensible. The image of the tall, burly young man's sweet face and twinkling brown eyes flashed through her mind. He'd been her sole focus since his father had died five years earlier. Blake's death had drawn them together . . . and apart.

Leigh read the paragraphs on the screen again. Her heroine was having a crisis of faith, brought about because she hadn't married the love of her life, whom she'd met in book one, *First Love*.

She stared at the screen, her mind blank. She didn't have any answers for her heroine right now. She minimized the document and walked back to the window.

Why wasn't he home? What was he doing at this hour? He'd said he was taking Jessica to the Wednesday night singles' group at Grace Bible Church. That would have been over by ten. Then they might have gone out for coffee. Still, that wouldn't have gone on until this hour.

Leigh turned off the light and sat on the edge of the bed. She should have asked more questions about this girl two months ago when Jeff had first mentioned her. But her son had never had a serious girlfriend and said nothing to indicate that this girl might be the first one. He believed in abstinence and had even spoken on the subject at the local high schools. She knew he didn't plan to get serious with a girl until he was ready to get married, and without ever discussing it, they both knew that would be after he got a job and was financially secure. There had to be a good reason why he was late.

She heard a car door shut and ran to the window, her eyes cutting to the driveway.

The gnawing fear in her stomach dissolved into relief, then bubbled up in anger. She folded her arms across her chest as she watched Jeff get out of the car and retrieve his backpack from the backseat. Casually throwing it over his shoulder, he walked to the keypad that opened the garage door, seemingly oblivious to the fact it was long past midnight.

He didn't even glance up at the window that he mischievously referred to as "Mother's perch." When she'd rented the house, he teased her that the location of the master bedroom window was why she chose this house instead of one of the others that had been available. Then he put his arm around her and hugged her. Letting her know he understood.

A smile tugged at her lips. Still, there was no excuse

for being this late and not calling. She glanced at the clock next to her bed. 1:15. Raising her eyes heavenward, she whispered, "Well, Lord, what do You think? Should I wait to talk to him about this tomorrow?"

She sat for a moment as her world righted itself. Her only son was home, safe and sound. Probably already flopped down on his bed in the basement bedroom. She pursed her lips. It would be better to wait until she got home from work tomorrow night to talk to him. Right now she was still too angry to have a reasoned discussion, and besides that, he needed his sleep.

Leigh slipped under the covers. And she'd find out more about this Jessica. An uneasy feeling swept over her as she recalled Jeff first talking about the girl. How she had a troubled past of drugs and alcohol, was struggling financially and looking for a place to live. But how that previous weekend she'd found God at the Gospel Mission and was determined to turn her life around. Jeff's gentle eyes had become serious. "She's a new Christian, Mom, and she needs support. If I hadn't happened to be sitting at Starbucks doing my homework on my laptop, we never would have met. I don't think it's any coincidence how that happened." He'd given Leigh a decisive nod, just in case she missed the obvious. It had been a "God thing."

She lay on her side, staring out the window into the starry sky. Yes, she had to agree, it wasn't any coincidence that a troubled girl who needed money and a place to live *just happened* to have found God a few days before meeting him. A boy with a future who had God at the center of his life.

And she'd picked the right one. Ever since Jeff had been a young man he'd had a heart for the less fortunate. Volunteering in the special education class in high school, going with the church outreach group to visit the homeless, even picking up a bum hitchhiking on a snowy night. She shuddered remembering that episode. It was a miracle nothing had happened to him. He had an innocent naiveté that allowed him to embrace people and their problems without judging them. Their pastor had once said to her, "Jeff loves the unlovely."

Leigh turned onto her back and stared at the ceiling. Jeff knew he didn't have time to devote to a girl right now. He'd introduced Jessica to other Christian young people in his church. Now he needed to stay focused on school, graduating, and starting his career. Nothing was more important than that.

Tomorrow night she would talk to Jeff about spending less time with Jessica and more time studying. She admired her son for the interest he took in others. But Jessica wasn't the kind of girl he would ever be seriously interested in. Right now, he needed to concentrate on getting his degree and a job and taking responsibility for the payments that would soon start on his student loan. The loan that was secured by her parents' home.

He needed to forget about Jessica. Jeff needed to move on.

❧

Jeff quietly opened the door from the garage to the back hall. He'd seen his mother's bedroom light go off just as he turned the corner to their street. Without a

16

doubt she'd been sitting on her perch waiting for him. She liked to say she was a mother hen waiting for her chick. He chuckled. Most of the time she seemed more like an eagle waiting for its prey. He hadn't dared look up to find out who was right tonight.

Passing through the kitchen, he stopped at the refrigerator and opened it. He quickly scanned the contents and located some leftover fried chicken on the back of the second shelf. He grabbed the plate, elbowed the door closed, and headed down the stairs. His cell phone vibrated in his pocket.

At least this time he was sure it wasn't his mother. A twinge of guilt pricked him. He shouldn't have ignored her calls earlier, but he was with Jessica and it would have been awkward. Jessica already thought his mother was too nosy and had told him so on several occasions.

He jogged across the small bonus room to his bedroom. It was time for the two women to meet. That would solve a lot of the problem. He set the backpack next to his desk and pulled the phone from his pocket.

Dropping onto the bed, he balanced the plate of chicken on his knees. He flipped the phone open and glanced at the screen. It brought a smile to his lips. "Hey."

"Hey . . . everything okay?"

He knew what she meant . . . he felt heat in his cheeks. When they'd first started going to church on Wednesday nights, he'd told her he had to be home by midnight. "Uh-huh. I'm going to start my homework in just a minute."

"Do you have to work tomorrow afternoon?"

Jeff swallowed the bite of chicken he was chewing. "No, but I was going to talk to my boss and see if I could get some extra hours." Two afternoons a week on the loading dock at Sears had been enough before he met Jessica. But now, extra gas and lattes for two left him short every paycheck.

"Maybe I could get you on here. They hire part-time."

Jessica worked nights as a caregiver, taking care of developmentally disabled adults. She did cleaning and checked on the clients during the night. That's one of the reasons he'd been late. He'd taken her to work and stayed to help her because the other woman on the shift, Helga, had been late to work. They'd moved a brain-damaged man from the living room to his bedroom. "Maybe. When will you be able to pick up your car?"

"As soon as I get the money together to pay the guy who fixed it."

Jeff heard her sigh into the phone. His heart went out to her. It seemed like she'd struggled all her life. Her mother abandoned her the day she was born, leaving Jessica at a hospital where no questions were asked. She'd been adopted into a home where she was physically and emotionally abused until she was old enough, and desperate enough, to tell someone. After that, she'd drifted from one foster care family to another, finally dropping out of high school to take a job as a babysitter and house cleaner, in exchange for a free room. Jeff admired Jessica for what she'd done with her life since then, getting her GED and a certification to be a nursing assistant. "I can help you get around until you get your car back."

Before she could answer, he heard a commotion in the

background. "Get back in bed." "No." "Piglet." "Where is Jessy?" "Jessica!"

"I've got to go now. It sounds like Helga's having some trouble."

"Who's Piglet?"

Jeff could hear Jessica breathing into the phone.

"Uh, just somebody who works here. Talk to you later."

"Wait, Jessica. Do you need a ride in the morning?"

"I'll get somebody here to take me home. Gotta go."

Jeff snapped his phone shut and tossed it on the bed. He finished the chicken, then settled into the chair at his desk. He had a quiz to study for and a project to complete. He looked at his watch. 1:45. If he could be in bed by four, he'd get a good three hours of sleep before he had to leave for school. He dug his class notes from his bag and spread them across the desk.

His mind wandered to the moment he'd said good-bye to Jessica tonight. He slowly closed his eyes. *Jessica.* Her pretty face, fair skin, and independent blue eyes were before him. He put his elbow on the desk and rested his chin in his hand. That sweet smile. Parted pink lips. A trill of excitement spiraled through his stomach. She'd kissed him.

And he'd kissed her back.

He leaned back in his chair. He'd never known a girl like her. She'd lived on her own since she was seventeen and managed to make a life for herself. There were things she'd done that she wasn't proud of. She'd told him about some of them. A girl without a family, without a home, and with nothing to eat had to do things to survive. He

19

didn't blame her. That was in the past and that was where it should stay. The Bible said that anyone who was in Christ was a new creation. "Old things have passed away . . . all things have become new." That was a verse he often gave to people he witnessed to. Powerful words that could set people free.

He heard Max's loud purr before he felt the big black cat rub against his leg. Scooping the animal up in his arms, he turned the cat on his back and scratched his chest. "Max, I've never felt this way before." He tilted his head and grinned. "She really is special. I can't wait to tell Mom about her. Mom's going to love her."

⌘

Jessica wiped the base of the toilet, then wrung the dirty water into the scrub bucket. Jeff was a keeper.

At first she'd thought he was a mama's boy. But over the past two months, as they'd become close, she'd realized Jeff allowed his mother to run his life because he had all kinds of misguided ideas about how the world worked. He'd spent his whole life tied to the church and bought into the lifestyle. She couldn't believe he'd never hooked up.

She didn't buy all the talk about abstinence. Every man wanted the same thing. When she was little, one of her foster mothers had told her that. At the age of eleven, one of her foster fathers had removed any doubts she might have had. A lump rose in her throat. She swallowed it.

Jeff was a keeper, but that mother of his wasn't. Jeff needed to move on.

2

Leigh pulled her Toyota into her parents' driveway and turned off the engine. It had been a long day in the office of Jan Jenks, the high-producing real estate agent she worked for. Jan's sudden decision to include her new listings in an advertising spread had forced Leigh to work through lunch. Glancing toward the front door of her parents' home, she murmured, "Only with Your strength, Lord."

She hurried up the walkway, hoping the required daily visit would be short. She was anxious to get home and talk to Jeff about Jessica.

The front door opened before she reached it. "It's you. I told your dad I thought I heard a car."

"Yep, Mom, it's me." As it had been nearly every afternoon after work since her father had come home from the hospital. "How's Dad doing today?"

Her mother's eyes teared up. "This last round of chemo has really taken its toll. Then he had an accident on his way to the bathroom this morning and that pretty much set the tone for the whole day. I even skipped my Bible study in case he needed me." She drew an unsteady breath. "I was hoping R.J. would call. That always puts him in a good mood."

The favored one, the golden boy, the son her father had always wanted. Leigh bit her tongue. Her younger brother, Robert Jr., never called unless he needed something. The charismatic opportunist, ten years her junior, who, as their parents began to struggle in the grip of old age, found his ambitions taking him to the sandy shores of Hawaii. There he could cultivate relationships that would insure he had financial security after their parents' deaths.

Their father's diagnosis of colon cancer last winter had prompted R.J. to call her. "I'm not that far from Idaho, Sis," he'd said. "Be sure to let me know if you need any help." But when she asked for his phone number, he told her he was between places and would stay in touch. R.J. needed the Lord in his life and she prayed for him. But it was hard.

It was hard because he burdened her with the full responsibility of their parents. It was hard because he flaunted how easy life could be without a moral compass. But most of all it was hard because all of his failings only magnified the darkness in her own heart. She didn't love her brother.

Leigh kissed her mother's cheek. "I can't stay long today. I have things to do at home, and I *have* to get some writing done tonight." Her stomach clenched. The days were passing and she was struggling with a glitch in the plot. Though the due date was months away, the deadline for her novel weighed on her.

When they got in the house, she followed her mother

to the family room. Her father was sitting in his recliner by the fireplace, an afghan thrown over his thin legs and a magazine in his lap. He bore little resemblance to the vibrant, active man who spent last fall drift-boat fishing and chukar hunting. The time and energy he'd spent fighting a steelhead on the end of his line was now spent fighting cancer.

He raised his head and looked at her. His dark eyes, alert and piercing, observed her from sunken sockets, on guard for any sign of pity. "Hi, Dad. What are you reading?"

"It's a travel magazine and it's got a big article about Hawaii in it. I got it at the doctor's office." His eyes scanned the open page in front of him. "Talks all about the fishing over there. Big game fishing. Blue marlin. Yellowfin tuna. That R.J. sure knows how to pick a place, doesn't he?"

"He sure does, Dad."

"Last time he called, he said as soon as I get better he'll send me a plane ticket and we'll charter us a boat."

Her mother took a seat on the couch across from the fireplace and Leigh sat on the hearth. "That sounds like a great idea."

She watched as her father's eyes drifted to the window, the pain lines etched in his face softening. He was on the open sea with his son.

"How's Jeff?" Her mother's voice cut in. "He started some kind of new medicine, didn't he?"

The question took Leigh by surprise. She hadn't mentioned Jeff's doctor had suggested he try a new drug. Her parents had never liked the idea of treating Jeff's

23

ADD with medicine. She didn't either. But when Jeff was diagnosed in the fourth grade, she had tried everything from the Feingold diet to biofeedback. None of it helped. "Are you talking about Strattera?"

"Yes, that's what he called it."

"When did he tell you that?"

"He stopped by the other day to visit."

Talk of Jeff brought her father back to the conversation. "That big, handsome young man should be playing professional football."

"Going to college and working part-time is all he can handle. That's one of the reasons he wanted to try the Strattera. It works for much longer periods of time than the Ritalin did. Now he doesn't have to plan his life around when his medicine is in effect." Since his diagnosis, his life, and *her* life, had been run on a timetable set by Jeff's medicine. School, activities, and homework were all scheduled based on when Jeff would be able to focus. Her life had had to take a backseat to his. Something she'd willingly accepted to give him his best chance at a productive, fulfilling life.

"I was hoping he would have grown out of it by now."

"Me too, Mom. Some kids do. He didn't."

"If you ask me, any problems he's having concentrating have a lot more to do with this girl Jessica than with his medicine." Her father chuckled. "Wouldn't you say so, Sally?"

Her mother grinned. "He seemed pretty taken with her, all right. Have you met her, Leigh?"

"No, but I don't think Jeff has any particular interest in her. You know how he is, he takes an interest in everybody. He's always been like that."

Her father raised his eyebrows. "It didn't strike me that way. I told him he ought to bring her by next Sunday after church."

"Dad, I don't think we should be encouraging him. He needs to finish school and get a job. You know as well as I do that the loan payments on the fifty thousand dollars we borrowed on this house to finance his education start the summer after he graduates."

"He'll do fine. When I was his age, I had a wife and two jobs and went to school too."

Leigh dropped the subject. They'd been down this road before. Her parents had never grasped the seriousness of her son's learning disability and how it impacted every aspect of his life. "Riva called today."

"Riva Stein?" Her mother leaned forward. "Your agent?"

Leigh nodded. "She's got some interest from Paramount Publishers for a possible contract. My second book is due October first. Then my contract's up with Little Press. Paramount says they think I'd be a good fit for the new inspirational imprint, Life Journeys, that they're going to be launching. This was completely unexpected because they haven't been taking on new authors. They've asked her to have me write a proposal and three chapters."

Her mother's eyes widened. "What does that mean?"

"It means they want a synopsis for a book. They're on the leading edge of Christian fiction. They want stories about real people involved in real issues. Stories that can touch and change people's lives. I've been giving it a lot of thought. I want to write the book of God's heart. A book that can make a difference in people's lives. But I have no idea what it should be."

"Don't worry, it'll come to you." Her mother clapped her hands. "My daughter, the author."

Her father nodded. "That sounds promising, Leigh. Did you ever send R.J. a copy of your first book?"

"Dad, it's inspirational fiction and a light, sweet romance. I doubt he'll be interested in reading it."

"A good book will hold a reader's attention regardless. I'd like to get his take on it."

Her mother nodded. "You should send it to him. He's not a believer and it just might speak to him."

Her father straightened in his chair. "He doesn't need speaking to. Nobody likes to be preached at." His words were clipped. He turned to Leigh. "Maybe you shouldn't send it. It might offend him."

"Next time I talk to him, I'll ask him about it." Leigh stood. "Well, I'd better be going."

She kissed her parents good-bye and started home. As she drove, her thoughts returned to the conversation about Jeff. Was it possible that Jeff was getting serious with this girl? Her mind filtered through the last two months. There was nothing that stood out. No change in his behavior . . . until last night. There was something about his coming home in the early morning hours that had been deeply unsettling, though she couldn't put her finger on why. She pursed her lips.

Slowly, dread filled her as long-buried memories worked their way out of hidden places . . . a lonely girl with an unloving father setting a trap for a handsome young man with a future.

Her heart lurched as things became clear. All the signs were there. It wasn't Jeff's behavior that had changed, it was far more subtle. The animation when he talked about Jessica, the tone of his voice on the phone with her, the immediate defense of her in response to Leigh's most casual suggestion that perhaps he was a little too involved.

It was what she had done to Blake.

And the natural consequences had been the birth of her son, seven months after her wedding day.

She set her jaw. This was not going to happen to Jeff. She hadn't found the Lord until years after that, but now she was forgiven. She prayed protection over Jeff every day. Surely God would honor a mother's prayers.

She blinked rapidly. But her prayers couldn't change the fact that Jeff had free will, and there was one who still stalked the earth, walking to and fro seeking to destroy all that was godly.

She would talk to Jeff tonight.

⁂

Jeff exited the freeway on the off-ramp that would take him to the house where Jessica was staying. As he pulled to a stop at the bottom of the hill, he saw an old man standing on the side of the road. Jeff couldn't see the man's face under the soiled hat and matted gray beard, but he held a sign that said "River Falls."

Jeff glanced at the clock on his dash. It was already after five, and he'd told Jessica he'd take her to pick up her car before five thirty. He frowned. There really wasn't time to stop and talk to this man, find out where he was going, if he was hungry, if he needed a place to stay. Jeff knew where all the shelters were because he often volunteered to help the homeless. He heaved a sigh as he drove past the drifter.

Once, when he'd first started driving, he'd picked up a hitchhiker. When his mother found out, she flipped out. She told him it was foolish and dangerous. Her exact words were, "When you step out from under God's wing and knowingly put yourself in harm's way, you don't have the benefit of His protection."

But she didn't understand. That wasn't the way Jeff saw it at all. He saw helping others as pulling them under God's wing with him. He wanted to live his life so it brought glory to God. He couldn't say why, but for as long as he could remember, he'd felt drawn to those in need. He felt a love for them that always brought to mind the words that Jesus spoke: "Seek first the king- dom of God." Love was the answer. Love was what God had called him to. He felt it in his heart. He'd told that hitchhiker about the love of God . . . and a lost soul had come under God's wing with him.

Jeff pulled up in front of the run-down house where Jessica lived. She waved at him from the window and moments later stepped out the front door. He jumped from the car and ran around to the passenger's side to help her get in. Then he got behind the wheel.

He glanced at her. "You look real nice."

She tilted her head and looked at him. Her pretty auburn hair framed her face, and her full lips curved into a smile. The memory of last night's kiss flittered through his stomach. He felt heat rising in his cheeks. Turning forward, he locked his eyes on the road ahead of him, started the car, and stepped on the gas. The car lurched into the street.

She reached over and rested her hand on his knee. "How was your day?"

The casual familiarity felt good. It wasn't like when his mother asked him. She always gave him the feeling that what she really wanted was an accounting, that there was an unspoken standard he was expected to meet.

"I got my project turned in for my technology class." He gave her a wide smile. "Got it done between two and four this morning."

"Bet you get an A. You're so smart."

He could feel her looking at him. He straightened in his seat and lifted his chin.

"But you must be tired. Do you usually stay up late like that to do homework?"

"No. When I took Ritalin I knew it would last about six hours. So I had to plan study time that wouldn't be interrupted. I took a dose at seven at night and then did my schoolwork until I was finished. But now I take Strattera and it works twenty-four hours a day."

Jessica patted his leg. "That must make life a lot easier."

Other than the counselor he was required to see every six months as a condition of renewing his prescription, Jeff had never really discussed with anyone how he felt about his medicine or his ADD. He thought for a moment. "Well, in one way yes. In one way no."

29

"What do you mean?" She withdrew her hand from his leg and turned toward him.

"It's hard to explain." He paused, unsure he wanted to talk about it. Still, Jessica had confided so much of her past to him. If anyone would understand, she would. "The more hours I have that I can focus and accomplish the things I want to do, the more it magnifies how worthless I am when I'm unmedicated and just myself." He glanced at her.

Her eyes met his. "Don't talk about yourself like that."

"I feel like there's a penalty for being who I am. I can't meet anyone's expectations, including my own." He suddenly felt a sweep of emotions and had to stop talking. Blushing, he turned his face away from her and glanced into the side mirror.

"It's okay." She gently pulled his right hand from the steering wheel and laced her fingers through his.

"It's been on my mind a lot lately. I've got one more year of college and then I'll be on my own. I'm moving to River Falls. I've got a job offer there."

"That's wonderful, Jeff. You're going to do great."

He looked at her. "I'm not sure. That's the problem. I'm just not sure. There are things I'm just not good at."

"Like what?"

"Reading people, for one."

"Why do you need to read people?"

"Lots of times people don't say what they mean. You're just supposed to figure it out. My counselor calls it 'social signals.' He says not being able to pick up 'social signals' is common with ADD."

"Give me an example."

30

"Like one time when I was a freshman in college, I asked a girl to go to church, and she said no. So I said, 'Okay, what about next Sunday?' She said she already had plans. So I asked if she could go out on Wednesday night. She said she was busy. This went on quite a few times, and finally I dropped it. When I told my mom about it later, she said the girl just didn't want to go out with me at all. That never crossed my mind."

Jessica grinned. "I think you're making too much out of that. Lots of boys don't understand girls."

"That's just an example. It's about being different, not fitting in. My senior year in high school I did a report on ADD for an assignment in health class. There have actually been studies done where they put a kid with ADD in a group of regular kids. The others target him and shun him within a very short time."

"Kids can be so cruel. I've had my share of that. I hated school."

"I'm sorry." Jeff squeezed her hand. "Grade school was the worst for me. The kids made fun of me because I was bigger than everybody else. And I got punished a lot for not doing my schoolwork."

"But you couldn't help it."

"Nobody knew that then. I went to a private Christian school, and they used to take me to the principal's office. I would get spanked with a paddle for not doing my work."

Jessica straightened in her seat. "That's terrible."

"They didn't understand." He shrugged. "They didn't know I couldn't help it."

"What did your mom say?"

31

"She went along with it and I even got punished at home. But when she found out I had ADD, she had a long talk with me. She apologized and asked if I could forgive her."

"Well, I hope you told her how much that hurt you. How humiliating. If you ask me, that's child abuse."

Jeff slowly shook his head. "No. It wasn't her fault. None of us knew what was wrong. I told her there was nothing to forgive."

"Doesn't say much for that Christian school."

"It wasn't their fault either. People put their kids in that school because it stressed academic excellence. Ninety-five percent of the students who graduate from there go to college. It was just the wrong school for me."

"She should have taken you out."

"She did as soon as the doctor made the diagnosis. But before then, every morning right when it was time to leave for school she would pray with me, 'Dear God, help Jeff do his work today.' But her prayers were never answered. Once she even asked me if that had made me think maybe there was no God."

"I agree. Why would God allow all that to happen to a little boy? Why does God allow children to be put through hell?"

The intensity of her voice caused Jeff to look at her. There were tears in her eyes as memories of her past spilled onto her cheeks. "I don't know why bad things happen, but I do know this, and it's what I told my mother. If there was no God, they never would have found out what was wrong with me. It was such a relief to find out there was a reason why I didn't do well in school. I thank God for that every day. Whenever I see people who are down-and-out, I know that could have been me. What if my mom and dad had given up? What if God hadn't cared about me?"

Jessica wiped her face with the back of her hand and looked straight ahead. "You were one of the lucky ones. It doesn't always work like that."

Jeff pulled into the parking lot of Andy's Auto Repair. "God cares about everyone, Jessica. He hears the prayers of His people. He's shown me that so many times."

"Maybe it's true." Jessica opened the car door and gave him a thoughtful, appraising look. "Maybe God does answer prayers, even if He waits until you've grown up."

Jeff smiled. "It's all in God's timing." He could see on Jessica's face that she was struggling. Being a new Christian, she wasn't sure about God's love. He'd learned long ago that God was the only one he could count on. In time, she would learn that too. But now she needed his support. A thought occurred to him.

"I'll wait for you. Go get your car and follow me home."

Jessica's face lit up and she started laughing. "What are you talking about?"

"Come and have dinner with me and my mom. She'd love to meet you."

3

Leigh wasn't sure how to start the conversation with Jeff without sounding confrontational. There was no need to put him on the defensive. He'd always been a sensible kid and they'd always been able to talk things out.

Max marched into the kitchen as she poured the meat sauce into the spaghetti. Stalking the savory scent, he jumped up on the dining table chair and stared at the pot.

There had been very few times while Jeff was growing up that he had to be disciplined. Though, whenever the occasion arose, it fell to her. Blake had never been close to their son. He wasn't able to accept that there was a medical reason for Jeff's struggles in so many areas of his life. Whether it was schoolwork, making friends, or playing sports, Jeff always fell short in his father's eyes. Once, driving home from a parent-teacher conference in the third grade, Blake told Leigh that having a child had been her idea, and now she could deal with it.

She released a deep sigh. That night she had realized two things: she should never involve Blake at the school again, and she must keep Jeff from ever knowing why. She had succeeded at both. Jeff adored his father.

Leigh hummed as she made a tossed salad, then quickly set the table for two. She and Jeff often found themselves on different schedules, but they always tried to meet up for dinner on Thursday nights. Whoever got home first started cooking. She paused. It would be only another year or so, and he'd be out on his own. Then it would be just her and Max. She wasn't looking forward to that.

The sound of the garage door opening caught her attention. "Perfect timing." She took two white ceramic bowls out of the cabinet and set them on the counter next to the stove.

The sound of the back door opening sent Max to his position at the entry to the kitchen.

"Jeff?"

"Hi, Mom. I've got a surprise for you."

Leigh heard a note of excitement in his voice. Maybe he'd lined up a summer job or gotten an A on a quiz. She decided to wait on filling the bowls, and instead quickly stirred the spaghetti and then put the lid on the pot. Clasping her hands in front of her, she faced the door he would come through. She could use some good news; plus it would be a great way to start the conversation.

As he stepped into the kitchen a smile spread across her face. Then her eyes shifted to the movement behind him. A young woman stepped from the shadows. A big girl, almost as tall as Jeff.

"Mom, this is Jessica."

Max bolted from the kitchen.

35

"Oh." Leigh tried to keep her composure. "Uh, hello, Jessica." Her hands dropped to her sides.

"Nice to meet you, Mrs. Scott."

The girl's skirt was askew and her sweater clung where it wasn't meant to. "Jeff, dinner's ready. Perhaps Jessica could visit another time."

"I didn't think you'd mind if she ate with us. There's always plenty."

Leigh lifted the lid from the spaghetti and looked into the pot as though checking for the first time to see how much she'd prepared. "Not really. Maybe we could plan something some other time."

Jessica lifted her chin. "That's okay, Jeff. I'm not that hungry anyway."

Jeff put his hand on her arm. "No, it's fine. You can have some of mine." He patted his solid chest. "Won't hurt me a bit."

The situation was getting more awkward by the minute, and there was no easy way out. Leigh knew her son well, and short of telling him Jessica wasn't welcome, he would doggedly pursue the idea of her remaining for dinner. Leigh took the tongs and stirred the pasta. "It's okay. It's fine. Really. I'll just add a few more vegetables to the salad and boil a few more noodles. It won't take me long."

Jeff smiled, clearly delighted that the three of them would have dinner together.

He shook off his backpack. "Let me help you."

Leigh's mind was racing. She needed time to get her thoughts together. "No, honey, why don't you two go sit in the family room. It won't take me a minute."

When she'd asked God the night before if she should wait to talk to Jeff, she'd never dreamed this would happen. Maybe this was God's way of telling her she'd judged the girl too harshly. Perhaps Jessica had had a spiritual awakening, and God had put Jeff in her life for His own purposes.

Give me wisdom, Lord. Let me see Your will in this situation.

As Leigh finished preparing dinner she could hear the two young people talking. Apparently Jessica was looking at the framed photographs on the wall behind the family room couch.

"Where was that taken?"

"That's me and my dad when we used to live in Montana, in the country. He bought me a football for my birthday and we practiced throwing it even before we had the cake. Mom grabbed the camera and took this shot."

Jeff's sixth birthday. The memory was suddenly fresh. Blake's excitement that day. Jeff's delight in his father's attention. But it hadn't lasted long. Blake was looking for his son's natural ability, hoping his boy was a budding star. Jeff wanted only the joy of being with his father. By the end of the week the ball lay untouched in the weeds of the front pasture, Blake saying some kids just don't have what it takes.

"Did your dad spend a lot of time with you?" Jessica's voice broke into her thoughts.

"Well, he was gone a lot. But I know he wanted to. I still have the football." His voice softened. "I'm going to throw it with my own son someday."

The football. A childhood afternoon preserved in a vinyl sphere, safe on a shelf in the center of Jeff's bookcase. Visited often and viewed through the filter of Jeff's love.

"You're lucky. I didn't even know who my dad was. My mom either, for that matter."

Leigh knitted her brows. *How awful.*

"And my foster parents never let me forget it. They always reminded me that nobody wanted me and I should be grateful they took me in."

She winced. *Maybe I was too quick to judge.*

Jeff's voice was gentle. "I feel like my dad is still with me. When he died, he left my mom a life insurance policy. She banked it so I could use it to go to college. I have to pay it back when I get a job because basically it's her retirement. But she said it's what he would've wanted. I know he'd be proud to see how I'm doing."

Leigh's stomach knotted. That had been the plan. The policy was something an insurance salesman had talked Blake into buying shortly after they were married. But Blake's intermittent jobs kept them living from paycheck to paycheck. When money was tight Blake wanted to let the policy lapse. She'd taken over the payments.

But the liver disease that led to his death was diagnosed when he was between jobs and they were without health insurance. It took her years to pay off the medical bills. And during those years, to keep a roof over their heads and food on the table, she'd had to borrow from the life insurance money she'd promised to her son. By the time Jeff was ready for college, most of it was gone. If Jeff had known, he would have insisted on getting a job to help take care of them. College would have become a missed opportunity. She'd turned to her parents for help, and they'd reluctantly agreed to mortgage their home for Jeff's sake. Leigh saw no point in giving him the details of how his education was financed—he knew he had to pay the money back, so what difference did it make?

As long as he graduates and gets a job.

She took another bowl from the cabinet. "Dinner's ready."

As they ate, Leigh noticed that Jessica spoke only when she was spoken to and volunteered nothing about herself. Leigh tried to draw her into the conversation.

"Where do you live?"

Jessica poked her fork at her salad. "I'm staying with a friend."

Leigh smiled at her, hoping she'd look up. "Waiting to find just the right place?"

"It seems like it takes a full-time job to keep my car running." Jessica speared a slice of tomato and put it in her mouth. "I couldn't pay rent if I wanted to."

"But it's running now." Jeff grinned at her.

"Is your friend someone you work with?" Leigh asked.

"No, she's someone I met at Planned Parenthood."

Planned Parenthood! Leigh glanced sharply at Jeff. He was looking at Jessica.

Leigh cleared her throat. "Did you work there?"

Jessica raised her head. "No."

Jeff turned to his mother. "Jessica's a certified nursing assistant at Haven House."

Leigh had heard of Haven House. She had a friend

39

whose brother had Down syndrome, and he'd lived in one of the homes for most of his adult life. "Have you worked there long?"

"Two years."

This was the first encouraging thing Jessica had said. She must have a compassionate heart to do such work. "That sounds like a rewarding job."

Jessica's face brightened. "You do get attached to the people."

"My friend's brother, Bob Steiner, is there. Do you know him?"

Jessica put down her fork. "When I worked swing shift, I helped bathe Bobby quite often. It was so cute. He would always sing songs in the bathtub from the Sesame Street videos. When I went to nights, they assigned me to a different house. I miss that guy."

Leigh took a bite of her spaghetti. Bob Steiner was in his fifties, and his sister had told Leigh he was difficult to care for because of his temper. That's why they had put him in private care.

Jeff picked up the conversation and turned it to the Wednesday night singles group. As he and Jessica talked, Leigh observed the young woman. There was a hardness to her eyes, and except for the few words she'd spoken about Bob Steiner, her manner was guarded. What Jeff saw in her was beyond Leigh.

The conversation stayed light, and when dinner was finished, Jessica and Jeff began cleaning up the kitchen. Leigh excused herself and went upstairs to her desk. She had just opened the file for her manuscript and read over the opening pages of her current chapter when she heard the garage door open. Good. Jessica was leaving. Now she could talk to Jeff. She waited a few minutes, then went downstairs. As she approached the kitchen, she heard low voices coming from the back hall.

Jessica giggled.

Leigh slowed her steps.

Silence.

Leigh hesitated. She hadn't heard the back door shut or the garage door close. Anger flashed through her. What was going on? She strode across the kitchen.

The garage door motor hummed. The back door shut. Jeff almost ran into her as he came around the corner.

"Did she leave?"

"Uh-huh." His face was flushed.

"Jeff, I want to talk to you."

"What?"

The abruptness in his voice surprised her.

Leigh pulled a chair away from the dining table and seated herself.

Jeff stood, looking at her.

"Would you please sit down?"

He took a seat across from her.

Leigh steepled her fingers under her chin. "It seems like you've been seeing a lot of Jessica, and last night you came home way past midnight."

Jeff straightened. "I wasn't really watching the clock. By the time I noticed it was getting late, it was too late to call."

"I'd rather be awakened by a phone call telling me when you'll be home than to wake up and wonder."

"Mom, I'm twenty-one years old." The edge in Jeff's

voice sharpened and he folded his arms on the table. "Do you know how embarrassing it would be to say to a group of adults, 'Excuse me, I have to call my mom'?"

"Don't give me attitude, Jeff. It isn't that you have to ask permission, or even tell me where you are, but I think I'm entitled to know when you're coming home. All I knew was that you and Jessica went to church. Every other Wednesday night you've been home by midnight. It was almost two o'clock in the morning. Why wouldn't I be concerned?"

His eyes held hers for a moment, then he lowered them. "It *was* late."

Leigh dropped her hands into her lap.

Jeff's eyes returned to hers. "I'm sorry I worried you." His shoulders relaxed. "It's just sometimes when I'm with Jessica I don't want to leave her."

Leigh felt a wave of apprehension rise in her chest. "What do you mean by that?"

"I just like hanging out with her. We have a lot in common."

Leigh's eyes widened. "Like what? She has a very troubled past, she's drifted from one foster home to another. In fact, from what she said, she still doesn't have a permanent address."

"That's why she knows what it means to feel like you never fit in." Jeff's gaze didn't waver. "She's overcome a lot of stuff in her life."

Leigh caught her breath. She couldn't believe what she was hearing. Yes, Jeff had had some struggles with his ADD, but she'd been by his side every step of the way. She'd shielded him from his father's rejection; she'd

42

monitored the teachers and the schools to be sure that he got whatever help he needed; she'd even borrowed from her parents to be sure Jeff could go to college and have an even chance for success in the workplace. She wasn't going to let some grifter come in now and destroy everything. "Jessica's trouble."

Jeff's mouth dropped open. "Why would you say that? You don't even know her."

"If she always acts the way she acted at dinner, I'll never get to know her. She wouldn't even make eye contact with me." Leigh hesitated. "And what was she doing at Planned Parenthood?"

Jeff pushed his chair back and walked away from the table. "I have homework."

Tears stung her eyes as she watched her son walk from the room. He'd never cut her off like that before.

Leigh felt the tears on her cheeks. She'd fought for her son all her life.

Her apprehension became resolve. She wasn't going to stop now.

⟡

Jeff stared at the client table on his computer screen. He'd spent the last two hours trying to figure out why the server wouldn't assign IP addresses for his virtual network. This was part of the semester final project and he had to get the program working.

But it was no use. The conversation with his mother kept intruding on his thoughts. She'd made it clear she didn't like Jessica. And Jessica had made it clear she didn't like his mother.

Slumping back in his chair, he folded his arms across his chest. His mother had made him feel like a fool the way she'd come running down the stairs while he was standing at the back door with Jessica. Heat rose in his cheeks again. Jessica had said she felt like she was in high school and pulled away from him. She hadn't even said good-bye.

Jeff picked up his cell phone from his desk and pressed Send. Walking to the doorway of his bedroom, he counted the rings. "Please answer, Jessica."

Her voice mail picked up. As he closed the phone, he heaved a sigh. He wasn't going to leave another message.

He flopped on the bed and stared at the ceiling. *Jessica.*

"She's trouble." His mother's voice echoed in his mind.

That was the kind of rejection Jessica had dealt with all her life. Anger flashed through him. He wanted to put his arms around her and shield her from the world. He wanted to kiss the tears from her eyes. He wanted her to know she didn't have to fight alone. She didn't have to fight at all.

Jeff closed his eyes. The memory of their kiss darted through him. An unsteady breath chased after it.

Jessica. He wanted to be with her.

Throwing his feet to the floor, he sat on the edge of the bed. He glanced at the computer screen. Then his eyes drifted to his phone. If only he could catch Jessica before she went to work. Clear things up.

Patting his pocket, he felt for his car keys.

Huffing a sigh, he let his hand drop to his side. There

was no way he could drive over to Jessica's house. If his mother found out, she'd go ballistic. It would just drive a deeper wedge between the two women. That was the last thing he wanted. First he needed to make amends with Jessica, then he'd find a way to bring the two women together. He loved his mother. Suddenly, he felt ashamed. He shouldn't have stalked out of the kitchen like he did. Tomorrow he'd apologize to her before he went to school. He rubbed his forehead with the tips of his fingers; his head ached, and he was tired.

Max jumped onto the bed and rubbed against him.

"Hey, you're cold. Been outside, eh?" He ruffled the big cat's cool fur. It felt good.

He rose, shoved his phone into his pocket, and picked his jacket up off the floor. He'd go for a walk. Then he'd come back and work on his virtual network. He walked quietly up the stairs, then slipped out the front door.

It was a beautiful night. The moon shone through the cloudy sky and the air was crisp and cool. He breathed deeply.

Reaching into his pocket he took out his phone, flipped it open, and pressed Send.

"Please answer." He counted the rings as he walked down the street.

His eyes wandered to the mountains. There was fog resting on the hills. The misty clouds stirred something in him. Something vague, distant.

"Hello?"

"Jessica?" Jeff's heart raced.

The silvery mist slowly rose from the mountains as he walked into the darkness.

Jessica fanned the smoke out of her bathroom window. She knew it was risky to smoke pot when she had to be at work in a few hours. But she didn't care. When she'd left Jeff's house, she had to go somewhere. And the numbing haze of the crumbled leaves in the baggie was the one place that always welcomed her. A safe place, where she didn't feel the pain.

Leigh thought Jeff was too good for her. Jessica had felt it. She folded her arms across her chest and leaned against the window frame. It wasn't the first time she'd been judged unworthy. She'd been stupid enough to think this time might be different. Even though Leigh treated Jeff like a child, he spoke highly of his mother. He'd talked about how supportive she was of his dreams, how he could talk to her about anything, and how her faith had taught him to never give up because God had a plan for his life. All things were possible with God.

Jessica had been curious about the whole Christian thing. When she'd first seen Jeff sitting at Starbucks, he'd been sitting with his back to her, typing on his laptop. She'd been at the counter buying a latte and saw only his back. He was wearing a black T-shirt with a gothic-looking cross on it that had some kind of medieval lettering across it. She'd just been switched to nights at work and was bummed out. Thinking he might be into heavy metal, and might be a contact for some weed, she'd approached him. If he had something to give her, she had something to give him. When she got closer she saw that the letters on the cross spelled "FORGIVEN."

She almost kept walking, but there wasn't any other place to sit. So she took the empty chair at his table and asked him about his shirt.

Jeff's quiet, patient manner had drawn her. His eyes were gentle and he constantly smiled as he talked about his faith. By the time he asked her if she knew Christ, she decided to tell him she'd just become a Christian. That's when he'd asked her to church.

God had never done a thing for her, but going along with Jeff's Christian ideas was a small price to pay to be with him. He treated her with respect, cared what she thought, and didn't care about her past.

She closed the window. What she wanted more than anything in the world was a family—a husband to love her, a house, and children—though she'd never shared her dream with anyone. One foster family had kept her locked in her room night and day. That's when she'd begun thinking about it in detail. When she was younger, she'd imagined she had a mother who braided her hair with ribbons and a father who called her Daddy's girl. Then as she'd grown older she'd imagined a big, handsome young man would come to rescue her. She used to pretend he'd seen her through the window and boldly knocked on her foster parents' door, demanding they let him in.

Jessica stepped away from the glass and drew the curtain. By the time she was seventeen she'd realized foolish fantasies weren't going to save her and had struck out on her own. She did what she had to to survive. During nursing school, she'd gone from selling drugs to selling her soul.

Then she'd met Jeff. And for the first time in years had dared to dream again. Until tonight.

Her cell phone had rung at least ten different times since she'd left his house, but she hadn't answered it. She didn't know what she wanted to say. Part of her wanted to run away. Part of her wanted to run to him.

The iniquitous, hazy fog of the sweet smoke drifted through her mind, wrapping itself seductively around her fears. She closed her eyes, enjoying the blessed assurance that there were places without pain.

Her cell phone was ringing. A big, handsome young man was knocking on her foster parents' door.

She walked to the bed and picked up the phone.

"Hello?"

All things were possible . . .

"Jessica?"

She smiled lazily. "Hey."

"I'm sorry things ended like they did tonight."

Lying down on the bed, she closed her eyes. The sound of his voice . . . his gentle eyes . . . his constant smile. She wanted to be with him. Always.

A tendril of smoke slithered its way through her memories. Reminding her of all she had learned about surviving.

It had been sheer luck she had met him and she would do whatever it took to hold him.

"I'm sorry too."

4

John Higheagle!

Leigh pushed aside her lunch bag and laid the newspaper on the table. Leaning over the paper, she studied the black-and-white picture on the front page of the "Local" section.

There wasn't a doubt in her mind. It was him.

The caption under the picture said "GOOD SAMARITAN RESCUES WOMAN FROM BURNING CAR." The article gave details of a two-car accident that had happened in downtown River Falls. One of the cars had caught fire and an onlooker, risking his life, had pulled the driver and her passenger to safety. The story detailed that John Higheagle had been in the car lot of White Water Ford when he heard the impact. Seeing the rising smoke, he'd rushed to the scene. Were it not for his quick thinking, the two trapped women would have died.

Leigh's eyes returned to the picture. Johnny . . . her inspiration.

Ignoring the feelings of sweetness and sorrow that rose in her heart, she glanced at the wall clock in the basement lunchroom of Hills and Homes Realty. It was past time to get back to work. She tore the page from the paper, folded it, and stuck it in her purse. After cleaning off the lunch table, she hurried back to her desk. There were flyers to make and escrows to check on for Jan. Clients were coming in to sign a counteroffer, and there were two houses she needed to get pictures of before the listings could be submitted to the Multiple Listing Service. The afternoon flew by. But John Higheagle was never far from her thoughts. By the time she got home, she could think of nothing else.

As Leigh pulled into the driveway, she saw Jeff washing his car. He stopped and waved at her.

Her grip tightened on the steering wheel. She smiled back and pulled into the garage. Jeff hadn't washed his car in months. Why now, on Friday night?

Jessica.

Jeff had come to her bedroom before he'd left for school. He'd apologized for the way he'd acted. But, she'd noticed, not for what he'd said. His attitude had been respectful but cool, and yet she'd felt the issue was still unresolved. Now she was sure of it.

Before stepping out of the car, she bowed her head. "Lord, You love Jeff even more than I do. Please give me wisdom in this situation. And please watch over my son."

She stopped at the back door and watched Jeff roll up the hose. As he neared the garage spigot, she called out, "What do you want for dinner?"

Jeff laid the hose on the ground and jogged over to her. "Didn't hear you."

"I was asking what you want for dinner."

"I'm getting ready to go out, so don't worry about me."

But she was worried, that was the problem. "Where you going?"

"Just out." He grinned at her. "I'll be home by midnight."

Leigh studied his face. He was trying to comply. His gentle eyes rested on hers, and his expression was relaxed, letting her know he wasn't challenging her authority.

She released a deep sigh. Without speaking a word, he was telling her he respected her. And that she should respect him.

"I hope you'll think about what I said last night."

"I understand, Mom."

Leigh turned and went into the house.

She took the newspaper article from her purse, hung her purse and coat on a hook in the back hall, then went upstairs to her desk. If Jeff wasn't eating at home, she'd have time to write. She laid the folded article next to the computer.

After hanging up her work clothes, she changed into leggings and a sweatshirt, then stepped into her slippers. Pulling her hair into a ponytail, she secured it with a scrunchie and padded over to the computer. She sat down and refolded the newspaper into a square that showed only the picture.

"Johnny." She traced the outline of his forehead, straight nose, and square chin. It had been twenty-five years since she'd seen him.

She closed her eyes . . . returning to the front yard of

her childhood home. She was in his arms, with only a thin cloak of darkness to protect them should her father decide to look out his bedroom window before going to bed.

"I love you." His voice was husky.

She pressed her face against his neck. "You don't have to go. My father can't stop us. We can make it on our own."

His arms tightened around her. "I can't take care of you right now. And with him against us, we wouldn't stand a chance. When I get out of the Navy, things will be different. Maybe we won't even have to wait that long. Once I know where I'm going to be stationed."

Living under the shadow her brother had cast on her life, Leigh was drawn to the independent and intense young man whose mixed blood made him a pariah to both cultures. They'd dated secretly all through high school, her father making it clear he wasn't going to allow a half-breed in his house, and certainly not in his family. The clandestine meetings, the glances exchanged when backs were turned, and the whispered goodbyes over four life-shaping years had forged a deep bond between them. She was closer to Johnny than to anyone else on earth.

"Don't go." Her tears came in earnest.

He took her face in his hands and kissed her. "We'll be together again. I promise."

And that was the last thing he said to her before he disappeared into the night.

She opened her eyes and gazed at the picture again. Her first and only love. She'd carefully preserved her memories through her marriage to Blake. Trying not to visit them too often. After she became a Christian, she tried not to visit them at all.

But when Blake died and she began to write, she'd allowed herself to remember. And soon her memories became notes, and the notes became pages, and the pages became chapters . . . and *First Love* became her first book.

She felt heat rise in her cheeks. She'd used her heroine to pour out her heart. Writing with abandon of her love for Johnny, sure that life had taken them so far apart they'd never meet again. She'd named her hero Patrick McFarland and given him an Irish brogue. When no one in her family had guessed the book's secret, she felt like the past had been put to rest. Until today.

She set the picture down. Did he live in River Falls? Did he work at White Water Ford? Was he married? She let her mind wander for a moment, then reached across the keyboard, picked up the telephone, and dialed information. "River Falls. John Higheagle." Her heart began to pound.

No listing.

She slowly lowered the phone into its cradle.

He had certainly forgotten her by now. He'd never tried to contact her after he'd been home on leave from technical school. He'd said he was being assigned to Bremerton, Washington, and would write her with the address. But he never had. She'd even driven there at one point, hoping to find him. But with no connections and no way to get on base it had been futile.

She blinked rapidly. That had hurt . . . for years. She straightened in her chair. Better to leave things alone.

Leigh jiggled the mouse. Chapter four of *Second Chance* appeared on the screen. The sequel to book one was due in September. She'd really been struggling, but suddenly she felt energized. Her heroine—sassy, smart Tina Ridell—had moved on from Patrick McFarland. Her second chance at love was with a handsome business-man who adored her. The faith thread of her plot let the reader know that God was in control. He'd brought the two together, and Tina need only wait for His plan to unfold and for her dreams to come true.

Leigh placed her hands on the keyboard, ready to give Tina her heart's desire.

If only she could have been as lucky.

❦

Jeff parked his car in front of Jessica's house. He paused for a moment, then bowed his head. "Lord, You know how I feel about Jessica. I've never felt this way about anyone. Is she the girl You have for me?" He waited, hoping to get a sense of confirmation in his spirit.

Jeff had made up his mind long ago that he wanted to live his life in a way that would bring glory to God. He'd even thought about being a youth pastor. But after thinking and praying about it, he came to believe that God had some other plan for him. Now, over the months he'd dated Jessica, he'd started to think instead about having a wife . . . and someday children. For a moment he saw himself throwing a football across a backyard into pudgy, outstretched arms.

Having kids would thrill his mother. She'd said more than once she couldn't wait to have grandchildren. She would come to love Jessica.

He stepped out of the car, grinning. Jessica had a special place in her heart for the people she cared for at Haven House. He could see himself and Jessica married and ministering together in the future. That would be heaven on earth. Before he got to the door, Jessica opened it.

His smile broadened. "Did you decide what movie you want to go see?"

She swung the door wide and stepped to the side. "Come in. I've got a surprise."

Jeff walked through the door.

"We've got the house to ourselves tonight, and I rented a DVD I'm positive you'll love." She clapped her hands. "And best of all, I don't have to go to work."

"Sounds great." Jeff followed her to the family room.

"Sit down while I set up the movie."

He watched her put the DVD in the player, imagining for a moment that they were in their own home.

She came and sat beside him on the couch. Turning to him, she put her arms around his neck and kissed him.

The familiar trill corkscrewed through his stomach.

He kissed her back.

She ran her hand slowly across his shoulder and down his arm until it rested on his thigh.

Yes.

He held the thought.

I love you.

This wasn't their first kiss and this wasn't the first time Jessica had let him know he was the one she wanted to be with. There wasn't a doubt in his mind how she felt about him . . . though she'd never really told him. She'd told him instead that she was afraid to love. Everyone she had ever loved had hurt her and then left her. She'd learned to keep a veil over her eyes and a wall around her heart.

He reached for her hand, picked it up, and brought it to his lips. *I love you.* He kissed her fingers.

Her eyes met his. Her pretty azure blue eyes. Heaven.

"I love you." He hardly heard his own whisper.

Her hand slid down to his hip.

Slowly, he pulled away from her. "No, Jessie. Not now. Not yet."

"Why?" She moved toward him.

"We've talked about this before. You know how I feel."

"What about how I feel?"

He picked up her hand again and rubbed the back of it with his thumb. "I care about how you feel. You know that. I care about what you think. I care about what you're doing every minute of the day." He leaned forward and kissed her forehead. "Come on. Let's watch the movie."

Jessica picked up the remote from the coffee table and pressed Play, then leaned back against the couch and folded her arms across her chest.

Jeff put his arm around her, pulled her to him, and kissed the top of her head.

Star Wars filled the screen. His favorite movie. He

grinned. "Now we're talking," he teased, squeezing her shoulder.

She didn't respond.

Jeff turned his eyes to the screen, but his mind was on Jessica. He glanced at her.

Tears were running down her cheeks, and she was looking at him. For just a moment, her eyes became defenseless and clear. The veil lifted. And he saw the pain.

Raw.

Ravaged.

He wrapped his arms around her and pulled her to his chest. Tears sprang to his eyes. The moment could not have been more intimate if he had seen her naked body.

She pulled away from him. Then rose and ran from the room.

He ran after her.

Before he reached the bedroom door, she slammed it in his face. He heard her trying to lock it.

Turning the knob, he held the latch back.

Finally, muted footsteps retreated. Inching the door open, he saw through the dim light that she was lying on the bed, hands knotted into fists, face turned into the pillow.

He moved quietly across the room and knelt beside her. "Jessie, don't cry." He stroked her thick auburn hair.

All she had told him about her past had not prepared him for the wounding he had seen in her eyes. A desire to protect her welled up within him. He would never let her be hurt again. Surely this was why God had brought him into her life. To take care of her, to treasure her, to show her the love of Christ.

"Why don't you want to touch me?" she choked out between sobs. "Is there something wrong with me?"

"No, there's nothing wrong with you." He pushed the hair away from her face.

"You said you loved me." She turned toward him.

"I do." How could he make her understand? "I do love you."

She held his gaze. Her sobs subsiding. "Hold me. Please hold me."

The cry in her voice pierced his heart. An overwhelming desire to be close to her, to comfort her, washed over him. He lay down next to her. Pulling her to him, he kissed the tears on her cheeks.

Her hands were on the back of his neck.

His lips on hers.

A starburst of emotion exploded in his chest. He was swimming through a haze of feelings and desires. Torn between torture and passion. Her heart hammered against his.

This is wrong.

As a war of emotions raged within him, his heart refused to believe what his mind was telling him. This couldn't be wrong. It felt so right.

He loved her.

He heard a breathy whisper. *It is right. You've waited all your life for the woman you love.*

As his heart pounded, the smoky voice grew louder and louder, until his heart and the voice whispered in unison. *It is right. This is the woman you love.*

Jeff slowly opened his eyes. As the room came into focus, he heard muffled voices.

He sat up. Jessica was asleep next to him. The clock on the nightstand said 11:22 p.m. His heart lurched as the events of the evening came back to him.

The bedroom door was closed, but he could see a light under it. Apparently, Jessica's roommate was in the family room with somebody. He slipped out of the bed.

He'd met Jessica's roommate, Gina, only a few times. He felt heat rising in his cheeks as he remembered inviting Gina to church.

The thought of walking out of the bedroom and seeing her filled him with shame. He walked to the window and pulled back the curtain. He paused a moment, then started to slide it open. A stab of guilt ran through his gut. How would Jessica feel when she woke up and realized what he'd done?

He looked at her, sleeping peacefully, her sweet face serene.

How many other men had seen her like this . . . had known her like this? The dark thought shocked him. He pushed it away.

Help me, God.

The words mocked him. Why should God help him when he'd just destroyed the plan he'd always believed God had for his life? To remain pure until he met the girl God intended for him, and then to become one with that woman in a union blessed by God. A bolt of fear flashed over him. What had he done? To himself? To Jessie?

"Jeff?" Jessica's sleepy voice broke into his thoughts.

He squatted beside the bed. "I'm here, Jessie." He took her hand and kissed it. "I've got to go now. I'll call you tomorrow." He loved her more than ever.

"Okay," she whispered.

He rose and walked out the bedroom door, closing it quietly behind him.

Tucking his chin, he walked down the hall. As he neared the family room he heard Gina's voice. "Do you really think they'll fire her?"

Jeff stopped, listening. A man spoke. "That's the rumor around Haven House."

Jeff's heart pounded.

"She's late a lot and just doesn't seem to get the work done."

He heard Gina giggle. "Besides, she's a piglet."

Jeff frowned, relieved that they weren't talking about Jessica, but troubled by the cruelty of their words.

Slinking past the entry to the family room, he headed to the front door. As he stepped outside, he took a deep, unsteady breath.

He jogged to the car, got in, and started it. He glanced at the clock on the dashboard. At least he'd be home by midnight and avoid a confrontation with his mother.

He clenched his jaw and shook his head. He'd never kept secrets from her, or anybody. Things suddenly were different. Complicated. Shadowy. "God, can You forgive me?"

As he drove home, his thoughts returned to Jessica. The way she'd clung to him. The way she'd needed him. How in that moment he'd believed he could soothe her wounds. But now in the cold reality of the aftermath, he realized how wrong he had been.

Jeff stared at the road ahead of him. Her eyes, filled with the wrenching pain of the hell that was her past, came before him. She needed the kind of love that set men free. The kind of love that could heal and change the heart of man.

He felt helpless. His heart ached for her. It would only be through the grace of God that she would ever find it.

⚮

John Higheagle turned off the light on his nightstand and climbed into bed. He'd have to be at the hospital by seven in the morning. A representative from Channel 6 had called, asking him about the rescue of the two women he'd pulled from a burning car. He'd agreed to meet a television crew at the hospital to do a live interview that would be broadcast on *Good Morning Idaho*.

He smiled. If he hadn't had a flat tire on his way home from work, he wouldn't have even been in the parking lot of White Water Ford. It had been the first place he could pull off the road.

He'd just stepped out of his truck when he'd heard the impact of the collision. Jogging to the edge of the street, he saw smoke rising from one of the cars, and he ran toward the scene. That's when he felt the presence of God. The familiar goose bumps on his arms and a certainty of purpose. He was being called.

Everyone had marveled at what he'd done. That he'd

disregarded the flames, not once but twice. And what a "lucky coincidence" that he'd happened by.

John Higheagle knew the Creator well. There was no such thing as luck or coincidence when one was in the will of God. God had taught him that long ago.

All things were subservient to the power of Christ.

The flames had never touched him.

5

Not wanting to miss the weather report, Leigh stepped out of the master bathroom and turned up the volume of the little television next to her desk. At breakfast Jeff had reluctantly agreed to help her clean up the yard later in the afternoon. Now it looked like rain.

Returning to the bathroom, she parted off a section of hair and wound it around a hot roller. Half listening to the morning news, she found herself thinking of Jeff. Her casual questions about his date the night before had revealed only that Jessica had rented *Star Wars*. He'd seemed distant. After eating a piece of toast, he'd gone to the basement, saying he had a project to finish.

Well, at least he was focused on his schoolwork. Praise the Lord for that.

Suddenly it occurred to her, maybe he and Jessica had had a fight. She quirked her mouth. She felt sorry for Jessica. The girl was a mess. She'd already put Jessica on her prayer list. And Jeff had done enough by guiding her to a good church and helping her make friends there. She huffed a sigh. He knew how she felt about the situation. Short of forbidding him to see the girl, there wasn't much she could do. Besides, forcing the issue could make it worse. Her eyes rested on her reflection in the mirror. She'd basically raised Jeff alone, and she knew like no one else could how critical it was that he get the support he needed in his day-to-day life. It made all the difference in the world for him. He deserved a girl who not only understood that, but was capable of meeting that need.

Sports scores droned in the background.

Her thoughts turned to her book. This morning her heroine would be going on her second date with the hero. It was fun writing romances, and the genre was wildly popular. But Leigh felt strongly that God was calling her in a different direction.

She hadn't accepted Christ as her Savior until she was in her thirties, and it had been only recently that she'd begun to understand the workings of the Holy Spirit. Grace Bible Church, where she and Jeff attended, spoke of the power of the Spirit and how it operated in the lives of all believers. But it was something she wasn't sure about, so she'd begun to pray, asking God to show her the Holy Spirit working in her own life. After that, the unexpected offer from Paramount Publishers had come.

She felt goose bumps on her arms and tears sprang to her eyes as the memory of her prayer time that morning returned to her. Believing the interest from Paramount was God opening a door, she had prayed He would give her the story that He meant for that opportunity. That He would reveal the book of His heart to her. She'd felt a quiet assurance in her spirit. And she'd been left with the strong impression God would show her His will.

"Sixty degrees—"

Leigh dashed out of the bathroom in time to see the weather graphic on the television screen: a big TODAY with raindrops on the bottom half of the letters.

She planted her hands on her hips. It looked like Jeff had lucked out. Walking to the window, she scanned the sky. The clouds were already thickening.

"—Mr. Higheagle."

Leigh whirled around and stared at the television.

There was a split screen. The news anchorman was in the studio and on the other side of the screen was a tall, dark-haired man standing next to a police officer.

The dark-haired man spoke. "No, I don't consider myself a hero. I just happened to be at the right place at the right time."

"You're being modest. You not only got them out of the vehicle, you put a tourniquet on the driver's leg, which kept her from bleeding to death before the paramedics arrived."

Leigh could hardly focus on what was being said. Without taking her eyes from the screen, she reached her hand behind her back and grabbed the desk chair. Pulling it in front of the television, she sat on it.

"That was just some training I learned in the Navy."

She closed her eyes a moment, then opened them again.

It was Johnny . . . and it wasn't.

He'd been a scrawny kid, not much taller than she, with a tough guy attitude. Somehow he seemed a lot bigger than she remembered, and his face was relaxed, his manner confident. And he was smiling. She used to tease him about how he never smiled.

The anchorman addressed a question to the police officer. Johnny, standing on the right side of the screen, turned toward the officer.

Some lettering on Johnny's coat caught her eye. Leaning forward, she saw the letters formed a half circle, partly hidden in the wrinkles of the jacket.

She craned her neck. "A--omot--e." She tilted her head. "--n Automotive."

The interview was coming to an end.

Johnny turned back toward the camera.

The anchorman continued. "Thank you for joining us." The right half of the screen disappeared and the newscaster spoke into the camera. "The two women were flown to the Harborview Burn Center in Seattle. We'll bring you more on this story tonight at five. Now it's time for a traffic update."

A long shot of Interstate 90 came onto the screen.

Leigh's mind was spinning. She turned off the television and stood. At this very moment, Johnny was somewhere in River Falls, Idaho, just twenty miles away. She folded her arms across her chest, her heart racing.

It had been about this time last year that she'd finished her first manuscript, saying in dialogue what she'd wished she'd been able to say to Johnny. Finally working through all the heartache, regrets . . . yearning. At least she thought she had.

Plopping down on the end of the bed, she put her elbows on her knees and her chin in her hands. Max jumped up on the bed beside her.

"Hey, bud." She stroked his fur. Max obliged her by arching his back under her hand. "What do you think?"

Max jumped off the bed, scampered across the room, and jumped onto the windowsill, eyes and ears intent on the street below.

Leigh laughed. "So you think I should just get in the car and drive to River Falls, huh?" She walked over and picked up the big black cat. "What if he's married and has a family? Did you think of that?"

Max ignored her question.

She giggled. "You'd like him. He's allergic to dogs."

Leigh set the cat on the bed and returned to the bathroom. As she finished fixing her hair, her mind filtered back through the years. Vignettes of her and Johnny flashed like snapshots, as clear as the moment they had happened. A trail as sweet as their romance, leading her to the truth.

She wasn't over him and she wanted to know why he'd walked out of her life.

She snapped off the bathroom light and walked over to her desk. Pulling the chair in front of the computer, she sat down.

She positioned the cursor on the browser bar and began to type:

n Automotive River Falls Idaho.

❧

Jeff pulled into the Starbucks parking lot. Jessica had called him three times while he was trying to get his virtual network running, telling him she had to see him. There was something she had to talk to him about. She'd said she didn't want to talk about it on the phone. The uncertainty he'd felt earlier returned. Was it about last night? Spotting Jessica's car, he took the space next to it.

Thank heavens it had started to rain. The calls had been awkward. The thought of telling Jessica he couldn't see her because he'd promised to help his mother in the yard made him feel foolish. But the thought of telling his mother he couldn't help her because something had come up with Jessica made him feel guilty. Ambivalence tinged with anger rose in his chest. His mother deserved respect and he'd made a promise to her. But Jessica deserved his support, and he loved her. He had to find a way to bring the two women together.

He got out of the car and made a dash for the coffee shop. Jessica was waiting for him at the table where they'd first met, drinking a latte. A second cup was on the table next to her. She rose.

Their eyes met and suddenly the intimacy of the night before was present. Jeff felt himself blushing. "Hi."

Jessica's face broke into a smile. "Hey." She sat down.

He pulled a chair around next to hers. Sitting down, he took her hand in his. "Missed you."

"Me too." She leaned toward him until their noses touched, then kissed him.

He reached for her other hand. "What's wrong?"

"Nothing." She straightened. "Why?"

"You said you had to see me."

"Oh. It's not that anything's wrong. I've got to find another place to live and I wanted to talk to you about it." She handed him the cup from the table. "I've been looking. Gina originally said I could stay with her for a few days, until I found something." She swirled the drink in her cup.

Jeff searched her face, waiting for her to continue. Jessica had lived there for as long as he'd known her.

"I've had some medical expenses, and with all my car problems and everything I just haven't found anything I could afford."

With no family, she had nowhere to turn. He squeezed her hand to let her know he understood.

"I was thinking." She looked into his eyes. "Your school's out next month. What do you think about sharing a place?"

"Share a place?"

"Yeah. You'll be able to work more hours without school. Between us, we can make it."

The thought of living on his own before he graduated had never occurred to him, and the idea of living with a woman before he was married had not even been in the realm of the possible twenty-four hours ago.

He'd been following a plan of school, church, and part-time work for three years. Summers were for building up his savings account. He wanted to be sure he could start paying back the money his mother had lent him for college, and he wanted to have move-in expenses for an apartment in River Falls when he graduated. He'd already saved several thousand dollars. He'd even built some credit by having a gas card and faithfully paying it off each month.

"I don't know, Jessica." He was the closest thing to family she had and he wanted to help her. He loved her. "How much would it cost?"

"I'll bet we could get a place for five-hundred and fifty a month." He could hear the excitement in her voice. "That would only be two-hundred and seventy-five apiece."

He grinned at her. "But that's two-hundred and seventy-five dollars more in bills than I have now."

"I thought about that." She fingered her cup. "You only work part-time at Sears. I bet I could get you on full-time, nights, with me. We could share a car. That would save on gas. And best of all, we'd be off at the same time." She squeezed his hand. "I want to be with you, Jeff. Isn't that what you want?"

Everything around them faded away. Only her sweet face and the fervent hope in her eyes remained.

I do.

◈

Leigh clicked Save and closed her manuscript file. Tina was tucked in bed, happily dreaming about the hero. Seventeen hundred and thirty-three words. It had been a good morning.

Her eyes drifted to the window. The rain was misting down, Jeff had shouted up the stairs that he was going out, and the rest of Saturday afternoon was suddenly open. She pursed her lips.

Her hand still on the mouse, she moved the cursor to the minimized Internet Explorer bar at the bottom of her screen and clicked. The same "1–10 of 166,328 matches" that had been retrieved earlier for "n Automotive" popped up. Only the first two were businesses: Cee N Bees Café and Splash N Dash Car Wash. Both were in

River Falls. She frowned. It was possible the name on Johnny's jacket had nothing to do with his job.

Maybe he'd just been passing through River Falls. Maybe he didn't even work there. Maybe she shouldn't even be looking for him. She sighed. Maybe. But the truth was, she'd thought about little else since reading the article in the paper. And watching the interview on television had only fanned the ember of possibility that had been sparked the day before. Maybe she would drive to River Falls and look around. She rose.

According to the paper, he'd been at White Water Ford when the accident happened. And he'd still been in River Falls today for the interview. It was only twenty miles north . . .

The ember became a flame.

Fifteen minutes later, Highway 95 stretched in front of her.

Leigh was familiar with River Falls. She and Jeff had driven around the midsize town when he first interviewed for the job at E-Solutions, and she recalled there was a row of car dealerships on the outskirts of town. Taking the city center exit, she turned onto the main street. As she drove, she looked left and right, hoping to spot a sign for an automotive business.

The buildings began to thin and soon she saw a Toyota dealership. Just beyond that was the marquee for White Water Ford.

She drove past it, made a U-turn, and parked across the street from the showroom. Looking through the drizzle, she scanned the car lot. Her breath began to fog up the window.

She sat back in her seat and lay her head against the headrest. She was acting like a schoolgirl. There wasn't any reason she should feel so hesitant about looking up her old friend. They were adults now. The meeting could be as casual as "Hi, I saw your picture in the paper. Just thought I'd stop and say . . . good job." She rolled her eyes. Sure. How about "Hi, I saw your picture in the paper and I've been thinking of you a lot lately, so I wanted to stop by and find out if you're available. Do you still care? Why didn't you write?"

She bit her lower lip. Wiping the window with her jacket sleeve, she peeked in the direction of the car lot. What if he was there right now? What if he'd seen her cruise by and then park across the street and wondered who the weird woman was? She surveyed the car lot again. Her eyes settled on a Service Department sign. There was a red arrow and a phone number under it.

Of course. Why hadn't she thought of it before? She'd call and ask for him.

Reaching across the seat, she grabbed her purse, pulled out her cell phone, and punched in the numbers.

"It's a great day at White Water Ford."

"Is John Higheagle there?"

"Excuse me?"

"Is John Higheagle there?" She held her breath.

"You must have the wrong number."

"I'm sorry. Thank you." She snapped the phone shut and exhaled. All the anxiety of the moments before vanished and the unsettling prospect of not finding him at all took its place. She drummed her fingers on the steering wheel.

Navigating through the traffic, she worked her way down the block and across the street, finally pulling into the lot. She wove her way toward the showroom through the rows of new cars and parked under the overhang. As a gray-haired man approached her, she rolled down her window.

He stepped up to the car. "What are you lookin' for today?"

"I'm hoping you can help me." She took a deep breath. "I read in the paper about an accident that happened near here yester—"

"Wasn't that somethin'? That guy who saved the two women was right here just before it happened."

"You saw him?" What a lucky coincidence.

"I was talking to him. He was changin' a flat tire."

"Oh. I thought maybe he worked here."

"John?" He tilted his head, giving her an appraising look. "No. But he brings in cars from time to time."

"Does he buy a lot of cars here?"

The man looked amused. "Could I ask why you want to know?"

Leigh felt herself blushing. "My name is Leigh Scott. John Higheagle and I were friends in high school. I lost touch with him. Then I saw his picture in the paper."

"Oooh. I understand." He grinned. "The cars he brings in here are on the back of a tow truck."

"Does he have a towing business?"

The man hesitated, then he leaned on the window ledge. "Leigh, I'm not sure how much I should be sayin'. You know what I mean." He gave her a conspiratorial smile. "But if you go to Dan's Automotive over in Ridge-line, they can tell you."

"Thank you. Thank you so much."

He nodded, then began to walk away. As she started to back up, he turned and called out to her. "Oh, tell him the next time he comes in to be sure to bring his sweetheart. The guys in the service department say they miss her since she stopped ridin' with him."

Leigh stared at him, too surprised to do more than nod. She rolled up her window.

Tears stung her eyes. He knew the whole time he was talking to her that John had a girlfriend. How humiliating.

As she pulled onto the main road, she looked for the green signs that would take her back to Highway 95 and home.

Sweetheart. She blinked rapidly. Stupid old man. Some lucky coincidence.

6

Jeff pressed the button to start the coffee, then opened the refrigerator and took out some bacon. This morning was as good a time as any to talk to his mother.

He lined up the strips of bacon in the skillet. It had been over a week since Jessica had asked him about sharing an apartment. He'd even looked at some places with her. But every time they met a property manager or a landlord, he found the situation uncomfortable. Without fail the conversation always seemed to point out that they were an unmarried couple that would be living together, something he'd always said he would never do.

He frowned. He'd gone over it and over it in his mind and had finally come to a decision. He didn't want to do it.

He'd already broken the promise of abstinence he'd made and that was bad enough. But what troubled him more was he didn't want that kind of relationship with Jessica. He wanted God's blessing on them. He wanted to graduate and get settled in his job and then, when he could take care of her, ask her to marry him.

He turned over the sizzling bacon. Still, that didn't help Jessica now. But last night when he'd been trying to study, he had thought of something. Something that would help Jessica, and help out his mom too.

"Good morning, Jeff. That sure smells good."

Jeff grinned. "I'll have breakfast ready in a minute, Mom."

Max bounded into the kitchen.

"Looks like you have another customer."

Jeff laid the bacon on a paper towel and cracked four eggs into the skillet.

His mom poured two cups of coffee. "I'll set the table."

As he finished making breakfast, she told him about a book signing she was going to have at Borders, and he told her about his upcoming finals. They hadn't talked much since Jessica had come for dinner. It felt good to have things back to normal. After he filled Max's dish with milk, he put the food on their plates and they sat at the table.

His mother folded her hands and bowed her head. "Lord, thank You for my son and this wonderful break-fast. Be with us today and let our lives be an example of Your love. Amen." She raised her head. "So what do you have planned after church?"

"I've got some homework and some other things I want to do. But, Mom, I want to talk to you about some-thing."

His mother took a bite of toast and looked at him.

"I shouldn't have stayed out late and worried you."

"Jeff, that's in the past, forget about it."

"I know, but I feel like it got you and Jessica off to a bad start."

His mother paused. "What got Jessica and me off to a bad start was what she said, and didn't say, when she had dinner with us." She put her hands in her lap. "What *was* she doing at Planned Parenthood?"

"I think she used to work there. Mom, Jessica's done a lot of things in the past that she's not proud of. We all have—none of us are perfect. But we can't just condemn someone for the rest of their life because they made some mistakes."

"I agree with you, Jeff, and I pray for Jessica. I pray that the Lord will continue His work in her life and she'll come to have a personal relationship with Him. But that doesn't mean it's your job to see that it happens."

"If not me, then who?"

She hesitated. "The church. Her other Christian friends. Aren't there some government programs that Jessica could go to for help?" She took a sip of coffee. "You should be nice to her and encourage her, but you have your own life to focus on. School and work . . . your future."

"That's just it, Mom. I've got everything going for me. She's got nothing going for her. It seems like we should help her if we can."

Leigh took a bite of her food, chewed it slowly, then swallowed. "I don't have any extra money to give her, Jeff. And I know you don't." Her voice softened. "Exactly what kind of help does she need?"

"She needs a place to live."

"She has a job. She should be able to find something."

"She can afford only about two hundred or so a month, and there's not much out there for that."

Leigh cut into her eggs. "Maybe I could ask around at work. Sometimes the agents know of places for rent."

Jeff took a deep breath. "There're two extra bedrooms upstairs. Why couldn't she live here with us until she gets some money saved?"

His mother glared at him, her fork midway to her mouth. "What?"

"Why not? She could pay two hundred a month, and it would help you out too."

"First of all, there aren't two extra bedrooms upstairs. One is a guest room and the other one is hardly bigger than a closet. And it's filled with stuff from our house in Montana that I'm keeping to give you when you get a place."

"Couldn't we put that in storage?"

"That costs money."

"Couldn't you use the extra two hundred dollars? I bet it wouldn't even cost that much. Or put that stuff in the basement family room. I only go through there to get to my bedroom."

"Jeff, this is a ridiculous idea. It doesn't make any sense at all." Her eyes narrowed, and the corner of her mouth ticked up. "When did she come up with it?"

Jeff sat back in his chair.

His mother set her lips in a firm, thin line.

He considered his words, then spoke quietly. "She didn't, Mom. I did. I haven't even told her about it yet. I wanted to check with you first."

His mother studied him. "Why are you getting so involved?" Her eyes never left his.

"I care about her." Blinking rapidly, he looked away. "A lot."

He heard her catch her breath.

She reached across the table, putting her hand on his forearm. "Jeff, you have to stop this and let her go her own way. She's no good for you. She can't live here." She pulled her arm away. "You can't solve her problems."

Jeff couldn't believe what he was hearing. His mother hardly knew Jessica and she wasn't even willing to give her a chance. He'd seen Jessica with the disabled adults she cared for and the compassion she had for them. He knew the kind of determination it had taken for her to get her GED and nursing certificate. And since the night he'd been with her and seen the pain in her eyes, he'd come to understand something more. She needed him. She trusted him. And no matter what, he couldn't let her down.

His mother rose, picked up her plate, and put it in the sink. "Jeff, when you're out of school and on your own, you can do what you want." She turned to leave the room, then looked back at him. "But for now"—her face was firm—"I'm asking you to stop seeing her."

❧

John Higheagle jumped from the tow truck and walked into the showroom of White Water Ford.

He approached the counter. "Hi, Sue. Here's the paperwork for the gray Taurus I just unloaded. It's in space seventeen. The owner will check in at the service department tomorrow morning when you open."

Her mischievous eyes sparkled. "Don't you love working on Sunday?" She took the papers from him.

"People seem to need help every day of the week." He winked at her. "Job security for me."

"John."

He turned to the voice that came from behind him. "Morning, Jake."

"Did that gal in the white Toyota get hold of you?"

John thought for a moment. "Don't think so."

"Said she was an old friend of yours from high school. Leigh was her name. Said she saw your picture in the paper and wanted to find you."

Leigh. A wave of emotion rolled over him. *Leigh Williams.* "Was she about this tall?" He raised his hand up by his ear. "And real pretty?"

"She was sittin' in her car, but the real pretty part fits."

There could be only one Leigh looking for him. "Did she leave a phone number?" His heart began to pound.

"No, I told her where you worked and I think she was goin' over there."

"She didn't. I was at the shop all afternoon." The thought that Leigh was looking for him rocked him to his core. "Did she say anything else? Did she give you her last name?"

"She said Leigh . . . ," Jake tapped his forefinger on his lip, ". . . Leigh . . ." His brows drew together.

"Think, man!"

"Scott. It was Scott. Leigh Scott."

"Anything else?"

"Nope, just said she wanted to find you." Jake tilted his head. "You want to find her?"

John hesitated. "Sure. Uh, yes. Yes, of course." He straightened. "Maybe she'll come by again." He turned to leave.

"Hey." Jake's hand was on his shoulder. "Did you bring your sweetheart?"

"No. She can't ride with me anymore. She's too big now."

Jake arched an eyebrow. "Bet she's not gonna take to you lookin' for this Leigh."

"I'd venture to say you're right about that."

By the time John started home to his house in Ridgeline, his head was spinning. Long-forgotten memories returned. Passing notes in study hall. Meeting secretly at the library. Their first fight. He chuckled, rubbing his chin absently. Boy, was she mad. Slapped him right in the face. But it had been worth it . . . it led to their first kiss.

But why would Leigh come looking for him now? She'd made a life without him and, as far as he knew, never looked back.

Shunned by the traditionalists of his father's tribe, and never fully accepted by his mother's people, he'd grown up believing he belonged to neither. Leigh had been the only ray of light, and he'd loved her as only an untried heart can.

And that love had lingered to this day.

He'd joined the Navy with the steadfast belief they would be together again. He counted each day away from her as one day closer to his dream of making her his wife. But when his carefully penned notes didn't receive replies, and phone calls weren't returned, his life began to spiral downward. Eventually, he'd learned the truth. And that had unleashed a hatred in his heart so strong it destroyed him.

He'd died . . . to be born again . . .

His first opportunity for leave since he'd been deployed more than a year before had been one week away. He'd planned to fly home to Idaho . . . and ask Leigh to marry him. He couldn't believe he was just seven days and a drag bag away from paradise.

What they had together was what had kept him going during the months he'd been at sea. He clenched his jaw. He was positive her father was the reason there had been no word from her. And that was why, if he had his way, they would be married before he had to return to the ship. He would arrange for her move to his home port. And if he never saw her father again after that, it would be too soon. The sound of the bell marked the end of his watch. After his relief arrived, he started down the passageway toward his berth.

He heard a familiar voice calling his name. Turning, he saw Harold Harns, the crewman who had the berth below him. "John, I told you you ought to go to mail call. You've got mail, buddy."

John quirked his mouth. "I haven't gotten a piece of personal mail since I deployed. Except once, from my mother telling me my grandmother died."

His friend ran his fingers along the edge of the envelope. "Well, this time I hope it's better news."

He took the large manila envelope. "Thanks, Harold."

His heart lurched . . . the return address was Leigh's house. "See you later."

He jogged the rest of the way to the berthing compartment. Jumping into his rack, he drew the curtain and tore open the packet.

Dozens of letters scattered on the mattress. Some still in unopened envelopes, others loose. A single sheet of yellow notebook paper drifted to the blanket. He picked it up.

Mr. Higheagle, my daughter married a good man and moved to Montana. She left these behind.

He read it again, the words not registering.

Married? He felt numb. "Married!" A hard pit formed in his throat. "No." The word tore from his lips.

Cursing, he grabbed letters and loose pages from the bed. His handwriting mocking him. *Leigh, I love you so much . . . I'll be home for you soon . . . I can't live without you.* His own words, uncensored passion direct from his heart. Read by her father and then spit back in his face.

He moaned. *Stupid Indian. Half-breed. Prairie nig.* Racial slurs, resurrected from the ashes of his youth, hissed in his ears. The words became louder and louder, until they awakened a seething self-hatred.

If only he weren't an Indian. If only he were worth something. But the voices raged on with authority—he was who he was and nothing could ever change that.

With trembling hands, he began to open the letters, reading each one, and then crumpling it. Methodically, page by page, he destroyed the professions of love. And the person who wrote them. The hate hardened into resolve. He knew with certainty what he was going to do.

He waited for night to come.

83

To end his life.

And he would have died that night were it not for the ship's chaplain, who had seen him jump. The same chaplain who later met with John and told him how he had not been able to sleep, how a still, small voice had prompted him to rise in the middle of the night, to get dressed and walk the deck . . . how there were no lucky coincidences when one was in the will of God.

He got goose bumps on his arms remembering how the chaplain had taken his hand and prayed for him. Asking Christ to heal his heart. The moment the man touched him, John felt an overwhelming sense of love. It was the first time in his life he'd felt such love. Compassionate and powerful. Accepting him just as he was, asking nothing in return. He'd broken down, sobbing. God loved him. God loved *him*. And for the first time in his life, deep in his heart he'd understood how Christ had suffered on the cross and chosen to die so the world might know His love. Accepting their rejection in exchange for His life. And that understanding had made John whole. He was no longer half Indian or half white. He was wholly God's.

John turned into the drive of his modest country home. That had been a long time ago, but the memory of it never failed to move him deeply. *Praise You, Jesus.*

He parked in the driveway and got out of the car. After picking up the newspaper, he went into the house.

He threw the paper onto the couch. "Sweety?" he called. "Sweetheart."

He listened. Looking around the living room, he could see she'd been rooting through things. He grinned.

84

A huffy grunt came from the direction of the back bedroom. A quick look confirmed she'd decided to take a nap in the pile of blankets that he left on the floor for her.

"Well, did I wake you up?" He squatted and rubbed her belly.

Her shoe-button eyes cut in his direction.

The black-and-white pot-bellied pig had come with the house. The sellers had been moving to Spokane and weren't able to take her with them. It had been love at first sight, and he'd agreed to keep her.

The odd black spot that surrounded her right eye was shaped like a heart, if you tilted your head just the right way. That's how they'd come to name her Sweetheart.

Rising, he took off his jacket and hung it up. Keeping the place clean with a pig as a roommate was a chore. Fortunately, Sarah, the college student who lived across the pasture, loved to help take care of Sweetheart. He'd even put in a gate between their properties and given Sarah a key, in case the back door was accidentally locked, so she could come back and forth whenever she wanted to.

As he made a pot of coffee, his thoughts returned to Leigh.

So much had happened over the years. When his commitment to the Navy was up, he'd moved to Seattle. Leaving everything behind . . . except his memories of Leigh. As the years passed he'd finally married, but the union had ended ten years later when his wife walked out, justifying an extramarital affair by saying she couldn't continue to live with a man who was emotionally absent.

There had been no children, and when the divorce was final, he'd packed his things and moved back to northern Idaho. He'd spent months in the mountains, alone, seeking God, and finally recommitting his life to his Lord and Savior. It was then that he also came to terms with the fact that he was still in love with Leigh Williams. That she had moved on with her life was something he needed to accept . . . and suffer alone. Still, he drew solace from the knowledge that all things were possible with God, and after pouring out his heart in prayer, he released the outcome to Him. It was then he felt God's call to minister to other Indians in the area. He'd taken a job that wasn't demanding and had given priority to spreading the gospel of Jesus Christ. He'd made a decision. He wanted God to take him deeper. And God had.

His gifting was something he'd never shared with anyone. Without fail, whenever God called on him to act, the person would say, "I was praying God would help me, and you just seemed to appear." Or, "I never really believed in God, but I called out to Him and then you were there."

He never embellished their experience with how he had heard God's call. He knew he was but a vessel God used to reveal Himself to others. The focus was to remain on God.

He walked to the far side of the kitchen to his computer area, sat down, waited for the computer to boot up, and typed in the URL for a search engine. A bar popped up. He typed "Leigh Williams Scott," then pressed Enter.

A hodgepodge of links came up. He scanned through them. Nothing looked like a match.

He typed in "Leigh Scott" and clicked.

A new column of links appeared. The first one was www.leighwscott.com. He clicked on it. A picture of Leigh looking straight at him, smiling, filled the screen. His heart lurched.

He leaned forward in his chair. She had hardly changed. Under her picture he read "Author of Inspirational Fiction." A smile tugged at his lips. So God had touched her too.

Settling his hand on the mouse, he scrolled down, reading about her debut book, *First Love*. As he read the blurb, he grinned. The heroine's father had apparently not liked the Irish hero, Patrick McFarland. He pursed his lips. Strange how art imitated life.

Under the blurb about the book, it stated Leigh lived in Cedar Ridge, Idaho, with her son, and cat, Max. He leaned forward, rereading the sentence. Beneath that was another picture of Leigh sitting at a desk. Even after all these years, it was hard to believe that she had just walked away from him.

Staring at the picture, something deep within him stirred. Pain . . . sorrow . . . and something else. A key in a lock.

He quickly moved his eyes to the bottom of the page. There was another link, "Meet Leigh." He clicked on it.

A picture of a book cover showing a young woman, eyes gazing into the distance, popped up. Bold letters across the top spelled *First Love*.

Under the picture in large font, he read "Book Signing, Borders, Cedar Ridge, May 13, 1–4 p.m."

John leaned back in his chair, staring at the date. "Next weekend."

He stood, turned off the coffeepot, and grabbed his coat.

So Leigh lived with her son and her cat . . . and she was looking for him.

He got in his car and headed for the mall in River Falls. There was a bookstore there. He wanted to learn more about this Patrick McFarland. The hero whom the father had chased away.

His foot pressed the accelerator. He wanted to find out if the heroine still loved him.

❧

The hostess led Jeff to a table by the window. He took the seat that gave him a view of the entry to the restaurant.

He'd agreed to meet Jessica at Mama Mia's for dinner. She wanted to tell him about the apartments she'd spent the day checking out. He hadn't told her anything about his conversation with his mother that morning. And he wasn't going to. It would only hurt her and deepen the rift between the two women. But he'd thought about little else.

He loved his mother. She'd always been there for him, supporting him in whatever he wanted to do. And he knew she would this time too, if only she'd give Jessica a chance. But after this morning, it seemed hopeless. He felt like she was making him choose between them. And the more he thought about it, the clearer the choice became. His stomach knotted.

"Two?"

He nodded as the waitress set water and a basket of French bread on the table.

His attention drifted to the view out the window. Jessica was walking toward the entry. She was limping.

Jeff stood and walked to the front of the restaurant, reaching the front door just as she did. Her cheeks were flushed and she was out of breath. He took her arm. "You okay?"

She pulled away and kissed his cheek. "I'm fine, silly. Just too much walking lately. I got a blister on the bottom of my foot."

He led her to the table, pulled out the chair that had the view, and helped her into it. Then he took a seat across from her. "You sure you're okay?"

"I saw two more places this afternoon." She took a piece of bread. "One of them is only a couple of miles from Haven House. I want you to see it."

He looked at his hands. "Jessie, it would be so much easier if you could find something small that you could afford."

Her brows drew together. "There's nothing out there, Jeff. I've looked. I know this isn't the perfect situation." She took a bite of bread, chewed it, and swallowed. "But I don't see anything else we can do right now. Gina's making my life miserable. She wants me out." Her eyes teared up. "I guess I could live in my car until I can find something cheap enough. I've done it before."

Thorny anger pricked him. If only his mother weren't so judgmental. He reached across the table and took her hand. "We'll work it out. Let's order."

As they ate bread and big bowls of pasta, Jessica told him about a position that was opening up on the night shift at Haven House. He would need only to get certified for CPR, first aid, and nurse delegation to be qualified for it. And the job paid ten dollars an hour.

"That's more than I make at Sears. But I don't have any of the training they want."

"Don't worry. They'll train you on-site."

"Really?" Suddenly the job sounded promising. "Ten dollars an hour."

"Yes. If we worked together on that shift, we'd be making twenty dollars an hour between us. That's more than enough to pay the rent *and* save. And you'd still have your Sears job." She affected a grimace. "They really don't like to hire couples because they think if there are problems at home, it'll carry over to work." She waved her hand, dismissing her words. "But that would never happen to us. Besides, when your school starts again, you'd want to drop the job anyway. I say just don't mention we're a couple. It probably won't even come up." Her eyes implored him. "Jeff, we can make it together. I want to be with you. Again."

The word sent a flash of fire through him. He loved her, had waited for her all his life. But this wasn't how it was supposed to be.

Still, he couldn't let her live in her car. Maybe he could take the job at Haven House for the summer and give her the money to pay her rent while he lived at home. Somewhere in his mind a voice suggested his mother would ask where all his money was going, and if he told her, she would insist he stop. It would never work. Besides, he didn't like the idea of misleading Haven House by purposely not mentioning their relationship when he knew Haven House would want to know about it.

The fire in his chest became a yearning. "I don't know what to do right now, Jessie. But the job sounds great. I'll figure something out."

They finished the rest of the meal in silence.

"Dessert?" The waitress looked from one to the other.

Jeff glanced at Jessica.

She shook her head. "No, thanks. I'm not feeling well."

"Just give us our check, please."

The waitress reached in her pocket, totaled up the slip, then laid it on the table and left.

"What's wrong, Jessie?"

"I don't know, I just don't feel good. My head feels heavy."

"Do you think you can drive home?"

"Yeah, I'll be okay. I'm just really tired all of a sudden."

She started to rise, then reached out for the table to steady herself. "I'm dizzy."

Jeff rushed around the table. "Here, sit down." He pulled her chair back.

She sat for a moment, then stood. "Maybe you had better drive me home."

After leaving the money on the table for the waitress, he helped Jessica to his car and opened the passenger door for her.

She grabbed the door. "Jeff, I've got to lie down."

"Go ahead, get in and I'll drop the seat back."

As soon as she was in the car, he moved the lever on the side of the seat, tilting it back.

"I'm going to take you to Urgent Care."

"No." The sharpness in her voice startled him. "Take me to Community Hospital, it's closer."

"Jessie, it isn't closer."

"Just take me to the hospital." Her voice trailed off. "I feel so sick. My legs ache."

"What do you mean?"

"I don't know. They feel kind of prickly."

Jeff put the car in gear and sped toward the hospital.

When they arrived at the emergency room, Jessica was transferred to a wheelchair. The admitting nurse took her insurance information, then directed them to the waiting area.

Jeff stroked her hair. "Feeling any better?"

She shook her head. "I wish they'd hurry up. It always takes so long here."

"Maybe we should have gone to Urgent Care." He grinned at her.

"I owe them money. They would have sent us here anyway."

"What happened?"

"I had to fix my car. I couldn't pay them."

"Jessica Braun." A nurse stood at the door to the exam rooms.

Jeff rose and, pushing Jessica's wheelchair, followed the nurse.

After taking Jessica's vital signs and asking her about the reason for the visit, the nurse left the room. Within a few minutes the doctor came in with a file. After questioning her further about why she had come in and what she'd eaten that day, he called the nurse.

He turned to Jessica. "Your symptoms are nonspecific, but I'm going to run a few blood tests. When I get the results back, I'll be able to make a recommendation."

The nurse drew two vials of blood.

An hour passed before the doctor returned.

He walked through the door and sat down. His face was stern. "Your diabetes is out of control."

"What do you mean?"

"Your blood sugar is over three hundred. You need to see your regular doctor about getting on some medication." He scanned the test results. "I'm going to prescribe some insulin right now, and I'll give you a prescription for some medication to hold you over until you can see your regular doctor."

Jeff leaned forward. "How serious is this?"

"As soon as her blood sugar is back to normal, she can go home."

Jessica put her hand on his arm. "It's going to be okay. One of the clients at work has diabetes, and we monitor her all the time. It's easy to take care of."

Jeff glanced at the doctor.

"Type 2 diabetes is manageable through diet and lifestyle modification. Your regular doctor will give you the information you need." The doctor rose.

Jeff stood and shook the doctor's hand. "Thank you."

As Jeff drove Jessica home, he tried to sort out everything that had happened. He looked at her, her eyes closed, resting peacefully in the seat next to him. Innocent and wounded. Had all of this happened because she couldn't afford the medicine she needed? How had she run up a bill at Urgent Care?

She'd never even told him she had health problems. But then, she wasn't used to asking for help, or getting it. She hadn't had a loving mother like his to help her fight her battles. Instead, she'd been thrown away when she was born, only to find herself placed with families who ridiculed, beat, or raped her.

He reached across the seat and rested his hand on her arm. *I love you, Jessie. You don't have to fight alone anymore.*

As he merged onto the highway, his eyes focused on the long, dark road ahead of him. He'd have to tell his mother. Soon.

7

"Please, have a seat." The property manager motioned to the two chairs facing his desk.

Jeff waited for Jessica to sit, then took the seat next to hers.

"We've run your credit and called your references. Jeff, your credit is excellent."

Jeff took Jessica's hand in his.

The property manager continued. "But you don't have enough income to qualify."

Jessica straightened. "What about my income?"

The manager gave a quick half nod. "We can use it, but the overall profile isn't strong enough." He paused. "If there were some way your credit could be left out of the packet, it would make it a lot easier for me to get this through. But without your income there's no way."

This was the third apartment they'd applied for in as many days. Each time they'd been denied because of Jessica's credit or rental history. Jeff glanced at her. He could see she was fighting to keep her composure. He rubbed the back of her hand with his thumb.

The apartment was only five hundred dollars a month.

The ad had read first month's rent, a security deposit, and a six-month lease. Even though it needed carpet and was in a rough neighborhood, the move-in costs were the cheapest they'd found. And since the money was going to have to come from his savings, he'd really hoped this one would work out. But the way the interview was going, it looked like another dead end.

As subtle as a whisper, an idea occurred to him.

"Sir, do you think we could talk to the owner?"

The property manager looked surprised. "What do you think you could tell him that would make a difference?"

Jeff thought a moment. "What if we gave some kind of extra deposit?"

The property manager waited for him to continue.

"When my mom rented her house, they said no pets. But she talked to them about our cat, and she paid an extra deposit so we could have him."

The manager's face seemed to soften. "Can you come up with an extra month's rent in advance? I mean pay the first month's rent and the next month's too. Plus the security deposit."

Jessica's grip tightened on his hand. That would eat up most of his savings.

He looked at her.

Her lips were slightly parted, her free hand knotted in her lap . . . eyes the color of heaven.

"Yes, I can."

Jessica turned to the property manager. "Does that mean we get the apartment?"

He paused a moment. "I'm not sure. I'll have to talk it over with the owner."

Jeff cleared his throat. "Would you tell him that Jessica had some health problems and medical bills, and that's a big part of the reason she got behind? I'm going to be getting a second job this summer. I give my word. We'll pay the rent on time."

The man gave him a long, appraising look, then spoke. "Wait here. I'll see if I can reach the owner by phone and work something out."

As they waited, Jessica talked excitedly about the prospect of moving in the coming weekend since the place was vacant. "We'll need to get the power turned on right away. We'll need to rent a truck to move our stuff. I get paid tomorrow. We can use that money to get moved."

The property manager returned to the desk. Jeff couldn't read his face at all.

Finally, he spoke. "This is your lucky day. It's a go if you bring me a cashier's check or money order for the total move-in costs and pay with a money order every month."

Jessica clapped her hands. "Yes. We will. We promise."

For a fleeting moment, Jeff felt a sense of panic, like a cold fist closing over him. He ignored it.

"Take this to the front desk." The property manager handed Jeff the file. "They'll figure the prorations and prepare the lease."

"Thank you." Jeff stood. He helped Jessica up.

Limping badly, she leaned on him as they walked to the counter. After the paperwork was completed, Jeff drove Jessica home.

"Are you going to be able to work tonight? You can hardly walk."

"I'll be fine. I'll stay off my foot the rest of the afternoon. I brought some boxes home from work last night, so I can sit on my bed and finish packing until I go in." She took his hand. "I love you, Jeff."

"Love you too." He kissed her lightly. "I've got to run now if I'm going to get to the bank and take the rental place the money before they close. And I want to turn in my application at Haven House."

He helped her into the house, then jogged back to the car. He slipped behind the wheel and started the engine.

As he drove to the bank, the reality of what he was doing hit him. It was no longer just talk about something in the future. Suddenly, it was actually happening. He was going to withdraw the majority of his savings, get a cashier's check, take it to the property management company, and move in with Jessica.

He took a deep breath, then exhaled. He and Jessica had talked about it a lot. It was all going to work out. He was sure of it, or he never would have given his word about paying the rent to the property manager. With two incomes he'd eventually be able to replace his savings. He had only one year of school left and then he'd be able to get a job that would support them.

A little trill of excitement rushed through him. He was going to ask Jessica to marry him. Now. There was no need to wait. She was as committed to him as he was to her. And . . . he hoped it would end the estrangement he'd felt from God since the night he'd slept with her.

His heart began to pound, and his stomach churned. There was only one thing he still had to do.

He had to tell his mother.

∽∾

Leigh had been waiting for an opening all week to talk to Jeff. But there hadn't been any opportunity since the blowup last Sunday. Every day, Jeff had left early, come home late, and gone straight to the basement. During the twenty-one years she'd raised him, they'd rarely had cross words, much less a full-scale argument.

"Thank the Lord it's Thursday, Max. Jeff's never missed our Thursday night dinners." She peeked into the oven and checked the lasagna. "And wait until he finds out what we're having."

Max meowed in agreement, then walked over to his plate and sat down, curling his tail around his front paws.

"He really should have been here by now."

Leigh absently glanced at the clock on the microwave again. It triggered the thought she'd dismissed earlier. What if he didn't come home for dinner? Her eyes drifted to the table. Two places set, salad in the center, no different from a hundred other Thursday nights . . . she wished. Turning, she walked into the family room and sat on the couch.

Every night since last Sunday, she'd lain in bed unable to sleep and thought about all that had happened. She sensed that somehow her son had changed. Besides the obvious fact that he was avoiding her, when they did speak, he was more reserved. His constant smile was gone and his easy manner muted. A subtle reminder that, though Jessica was never in view, she was always present.

Leigh had poured out her heart to the Lord, praying that He would intervene and put a stop to the relationship. And, as she knew she should, she'd prayed for Jessica too. Asking the Lord to work in the young woman's life and reveal the plan He had for her. One she was sure did not involve Jeff.

Tears stung Leigh's eyes. She loved her son so much. She hadn't been able to give him much growing up, but she'd done everything in her power to insure he would be able to make a life better than the one she'd had. And now, with only one year left in college and the promise of a good job, everything seemed to be in jeopardy. She swallowed the fear that rose in her chest, then took a deep, steadying breath and straightened. She wasn't going to let Jeff's dreams slip away.

The sound of the garage door motor caught her attention.

Leigh sprang from the couch. He was home. *Praise You, Lord, for Your faithfulness.* She rushed into the kitchen and opened the oven.

Jeff walked into the room from the back hall. "Smells good."

She set the lasagna on top of the stove. "Wash up, dinner's ready."

As Jeff washed his hands, she put food on the plates and the plates on the table. Then they took their seats.

"Jeff, would you say grace?"

Jeff looked at her. "Would you mind saying it tonight?"

"Sure, honey."

She bowed her head. "Dear Lord, bless our time together and this meal. You are our strength and our salvation. Amen."

She glanced at her son. Jeff was staring at his plate. "Eat. It's one of your favorites."

He took a bite, chewing slowly.

Leigh scooped some salad onto her plate, trying to ignore the flicker of apprehension that coursed through her. "School will be out soon. Have you talked to Sears about giving you some more hours?"

Jeff swallowed. "Uh, no. I've got a lead on another job. It would be full-time, nights."

Leigh frowned. "I hate for you to work nights. You won't have any time during the day to have fun. You work hard all year, you deserve some free time. The church is setting up a mission trip to Mexico again in July. Do you think you'll be able to get the time off?"

"Probably not."

She passed him the salad. "Where is this new job?"

Jeff put down his fork. "Mom, I've got to talk to you about something."

Leigh felt herself stiffen. "Yes?" She put her hands in her lap.

"The job I applied for is at Haven House."

"With Jessica?" The question slipped out. Of course, it was with Jessica. This was just one more way she had come up with to get close to Jeff. One more way to trap him.

Jeff nodded.

She clenched her hands. She needed to stay calm.

Another confrontation would just drive him further from her. He'd always been levelheaded. They could talk this through.

"What would you be doing there? You don't have any training for that kind of work."

"Oh, they train you and it pays ten dollars an hour."

"Well, that will help you build your savings."

Jeff sat back in his chair. "Mom, I took the job to help Jessica get a place to live."

Leigh pressed her lips together, willing herself to remain calm. "How do you figure that would work?"

"I can share rent with her."

The enormity of his words left her gasping for breath. "Exactly what are you saying, Jeff?"

"We rented an apartment. I want to move this weekend."

For a moment she thought she was going to throw up. She gripped the edge of her chair.

His eyes sought hers. "I'm sorry, Mom. I dreaded telling you this."

"If you dread it, don't tell me. Don't do it, Jeff." She searched his eyes for the boy she knew. The steadfast, good boy who was her son. "What's happened to you?"

He blinked rapidly. "Mom, I've thought about it a lot. I love her. I want to be with her."

Leigh swallowed the hard pit in her throat. His voice was pleading, not angry. Maybe there was still some way to save him. "Think. This doesn't make any sense. Why would you throw away everything you've worked for?"

"I'm not throwing anything away. I'm going to finish school and get a job. Nothing's changed. But now Jessica's going to help me."

"Jeff, she can't help you. She can't even help herself. And you can't live with her. It's wrong."

His eyes held hers.

Suddenly, she knew what he was going to say. She looked away.

"I'm going to ask her to marry me."

The words exploded in her ears, fracturing her world.

Suddenly she was but an observer of her own life. Everything she'd believed was brought into question. She'd raised her son in the church; she'd prayed for him daily; she'd faithfully taught him godly principles. But none of that had worked. Instead, it had brought her to this situation, this day, this moment. She desperately searched her mind for a verse, a prayer, something spiritual to say. But wisdom eluded her, and anger took its place.

"Don't marry her, Jeff. That will only make a bad mistake worse."

His mouth dropped open. "How can you say that?"

"I can say it because I know what a bad marriage is."

His face contorted. "What are you talking about? Dad was a good man, a great father."

The pain on her son's face caused her to pause. She was hurting Jeff, just like he was hurting her. She began to tremble. Where had it all gone wrong? She rose.

"Jeff, if you have any respect for me at all, don't do this."

"Mom, it's the right thing to do."

Something in his voice, something about the force of his words. She knew. He'd crossed the line with Jessica and now he felt there was no turning back.

"You *don't* have to marry her. It's not too late to get your life back on track."

Jeff stood. "Don't you understand? I love Jessica. Can't you love her too?"

The simple honesty of his question condemned Leigh. She was a Christian, seeking God's Holy Spirit, reading His Word, asking Him to give her the book of His heart.

"I can love her. But not for you." The next thought came quickly and she gave it voice. "I can see your mind is made up to move in with her. But you don't have to marry her." Her voice cracked, and the tenuous hold she'd had on her composure vanished. "I can accept a lot." She choked the words out. "But don't marry her."

She ran out of the kitchen and up the stairs.

When she reached her bedroom, she closed the door behind her. She leaned against it, then slid to the floor. Wrapping her arms around her knees, she wept.

Deep, racking sobs shook her as sorrow turned to mourning. Their lives would never be the same. Jeff had broken her trust and her heart.

When she finally lifted her head, the room had darkened, evening turning to night. She was cold and alone.

She stared into the silent darkness. The son she had known was dead. And part of her had died with him.

God, why did You allow this to happen?

Jessica lay in her bed, staring at the ceiling. Why did Leigh have to make such a big deal out of Jeff getting his own place? He was twenty-one years old.

When Jeff had called, he'd been so upset about the argument he'd had with his mother that Jessica hadn't been able to bring herself to tell him she wasn't going to work. The blister on the bottom of her foot had started bleeding, and Gina had driven her to the emergency room. The doctor had said that because of her diabetes, she'd have to have a cast on her foot to keep constant pressure on it. And she needed to stay off it for four to six weeks. Thank goodness Jeff had paid the rent two months in advance. She'd be back to work by then, and they could work out some kind of payments with the landlord.

She snuggled under the covers and closed her eyes. Jeff wasn't like any of the other guys she'd lived with. She drew her hands up under her chin, remembering the intense but tender way he'd cradled her.

She turned her face into her pillow, seeking the spot that still held his scent. It stirred a yearning in her heart.

Tears stung her eyes. She squeezed them shut and turned her face back to the ceiling. No one had ever loved her . . . she had never loved anyone.

And she didn't want to.

8

Leigh stood at her bedroom window looking at the pickup parked in her driveway. "Don't go. Please, don't go," she whispered through the window.

She and Jeff had hardly spoken since Thursday night, other than when he'd told her he'd be moving Saturday morning. She'd expected him to ask her about the furniture in the spare bedroom. But he didn't. It was just as well. She didn't know what she would have said. She didn't know anything anymore.

She watched Jeff and a boy she'd never seen before load Jeff's dresser into the back of the truck. At least her son had had the courtesy not to bring Jessica with him.

Dropping her eyes, she walked to her bed and sat. Max appeared beside her, gently rubbing against her. She picked the big cat up and cradled him in her arms. "I don't want him to leave. Not like this, Max."

If only she could run down the stairs and outside and tell him she'd been wrong. That she understood his decision and it was okay.

But she couldn't.

It was against everything she believed, it was wrong on every level . . . and she couldn't give up that ground to Jessica.

She set the cat down and picked up her Bible. Thumbing through the pages, she read a verse here and there, searching desperately for meaning behind the words. But they gave her no comfort.

"Mom?"

She turned at the voice behind her.

"I'm leaving now." Jeff walked over to her.

She clasped her hands on top of her Bible.

Jeff bent down, put his arms around her, and hugged her. "I'm sorry, Mom. This is just something I feel I have to do."

He stood, pausing for a moment. When she didn't speak, he left the room.

Leigh sat listening. Within minutes she heard the truck start.

She ran to the window just as the truck pulled out of the drive. *Come back. Please, come back.* She watched as twenty-one years of her life disappeared down the street.

He was gone.

For a long time she stood at the window. Suddenly she realized she didn't even know where her son lived. Had someone suggested such a thing to her a week ago, she would have laughed.

The phone rang and she quickly ran to her desk. Maybe Jeff had just realized the same thing and was calling to give her his new address. "Hello."

"Good morning, dear."

Her mother.

"You didn't come by yesterday after work."

"I know, Mom. I'm going to come over before I go to my book signing. First I've got to do some writing though."

"Okay. We'll see you then."

Leigh hung up the phone and sat at her desk. She had to tell them. They would be deeply disappointed. Especially her mother, who had overseen the nurturing of Jeff's spiritual life since the day he was born. Fortunately she hadn't let Leigh's indifference to the church in his early years infect her new grandson. And as Jeff grew older, the two had become prayer partners. Something her mother credited for Leigh's salvation. Maybe if she'd committed her life to the Lord earlier, this wouldn't have happened.

Her mother called Jeff's love of the Lord and other people God's secret weapon. Jeff often enlisted his grandmother's prayers for someone he had met who was living on the street or in a shelter and who didn't know God.

Leigh heaved a sigh. Jeff certainly wouldn't be teaching anyone anything about God now. At least, not by the way he lived his life.

Her father would be more philosophical.

Her father.

The mortgage.

She caught her breath as fear swept through her. It had all happened so fast she hadn't thought beyond stopping Jeff from leaving.

What if he couldn't repay the loan she'd arranged for

him? What if he didn't finish school and get the job in River Falls? Dozens of scenarios crowded into her mind. All of them with disastrous consequences for her and her parents.

She looked at the blank computer screen. She'd already received half of the small advance for her second book. The only other possible source of income would be from coming up with a book proposal that really wowed Paramount Publishers.

Her shoulders slumped. That was a complete unknown at this point and would be for months. Not to mention she didn't have any ideas for a new book. She sighed. Maybe she'd have to give up her dream of writing and get a second job. If that's what it took to make sure the payments were made on her parents' house, she'd have to do it. She wiggled the mouse. Surely Jeff wouldn't do that to her. He knew he owed the money.

The paragraph she was working on popped up on the screen. It was dialogue in a light, funny scene. She stared at the words, her mind blank.

Scrolling back a few pages, she found the beginning of the chapter and reread it, trying to capture the mood she'd set up. The words seemed wooden and trite. She spent the next hour trying to think as her sassy, smart heroine, but the crisis in her own life kept intruding. Finally, she gave up and turned her attention to what was really on her mind.

She dressed quickly for her book signing, then headed to her parents' house.

When her knock on their front door went unanswered, she opened it. She could hear their voices in the family room. As she walked to the back of the house, she called out, letting them know she'd arrived.

Her father was in his favorite chair, reading the paper. Her mother stood by the couch with a laundry basket next to her feet, folding clothes.

"Hi, honey. I didn't expect you so soon," her mother said.

Leigh patted her mother's back as she stepped around her and sat on the other end of the couch. "I had a little extra time and I thought I'd spend it with you."

Her father dropped his paper and looked at her.

"How you feeling, Dad?"

"I'm finally getting my strength back after that last round of chemo."

Her mother rolled a pair of socks into a ball. "Dr. Lang is really pleased with his progress."

"When do you have to go—"

Her father's voice cut in. "Your brother called last night. He's moving back."

Leigh leaned forward. "R.J.'s moving back here?"

"Well, no. But at least he won't be way out in the middle of the Pacific. He's moving to Newport Beach." The excitement in her father's voice was obvious. "Has a lead on a job, he said. Acting."

Leigh and her mother exchanged glances.

"Said they were filming a movie over there on the big island, and he met some director at a party and . . . well, I guess one thing led to another." Her father clucked his tongue. "That boy is something else. Naturally gifted. I have a feeling we might be seeing him on the big screen."

Her mother snapped a pair of pants in front of her. "I wish he was just a little more responsible." She folded them in half. "Like Jeff." She looked at Leigh. "You've done a good job with that boy. We're so proud of him."

Leigh looked at her hands.

"Mom and Dad, I need to tell you something."

Her mother's hands dropped to her sides. Her father closed the paper.

"Jeff moved out this morning. He got his own place."

"Well, well." Her father chuckled. "Good for him. It's about time that boy got out on his own."

"There's more to it."

Her mother pushed the clothes basket to the side and sat on the edge of the couch. "What do you mean?"

"He moved in with a girl."

Her mother knitted her brows. "Lots of boys and girls share apartments these days. They have to, to make ends meet."

God bless her mother, she loved her grandson. "It wasn't that kind of arrangement. It was with Jessica."

"That's the girl he told us about." Her father straightened in his chair, looking pleased. "I knew it. I told you I thought he was sweet on her."

"Dad, she isn't a nice girl. She's had all kinds of problems."

"Like what?"

"She dropped out of high school, she's gone from one foster home to another, she hardly makes enough money to survive. She doesn't even have a permanent address."

Her father grinned. "Well, she does now."

"Dad, how can you be so glib? It's immoral."

"Oh, Leigh, stop it. The way you're acting you'd think he was playing house with a man. Now that would be immoral. He's a nice young boy and he's just feeling his oats. I'm sure R.J.'s lived with a woman or two along the way. The only difference is, he probably kept it from us for your mother's sake."

Her mother reached across the couch and patted Leigh's arm. "I'm sorry, honey. This *is* disappointing and upsetting. Maybe I can talk to him."

"Believe me, I tried. It's too late, Mom."

Neither one of her parents were grasping all the possible implications of Jeff's move. And she saw no need to alarm them. Somehow her father's words had taken the razor edge off the situation. Maybe she was just borrowing trouble and things were going to work out.

Leigh turned to her mother. "I need your prayers."

Her father picked up the paper and shook it out. "Nonsense."

Leigh rose. "I've got to run. I want to get a bite to eat before I go to Borders."

Her mother stood and walked with her to the door, then hugged her. "I understand completely how you feel." She paused. "He is going to finish school, isn't he?"

The concern on her mother's face told Leigh the loan on the house hadn't been overlooked.

Leigh wanted to break down and pour out her fears, but what good would it do to have two people despairing over a situation they couldn't control? Instead, she smiled. "Of course he will."

She kissed her mother on the cheek and left.

After stopping at Safeway and buying a deli sandwich and drink, she returned to her car. As she sat eating her lunch, she watched the people going in and out of the store. An elderly couple, a man with two children . . . a young mother holding the hand of a little boy.

Leigh put her sandwich down and watched the mother and child disappear into the building. The image transported her through a hundred walks to the grocery store, holding the hand of a little boy.

She sat silently for a few moments, then dropped her sandwich back into the bag, started the car, and pulled out onto the main road. She drove aimlessly, struggling to breathe through the vise of loneliness and loss that squeezed her chest.

As the road took her away from the store, she found the streets becoming familiar. She turned right at a yellow house with the swings in the front yard, left at a big, two-story Victorian, and then left at a playground.

She pulled into the empty parking lot of the elementary school Jeff had attended. She stopped the car and got out.

Her eyes drifted to the spot by the entry where her son used to stand when she came to pick him up. "The Winner's Circle." She'd devised a name and a reward to encourage him to remember, to focus, and it had worked. Every afternoon, with a grin from ear to ear, he'd watched for her, managing to keep at least a part of one foot in the circle.

For one heartbreaking moment she saw him there.

She turned away, wandering toward the playground. As she approached the chain-link fence, she saw the gate

113

was locked. Shut out, she walked the perimeter, stopping near the jungle gym and slide, then slowly moving on to stand under the trees that arched over the fence toward the lunch area. Finally, she circled back around to the front of the school to the spot where she used to pick up Jeff. She stepped into it.

Closing her eyes, she slowly extended the fingers of her right hand. With tears coursing down her cheeks, she allowed herself the memory of a little hand slipping into hers. And with it, the innocent, sweet, pure promise of a life yet to be lived.

She closed her fingers around the promise. Clinging to it.

How many times had he said he wanted to live his life to bring glory to God? She remembered the first time he told her. He'd just returned from a church camp, on fire for the Lord. "Mom, I'm a warrior in Christ's army."

She wiped the tears from her eyes.

If so, the Enemy was winning.

⟨∾⟩

John Higheagle backed his Ford pickup into one of the empty spaces across the parking lot from Borders. He turned off the engine and settled back in his seat. A glance at the dash told him it was 3:30.

He reached across the cab and picked up the copy of *First Love* lying on the passenger's seat. He'd bought it and read it the same night.

A grin tugged at his lips. Leigh's heroine was deeply in love with the Irish rebel. And the young woman didn't whisper a single word of affection that he himself had not heard when he'd held Leigh in his arms. He shifted in his seat. Even after twenty-five years it took little reflection to bring those memories back to life.

He laid the book back down. Maybe he was finally going to get an explanation from her. Maybe this was the reason she wanted to get in touch with him, to tell him why she'd walked away. And he had to admit, after reading the book and thinking things through, he'd allowed himself to consider the possibility that she wanted to clear the air because she still had feelings for him. *Praise You, Jesus. You know my heart.*

He looked at the clock. 3:45. It was time to go to the book signing. He craned his neck to check his hair in the rearview mirror. Satisfied, he pulled the keys from the ignition.

He stepped out of the truck and took a deep breath, then walked across the lot and into the store. Immediately to his right was a sign with an arrow and the words Featured Author.

Instead of following the arrow, he circled around in the opposite direction, through the coffee shop, scanning the store for the "Featured Author," finally catching a glimpse of the table, and the woman sitting at it. Even from the back, there was no doubt it was Leigh. His heart began to pound.

He slowed his steps and positioned himself at the end of a long, tall shelf displaying cookbooks. Then tilted his head to the left, bringing her into full view.

She absently brushed her hair away from her face.

A wave of emotion hit him. Love, anger, joy, despair.

He was standing in the shadows of her father's yard, waiting for her.

A smoky voice whispered to him. *Loser. Half-breed.* Tears stung his eyes.

He clenched his teeth and gave his head a quick shake, shocked by what he was feeling. That life was dead and buried. He knew who he was in Christ. And God had favored him mightily.

His eyes returned to Leigh. She was beginning to stack the books, preparing to leave. He took a deep breath and stepped into the aisle. *Here we go, Lord.*

She didn't see him approach the table, so he stood silently waiting for her to look up. For an instant, bittersweet and poignant, the naive young love he'd once felt for her returned as an ache in his heart. He pushed it away. *Slow down, buddy.*

She raised her head and their eyes met.

He heard her catch her breath, then her lips parted, forming a silent *O*. "I'd like to buy a book."

"Johnny!" She rose.

He winked at her. "Heard you were looking for me."

She didn't speak as color rushed to her cheeks.

Suddenly, he was enjoying himself immensely.

She started to extend her arm, then dropped it by her side, then lifted it again.

Stifling a chuckle, he reached out and shook her hand. "You're looking good. How are you?"

Her hand dropped to her side and she stepped back. "I'm . . . I'm fine." She fingered the top button of her blouse as a broad grin worked its way across her face. "How are you?"

He nodded. "Good." *Better than I've been in a long time.*

They stood in silence looking at each other.

The nearness of her brought heat to his cheeks. "Did you sell some books today?"

Leigh looked at the stack on the table. "A few."

"Well, I want one." He picked up a book from the display. Turning it over, he read the back of it. "Sounds real interesting."

Leigh sat behind the table. "Let me sign it for you."

He glanced at the stacked books. "Looks like you were getting ready to leave. Why don't you finish up? I'll go pay for this and meet you in the coffee sh—"

"Okay." She held her hand out for the book.

"I was going to say, as soon as you finish up, I'll meet you in the coffee shop, and you can sign it there."

She snapped her empty hand back to her side. "Oh, of course. Fine. Yes. Um, I'll meet you over there in a few minutes."

As he walked to the cash register to pay for the book, he smiled to himself. It couldn't have been more obvious. She wanted to make amends with him. She was as nervous as could be about it.

He'd make it as easy for her as possible.

⚬⚭⚬

Leigh leaned toward the bathroom mirror and applied her lipstick. So Johnny had found out she was trying to find him . . . and he'd decided to make sure she did.

She smoothed the lip color with her finger. Surely he wouldn't have made a point of coming to meet her for

117

no reason. It had to be that he wanted to clear the air and explain why he'd left her. She took a paper towel and rubbed the lipstick off her fingertip. Maybe his relationship with his sweetheart wasn't as serious as she had assumed.

She didn't dare let herself dwell on that thought. Dealing with the loss of Jeff was more than enough to handle right now. She wasn't about to set herself up for more heartache.

Stepping back, she gave herself a final, quick inspection, then rushed out the door, hurrying to the coffee shop.

Johnny was waiting for her at the counter. They each ordered a Coke, then seated themselves at a table.

Now, sitting just a few feet from him, she suddenly realized she'd hardly thought about what she would say if they met. She stole a glance at his left hand. He wasn't wearing a ring.

She looked at him and immediately realized he'd seen her looking at his hand. Unwelcome heat crept into her cheeks. "I saw your picture in the paper."

"That's what I heard."

So it *was* her visit to River Falls that had brought him here. "That was a great thing you did. Saving those two women."

"Just lucky I happened to be there."

She studied his face. He seemed so different from the tough, angry kid she'd fallen in love with. He was relaxed and had a quiet confidence about him. But more than that, it was his eyes. The rage that had always simmered there was gone.

"Have you heard how they're doing?"

He fingered his straw. "Nothing new. I understand they're recovering though. When did you start writing?"

"I committed my life to God about ten years ago. It was shortly after that that I began to feel He was calling me to write. I started taking some classes, volunteered for the church newsletter, and finally decided to try writing a novel. I have to say, God's blessed my socks off. I got an agent and a contract for two books."

Johnny slowly nodded. "Yep, He can be pretty awesome, all right. Where do you go to church?"

She lowered her head and took a sip of her Coke. So Johnny Higheagle was a believer. That explained a lot. "We go to Grace Bible here in Cedar Ridge. How about you?"

"We?" His voice went up an octave.

Leigh hesitated. The natural reference to Jeff now felt awkward. "My son and I."

"How old is he?"

"Twenty-one. How about you, do you have children?"

He shook his head.

She waited for him to continue, but he didn't. Instead he turned the conversation back to her, and she found herself telling him about her job as a real estate assistant. She kept trying to create some kind of a segue to make it easier for him to bring up their unresolved past. But all that brought about was a casual comment that he hoped her parents were in good health.

"Leigh?" His voice was tentative.

Finally. She watched his face. He seemed to be choosing his words carefully.

"Would you like to go to church with me tomorrow?"

"Church?" That was the last thing she'd expected him to say. "What about your girlfriend?" She couldn't believe how she'd blurted out the words.

"Girlfriend?" He looked as surprised as she felt. "What are you talking about?"

"Your sweetheart. The guy at White Water Ford told me you had a sweetheart."

At first his face was blank. Then slowly his expression became mischievous. "Oh. So you know about her."

"Yes, I do. Were you planning on taking both of us?" She grabbed her purse.

"Whoa. Wait a minute." He reached across the table and put his hand on her arm. "Trust me, she doesn't like to go to church. She won't mind one bit if I go with you. In fact, if you like, after church I'll take you home and introduce you to her."

She saw the twinkle in his eye. So, this was some kind of a private joke. Well, she was game. "What time does church start?"

"It's called His Place and it starts at ten. Should I pick you up?"

She arched her eyebrows. "I think I'll meet you there, if you don't mind."

After he gave her directions, they rose.

He walked her to her car and opened her door. "I'll see you tomorrow."

"Ten o'clock." She closed the car door and waved at him through the window.

As she drove home she reflected on the time they'd spent together. It had to be difficult for him to own up to what he'd done to her, but she'd really expected him to try to clear the air right away. If he didn't bring it up tomorrow, then she would.

Leigh turned onto her street. As she approached the dark house and the empty driveway, Jeff's absence held a fresh sting.

She'd never involved herself with outside activities, or made close friends. For the past ten years, her life had revolved around caring for her sick husband, raising her son, and, more recently, concentrating on her writing, caring for her parents, and trying to make ends meet. Since becoming a Christian, she'd always tried to do what was right, and she'd believed God would honor that. But somehow it hadn't worked out that way.

Leigh pulled the car into the garage and turned off the ignition. Dropping her hands into her lap, she sat staring into the darkness. She dreaded going into the house.

Why did God seem so distant when she needed Him most?

She pulled the keys from the ignition and stepped out of the car, her thoughts returning to Johnny. For just a moment she allowed herself to remember what they'd had together so many years ago.

Just the two of them against the world.

What a lucky coincidence she'd seen his picture in the paper.

9

John slowed his truck, looking in the rearview mirror to make sure he hadn't lost Leigh at the final turn onto the country road that led to his home. As her car came into sight, he stepped on the gas.

Seeing Leigh yesterday had only confirmed that she was the one God had intended for him. It had rekindled hope in his heart . . . and more.

He'd spent most of the night trying to ignore it, afraid to believe it, and finally surrendering to it. He still loved her.

He'd risen before dawn and hiked through the trees that bordered his five-acre property, finally emerging into a clearing on the ridge. It was the place he went every morning, whether the heat of summer or the biting cold of winter, to meet with the Lord. The magnificent, pristine views of the pine-covered mountains were like a gateway to heaven. The land God had given his tribe. Sometimes the time he spent there was so intimate and so profound that he felt like he was standing on holy ground. And today, as certain as the sunrise that had begun, the Lord had been waiting for him.

He knelt, and as he always did before prayer, he worshiped God. At times singing, at times just sitting quietly. Then he prayed what he believed to be God's will, asking God to use him to spread the gospel of Christ and His message of unconditional love.

When he finished he sat quietly again, thoughts of Leigh filling his mind, and his heart, knowing he would be seeing her again in a few hours. Excitement winged through his chest. *Leigh.*

Turning his face to the cloudless blue sky, he closed his eyes, and for just a moment allowed himself to imagine what it would feel like to hold Leigh in his arms. Did he dare to dream again?

Silently, willfully, he released the outcome to God. Then he rose, at peace, and headed back down the mountain to dress for church.

John's thoughts returned to the present as he pulled in front of his garage. Leigh pulled in next to him.

They got out of their vehicles and walked together to the front porch. It was all he could do not to take her hand in his. He stopped at the front door and turned to her.

"Ready to meet my Sweetheart?" He couldn't stop himself from smiling.

Leigh straightened. Holding her purse primly at her waist, she said, "I'm ready if she is."

John opened the door and Leigh followed him into the living room. He could see her trying to look right and left without moving her head.

"Sweetheart," he yelled.

The familiar grunt came from down the hall.

Leigh's eyes widened.

"Sweetheart," he yelled again. "She's probably still in bed. She's kind of a pig."

Leigh looked at him with stunned horror.

He burst out laughing.

Just then scratchy clicks and clacks sounded in the planked hall, and Sweetheart emerged, her ears forward, her little piggy nose up in the air, and her bright eyes turned toward Leigh.

Leigh's hand flew to her chest. "Oh, she's adorable."

She squatted down as Sweetheart moved toward her.

"Scratch her behind her ears." He caught the scent of Leigh's perfume as he knelt beside her.

Leigh rubbed the pig behind her ears, and giggled when Sweetheart flopped over on her side.

"She wants you to rub her tummy."

Leigh obliged her.

So near Leigh . . . alone in the house . . .

John rose. "Can I get you something to drink? Tea, coffee, Coke?"

"She's just darling." Leigh stood. "Do you have Diet Coke?"

"Sure do. Why don't you put your purse down and go sit out on the porch? I'll be right there."

He watched as she stepped through the front door, then spun on his heel and went to the kitchen. After fixing their drinks, he joined her outside.

She took the glass from his hand. "Do I hear water?"

John nodded toward the side of the property. "There's a year-round creek down there." He took a sip of his Coke. "Would you like to see it?"

She paused. "Johnny, first I feel like we need to talk about something." Her face clouded over. "I think you know what it is."

He nodded slowly. "I figured that's why you were looking for me." He waited patiently for her to continue, wanting to know why she'd left him. But more than that, he wanted to forgive her.

Leigh set her glass down by her chair. "Go ahead."

He leaned forward. "Go ahead and what?"

"Go ahead and tell me why you walked out of my life." Her lips were set in a firm line.

He drew back. "What are you talking about?" Mixed feelings surged through him. "I sent you my new address as soon as I returned from leave and found out my home port wasn't going to be in Bremerton. And when you didn't write back, I still wrote to you for months."

She blinked slowly, her expression blank.

"One afternoon, out in the middle of the ocean, I got a package from your father." He could hear the anger in his own voice. "It was filled with my letters. Even the ones you opened."

Leigh's face was ashen. "I never received a single letter from you, much less opened one."

John stared at her as the pieces fell into place.

He felt like he was breathing through mud. Twenty-five years of deception. Her father had destroyed his dreams and changed the course of his life. A scab torn off a wound.

Anger rose in his belly.

John hated him for it.

He rose and strode off the porch, not trusting himself

to speak. Breathing heavily he kept walking, down the hillside and across the stream. Blind to everything except his pain and the smoky voice that whispered.

Stupid Indian. Half-breed.

❧

More than an hour had passed when Leigh saw John in the distance.

The minute he'd spoken, she knew it was the truth. She felt overwhelmed by the enormity of what her father had done and all the grief it had spawned. And what had her mother known? Had she kept his secret all this time?

Leigh stepped off the porch and began to walk toward Johnny. As she neared him, she broke into a run. "I'm so sorry."

Looking up, he stopped, waiting for her. Lips pressed into a firm line, jaw clenched, he wrapped his arms around her and drew her into his chest.

She could hear the hard beat of his heart. "Can you forgive me?"

A few moments passed, then he leaned back from her and smoothed her hair. "It wasn't your fault."

Her eyes sought his, but he turned his face from her and pulled her back into his arms, holding her so tightly she could hardly breathe.

Finally, he slowly released his grip on her. Then without speaking, he took her hand and they walked back to the house.

When they reached the porch, he sat on the step, pulling her down next to him. With her hand in his lap and his eyes cast down, he spoke. "I just can't believe it."

His voice became husky. "When he sent me my letters, he wrote you'd married and moved to Montana. When I finally got back here, I found out it was true. That's when I accepted the whole story. I never looked for you again."

His pain, interlocked with her past, stirred her own memories. Devastated by his rejection, she'd set out to find a husband, finally landing a handsome, smooth-talking man. And all the trouble that came with it. A voice from the past whispered to her, *If a half-breed Indian doesn't want you, who will?* Shame colored her cheeks. It had *all* been a lie. She squeezed his hand. "I'm sorry."

"Your father's the one who should be sorry." He raised his eyes to hers.

Thank God he couldn't read her thoughts. "He's been very ill."

Johnny's gaze didn't waver.

"He had colon cancer. He's been through chemo for months, though, right now, his prognosis is good."

Johnny released his grip on her hand and rubbed his palms on his jeans. Stretching up, he inhaled deeply, then released a long sigh. He rested his forearms on his thighs and let his eyes wander to the distant mountains.

Leigh sat silently.

Finally he spoke.

"It's over. It happened a long time ago and what's done is done." He gave her a weak smile. "I'm glad you're here."

"Johnny, it isn't that simple to me. It's not something I can just forget about. I see him every day. How do you think I'm going to feel now, knowing what he did?"

127

"That's the *only* difference between today and yesterday." His voice was gentle. "Now you know."

"It changes everything. I spend time with my parents every day, and I have to see him and talk to him."

Johnny turned toward her, his knee touching hers. "Leigh, I go to God every day, and He knows everything about me. Every wrong thought, every sin. And He not only sees me and talks to me, He welcomes me."

Leigh felt tears sting her eyes, his quiet reprimand hitting home.

"I feel so confused. Not just about this, but everything in my life." A sense of lonely desperation rose in her heart as snapshots of the previous morning replayed in her mind. Watching Jeff load the truck—seeing him drive away—walking the perimeter of the school yard.

Looking away, she took a steadying breath.

His fingers gently rubbed her back, his hand moving in a circular motion. "Do you want to talk about it?"

Oh, yes. Yes . . .

"No." It wasn't fair to burden him with her problems.

"I understand." His voice was gentle. "Tell me about your writing. I didn't know you liked to write."

The reference to their shared past rekindled a sweet familiarity, a balm on raw emotions. His arm slipped across her shoulders.

She leaned into him, resting quietly for a moment. "I feel it's something God's called me to do. He's opened so many doors for me. An agent, a contract for two books."

She straightened and turned to him. "And one of the biggest publishers of inspirational fiction, Paramount, has asked me to write a proposal for a third book. Having them behind me could really launch my career."

His face broke into a broad smile. "Wow. That's great."

"Well, it is and it isn't." She hesitated. "I mean, of course it is. But I have no idea what that book should be about. It's a complete departure from my first two books." A twinge of excitement pinched her. "I feel like God's moving me to the next level, but somehow . . . I don't know . . ."

Pausing, she clasped her hands in her lap. Would he think she was crazy if she told him she'd been asking God to reveal the book of His heart, and she thought the Holy Spirit would be His messenger? Did he even believe in signs and wonders, the awesome power of the Holy Spirit? The Gift.

"I'm hoping the Holy Spirit will show me the book of God's heart." She grimaced. "Do you think that sounds crazy? I mean, the Bible says God speaks to His people. I think He does today, just like He did then. Don't you?"

John took her hand into his, his eyes filled with a tenderness and peace so sweet she lowered her gaze. "I don't think that sounds crazy at all, Leigh. God's calling you to a deeper walk with Him."

"Oh, Johnny, do you think so?" His words sent a flurry of anticipation through her. "Well, Paramount won't be asking for it until after my second book is turned in, which will be September. I hope God shows me something by then."

John squeezed her hand. "He will."

"Hey." She poked him. "I didn't sign your book yesterday."

His shoulders relaxed, and he grinned. "That's right." He rose. "Come on. It's in the house."

She stood and stretched. "I probably should be heading home after that. It's a little bit of a drive and the mountain roads can be tricky enough in daylight."

She followed him into the living room, and he disappeared toward the back of the house.

Sweetheart scampered out of the kitchen. Spotting Leigh, she gave her a snooty look, then marched down the hall after John.

As Leigh waited for him to return, she glanced around the room. Well-worn, but comfortable-looking furniture sat on shiny hardwood floors. A short bookcase, filled with books, took up one wall. She walked over to it.

The whole top shelf held Bibles. Two King James versions, a Living Translation, a New American Standard, a study Bible. They looked as if they'd been used often.

On the next shelf there was a *Strong's Exhaustive Concordance* and several small books, all by an author named Nee. Mixed among them were books on prayer and the Holy Spirit.

She raised her eyebrows. There was a lot more to John Higheagle's faith than going to church on Sunday.

She heard his footsteps in the hallway and stepped to the center of the room.

"Here you go." He held out the book and a pen.

Leigh stepped over to the couch and sat on the edge

130

of the frame. Opening the book to the title page, she balanced it on her lap.

She tapped the pen on her chin. *To Johnny . . . to a dear friend . . .* She glanced at him.

His eyes sparkled and he grinned mischievously.

"Why don't you put, 'To Patrick McFarland'?"

At the mention of the character in *First Love* a shock wave zigzagged through her. He'd read the book. Was he saying he'd seen through her writing and guessed the truth about the Irish hero? She felt heat rushing to her cheeks.

She put her head down and scribbled *To Johnny—Best Wishes, Leigh.*

She closed the cover of the book and handed it to him. Grabbing her purse, she stood. "Well, I'd better be going."

Leigh headed for the door with quick, self-conscious strides, tripping over one of Sweetheart's blankets on the way.

He reached out to catch her and she found herself lifted in his arms, his clear, dark eyes inches from hers, observant and magnetic.

He was smiling ear to ear. "What's your hurry?"

Her knees felt weak as the sweet familiarity she'd felt on the porch sparked to something more. She pushed against his chest and he released her.

"It's getting late, and I need to start home."

He opened the door and stepped to the side. "Let me walk you to your car."

When they reached the car, he touched her arm. "I'd like to see you again."

Things were happening too fast. He'd as much as said he knew she was still in love with him when she wrote the book. She looked down.

He put his finger under her chin and gently lifted it. "I'd like to see you again." He tilted his head, looking at her, his face contrite.

Frowning, she stepped away from him. She ought to just leave and make him worry.

But then he smiled at her.

Maybe not.

Leigh opened her purse. Taking out one of her author cards, she handed it to him. "I'd like that too."

He took the card from her and helped her into the car. "Drive carefully."

Leigh watched him in her rearview mirror as she drove away, her mind spinning. She rolled her eyes. How embarrassing.

He was a very different person from the angry, troubled boy she'd known. Now he was kind, considerate, and apparently quite sure of himself.

Her thoughts returned to her father and what he'd done. Maybe Johnny could just put it behind him, but she couldn't. It was unforgivable, and she was going to confront him. She looked at her watch, angry tears filling her eyes. It was early enough to go to their house now.

She drummed her fingers on the steering wheel. No, she would wait. Things felt too raw right now. She would take the time to think things through, and when she talked to him it would be on her terms, at the time of her choosing.

He'd had no business interfering in her relationship with Johnny. Johnny was the one she'd wanted to marry. Her father should have stayed out of it.

She wiped her eyes with the back of her hand. She'd think about it later. She was just glad they'd reconnected. Better late than never. Johnny had a deep interest in the Lord and the Holy Spirit. She wanted to talk to him more about that . . . and the story that eluded her.

Slowly shaking her head, she marveled at how it had all happened. Seeing his picture in the paper, then the TV interview, then Johnny finding out she was looking for him. It was almost as if God had orchestrated it.

For the first time in a long time she felt special.

Lucky.

❧

John sat on the porch step, his chin cupped in his hand, gazing into the night sky.

Leigh confiding in him how she was seeking the Holy Ghost had touched his spirit. God was going to use her writing in a mighty way. He could feel it.

And he felt something else. A growing conviction about why God had brought Leigh back into his life. He was to pray for her.

He bowed his head. "Lord, prosper what You have begun in Leigh's heart. Use her writing to spread the love of Christ and take ground for Your kingdom."

A tremor passed through him as the Spirit showed him more. God knew the end from the beginning.

Deep concern rose in his chest as divine certainty filled him.

There were no lucky coincidences when one was in the will of God . . . or the will of the Enemy.

But it took the wisdom of the Holy Spirit to know the difference.

10

Jeff couldn't believe he'd actually dozed off in his first class of the morning. Finals were next week and this week was critical for review and study. He released a deep sigh as he turned from Fourteenth Street into the parking lot of his and Jessica's apartment.

Moving had been exhausting. Not only had he moved himself, but he'd moved Jessica too. With her leg in a cast and unable to manage her crutches, she hadn't been able to help at all. He'd even had to finish her packing. Then her car had broken down again as they were making the last haul to their new place. It had died, and when he couldn't get it started, he'd ended up pushing it into their carport. He was pretty sure it was the starter.

His cell phone began vibrating in his jacket pocket. Retrieving it, he flipped it open. "Hello?"

"This is Betty Lundgren at Haven House. Is this Jeff Scott?"

The job application. "Yes."

"We'd like to schedule an interview with you."

He tightened his grip on the phone. "Great. When?"

"When are you available?"

"Any afternoon this week." He pulled into the unassigned parking space nearest the apartment and turned off the car.

"How about one o'clock today?"

That was in an hour and a half. "I'll be there."

She gave him the directions and he hung up.

Wait till Jessica heard. Grabbing his backpack, he jumped out of the car, jogged across the parking lot, and dashed up the stairs to their unit. He burst through the door.

Jessica started, grabbing the arm of her chair. "What's wrong?"

He dropped his book bag on the floor and took two big steps across the room, dropping to his knees in front of her. He folded his arms over her lap. "Nothing's wrong. Haven House just called me for a job interview and I've got an appointment at one."

Her face broke into a wide smile. "What perfect timing. You're out of school next week, aren't you?"

"Yep, as soon as I take my finals." It was true, the timing couldn't have been better. Maybe God was going to give him grace. A little twinge of guilt pricked him. He hadn't really spoken to God much since he'd left home.

Jessica put her arms around his neck and kissed him. "Why don't you take a nap? I'll wake you up at twelve thirty."

"I wish I could, but I've got to study."

"Oh, stay with me." She stuck out her lower lip in a mock pout. "Stretch out right there on the couch and rest. You can study later."

He looked at the mattress and box springs pushed

136

against one wall of the small living room. With the bedspread draped over it and the decorative pillows that had been scattered on Jessica's bed lined up like a cushion back, it did look inviting.

He turned back to her. "I really need to study."

"You can study later. How much could you get done in an hour, anyway? You'd just get started, and it would be time to leave."

That was true.

Jessica pointed the remote at the television. "I'll turn this down and you rest."

He eyed the couch again. He'd been fighting sleep all morning. Maybe this would let him catch up so he could study late.

"You win." He took her face in his hands and kissed her lightly, then crawled the few feet to the mattress and rolled onto it.

Jessica woke him at twelve thirty. He quickly washed his face and combed his hair. After giving her a kiss good-bye, he bounded out the door.

Jessica's voice followed him. "Remember, don't mention we're a couple."

Her warning slowed his steps. By the time he got to his car, he'd decided it probably wouldn't come up. If it did, he'd deal with it then.

As Jeff drove to the job interview, he found himself thinking of his mother. He hated having this rift between them. He understood his mother's disappointment in how things had worked out, but it was only temporary. He and Jessica would be getting married soon. Then his mother would see that he and Jessica loved each other. They would earn her respect as they built their life together. And someday they would have children. He smiled. The thought of having a little boy or little girl of his own gave him goose bumps.

Jessica getting laid up for a month was something they hadn't planned on. But if he could land this job, it would solve that problem. He could start working as soon as finals were over. Then when Jessica went back to work they could start saving and replace the money he'd taken from his account. Their only big expense was rent. No car payments, no credit cards. They could make it if they were careful with their spending.

Right now he needed to get school behind him and get some money coming in. His grades had slipped a little over the past month, but he would be able to bring them back up by doing well on his finals.

He smiled. That's what he'd do. He'd wait to get his grades, then he'd visit his mom and tell her about them and his full-time job. That would prove to her that everything was going to work out. His mother would see that he and Jessica were a team. He took his foot off the accelerator, watching the street signs for the turn to the Haven House office.

Jeff located the company's business office on one side of a well-maintained four-plex. He parked the car, went in, and introduced himself to the woman sitting at a desk in a reception area.

She gestured to a row of chairs. "Take a seat. I'll tell Betty you're here."

Before he could pick up a magazine, his name was called.

A small, gray-haired woman with glasses approached him, her hand extended. "Good afternoon. I'm Betty."

The firmness of her grip surprised him. "I'm Jeff Scott."

"Come with me."

Jeff followed her to a bedroom that had been converted to an office. He sat in a chair across from her as she seated herself behind a desk.

"It looks like you'll need some training."

Her warm smile immediately put him at ease. "I will. But I'm a quick learner."

"Yes, I see you're a student. What's your major?"

"Computer sciences."

"That's a wonderful field for a young man." She gestured to the computer on her desk. "We have a small network here. We seldom have problems with it, but if we do, maybe you could take a look at it?"

Jeff hitched his chair closer to the desk. "Sure."

This *was* God's grace. Who would have guessed this interview could lead to computer work? God knew. God always knew the end from the beginning.

"This is a full-time position. Are you planning to work this job when you're back in school?"

That wasn't the way he and Jessica had planned it, but if he said no, they might not hire him at all, and then there'd be no chance for the computer work. "I hope to." With Jessica laid up they really needed the money right now. He licked his lips. "I plan to."

She made a mark on his application. "How familiar are you with what we do here?"

Jessica's warning echoed in his mind.

139

He thought a moment. He really knew nothing about Haven House firsthand . . . other than what he'd seen that one night he'd helped Jessica. "Not too much."

Betty folded her hands in front of her. "Well, most of our clients are developmentally delayed. Some have Down syndrome, others have autism. And there are various levels of functionality from one individual to the next."

Jeff nodded.

"Some of the individuals you will be caring for are incontinent. You'll be expected to maintain their health and safety. Do you think that will bother you?"

He shifted back in his chair. "No."

He hoped.

"You'll also be required to routinely lift people weighing over one hundred pounds." Smile lines wrinkled around her eyes. "It doesn't look to me like you'll have any problem with that."

Jeff shook his head and grinned.

She spent the next few minutes going into detail about what would be required of him on a typical shift, finally concluding, "The reason your application rose to the top is because your references were outstanding, especially regarding the length of time you've been on your job at Sears and your lack of absenteeism." She tilted her head. "Frankly, we don't get many college-educated applicants asking for swing shift. I was so impressed with your application I went ahead and checked your references. Sears is quite impressed with you. *Honest* and *hardworking* are the words they used."

Honest. It sounded like she'd shouted the word.

"We have a trial period of three months. You'll get full benefits after that. We like to give new employees time to get to know the job and be sure they're capable of doing it. It's a time when either party can give a short notice. We understand the job is demanding."

A trial period? Suddenly, Jeff felt better. The end of the trial period would be when school started. If he gave his notice then, it would fall within the parameters they'd set. It wouldn't really be like he'd misled them. It would be like he tried it for three months and it didn't work out.

"Would you like the job?"

"Yes, very much."

"Could you start training tomorrow night?"

"I've got finals next week. Could I start in two weeks?"

"The training takes about a week. That would put you three weeks out." Disappointment clouded her face. "We're very short-staffed right now. I really can't wait that long."

His mind raced. The idea of working part-time at Sears, finals, and training for a new job was overwhelming. "I—I don't know."

She waited for him to continue. When he didn't, she said, "Are you sure you can't juggle things? It would only be for two weeks, and you get paid for it."

"It's my finals I'm worried about."

Jeff's heart sank as she picked up his application and put it in the file.

She nodded. "Of course. I understand. Why don't you check back with us when you're available? If there's still a position open, we'd love to have you."

The memory of pushing Jessica's car into the carport flashed through his thoughts.

"Would it be possible to maybe train just one night this week, and then on Friday I could start coming in regularly?"

Betty reached across her desk and picked up a stack of papers. She thumbed through them and pulled one out.

He could see she was looking at a weekly schedule.

"Could you come in tomorrow night *and* Thursday night, then start full-time next Monday?"

Jeff straightened in his chair. That would give him several nights and all next weekend to study. If he wasn't ready for finals by the time they started, he probably never would be. "I can do that."

She looked genuinely relieved. "That's wonderful." She laid the grid down in front of her and wrote his name in two of the squares.

"You're going to be training with Helga on the swing shift. One of the employees who works with her is on leave right now." She opened a drawer, retrieved a booklet, and handed it to him. "Read through this. It has all our policies, the list of classes you need, and how to schedule them." She stood. "Come a little early tomorrow night, and if you have questions, we'll be glad to answer them."

After shaking her hand, he turned and left. As he walked to his car, apprehension dogged his steps. At the mention of Helga's name he knew the house where he'd be training was the same house where Jessie had worked. He hadn't been honest with Betty. He was

142

Jessica's boyfriend. He'd once been at the house she was sending him to, and he probably wouldn't continue with the job after school started. He found himself fighting a strong desire to go back and level with her about everything.

When he reached the car, he turned and faced the building.

A flash of fear zigzagged through him.

It was too much of a risk. Better to take the job and, at least through the summer, have the security of two incomes. Suddenly anxious to leave, he opened the car door, slid behind the wheel, and started home.

As he drove through town, he realized he was only a few blocks from the mechanic who had worked on his car in the past. He took the next turn and wove his way to Al's Auto Repair. Al was just walking from the garage to the office when Jeff pulled in.

Jeff honked and rolled down the window.

Waving, Al walked over to the car. "What's up, buddy?"

"I think the starter's out on my girlfriend's car. What would it cost to fix it?"

"What kinda car?"

"1992 Nissan."

Al's brow wrinkled. "Around three hundred fifty bucks."

Jeff drummed his fingers on the steering wheel and swallowed hard. "Thanks, I'll get back to you."

As Al walked away, Jeff rolled up his window. Then, reaching into his pocket, he took out his phone. He glanced at the policy manual on the seat next to him and punched the phone number of Haven House into his cell.

❧

Jessica tossed the emptied box toward the front door. Balancing on the edge of her chair, she finished stacking the books in two short towers, spines out so they could be identified if Jeff needed them. Then she wiggled back on the chair seat and propped her injured foot up on them. She gave a quick half nod. The heavy textbooks made a perfect footstool.

She folded her arms across her chest and looked around the apartment. They'd used Jeff's bedroom furniture for their bedroom and put her small chest of drawers in the living room to set the television on. Jeff had put his desk, chair, and bookcase in the second bedroom so he could have his own place to study. They'd stored her bed frame in the small closet at the end of their carport and used her bed for a couch. Other than the chair she was sitting on, that was pretty much it. And it looked great.

It looked like . . . a home.

She admired the pillows she'd lined up on the mattress to give the "couch" a back. That had been her idea. Jeff said he bet she had a natural talent for decorating.

Watching the Home and Garden channel was more likely the reason. She'd often dreamed of having a place of her own and had decorated this apartment a thousand times while locked in her room as a teenager, and many times during lonely hours since then.

She leaned forward, knotting her hands under her chin, and studied the open area. Peach and green . . .

144

that would be pretty. Yellow and white . . . she frowned, too feminine. She had a man in her life now. Taupe and burgundy . . . yes . . . that was elegant.

The carpet was pretty rough, but the area rug that had been at the foot of her bed could be put on top of it. That would hide a multitude of sins. A couple of yards of burgundy cotton draped over her dresser would turn it into a skirted table. She'd leave a pleated opening in front so she could still use the drawers. She smiled. Maybe she'd surprise Jeff when he was back in school. She'd buy the fabric and work on it when he wasn't home.

They'd have to buy some things. Two floor lamps would take care of the lighting. They could sell the "couch," and then go hunting at garage sales for a love seat. That's where the taupy browns would come in. Warm and inviting. That's how her home would be.

She slowly closed her eyes . . . She was preparing dinner. The table was set and she had just finishing arranging flowers in a vase for the center of the table. She glanced at the clock. Jeff would be home from his new computer job any minute.

She silently tilted her head, listening. And for one sweet moment she heard it.

A child's voice. That precious small voice of her dolls, her dreams, the yearning of her heart, calling her.

"Mama."

A tear slipped down her cheek.

She brushed it away with the back of her hand. No point in thinking about that. She willed her thoughts back to the room . . . and to the truth.

The end of the living room next to the kitchen had a

145

light fixture in the middle of the ceiling, positioned for a dining table. That, and some chairs to go with it, would be another garage sale item she needed to buy.

Neither one of them had any kitchen utensils, plates, silverware, or pots and pans. Other than the major appliances that came with the apartment, they needed almost everything else.

Her hands dropped into her lap. It was going to take some money to get the place in shape. She pressed her fingertips together. There probably wasn't much left in Jeff's savings, and she didn't know anyone she could ask for a loan.

There was no way she'd ever let Jeff ask Leigh to help them. That would be the same as saying they couldn't make it on their own. She lowered her eyes to her hands. Not that she cared what Leigh thought about her and Jeff.

Jessica dropped her foot from the stack of books. Pushing up on her good leg and balancing with one hand on the chair, she managed to work another packed box close enough to her to get a firm grip on it. She pulled it around in front of her and opened it.

More of Jeff's things. She dug into the box.

Books . . . DVDs . . . a football. Her stomach churned. The memory of Jeff telling her how he'd saved it for the son he hoped to have someday flashed in her mind. She quickly pushed the ball aside.

A Bible.

She hooked her finger under its spine and pulled it out. She ran her hand across the top of the dark leather. She'd never owned a Bible. And before she met Jeff she'd never even looked in one. Though she'd led him to believe she had.

On the lower right-hand edge, in gold print, was Jeff's name. She opened the cover. The first page had a heading, Presented To: followed by black lines that had been written on.

She read.

To Jeff. I am so proud of you. You are the light of my life. It is my prayer that God will bless you abundantly on this graduation day and always. Matthew 7:7. Mom.

The handwriting had been set on the page carefully, each letter formed perfectly. Jessica stared at the words.

Graduation day.

She'd had a graduation day. That's what her foster father had called it the first time he'd used her, then thrown her away. It had been the last day of sixth grade. His stinking breath and yellow teeth inches from her face. She swallowed the spit that poured into her mouth as her stomach roiled. The years of abuse suddenly palpable.

She held her breath and willed her eyes to move on.

Matthew 7:7.

Shaky fingers fanned through the pages of the Bible. The third pass through, Matthew caught her eye. She quickly stopped. Matthew 3. She picked through a few pages. Finding chapter 7, she ran her finger down to the verse in the inscription.

Ask, and it will be given to you; seek, and you will find; knock, and it will be opened to you.

She'd heard this verse before, in church with Jeff. She hadn't believed it then and she didn't believe it now. Asking God for things was useless. She'd cried out to God a thousand times, asking Him to rescue her, to stop the hurting. And to give her a family like other kids had. A real family . . . a family who loved her.

She slapped the cover shut and threw the Bible back into the box.

. . . *that God will bless you abundantly.* Did God hear a mother's prayers? She tossed her head. She had no way of knowing.

Mama.

And she never would.

She couldn't have children.

11

Jeff had started at Haven House the day after the interview. His call from Al's parking lot had caught Betty before she'd left, and she'd been more than happy to accommodate his change of heart.

In a few hours he'd be off for the weekend, and even though he'd have to work at Sears both Saturday and Sunday afternoons, he'd finally have some time to study for finals. But for now, he needed to focus on the task at hand, getting Ed ready for bed.

Ed was in his twenties and had autism. Helga had gone over the steps of Ed's bedtime routine with Jeff, and then left them so she could help one of the other clients bathe.

Step one. Jeff folded Ed's pants and put them on the chair next to the dresser. "Come on, Ed, time to go to bed."

Ed sat on the edge of the bed. His brow creased as he watched Jeff pick up his shirt.

Step two. Jeff hung Ed's shirt on the back of the chair next to the dresser.

Step three. He picked up Ed's tennis shoes and put them next to the chair.

Tonight Jeff would be home by eleven thirty. He'd hardly seen Jessica all week and he was looking forward to spending some time with her. They needed to talk. Now that a week had passed, the full impact of her being temporarily out of work had settled in. What was left in his savings was barely keeping their heads above water. They'd bought food and made her car payment. He slowly shook his head. Haven House paid on the fifteenth and the end of the month. But during his training period he was earning only minimum wage. So this time his check wouldn't be much.

"Ouu. Ouu."

Ed's voice cut into Jeff's thoughts.

Jeff stepped toward him. "Let's go to bed, buddy."

Before he could move any closer, Ed rose from the edge of the bed, his voice growing louder. "Ouu. Ouu."

"It's bedtime." Jeff gently took Ed's arm and tried to redirect him to the bed.

Ed faced Jeff, slapping Jeff's hand away. "Ouu. Ouu."

Unsure what to do, Jeff took a step back.

Ed began flapping his arms and making guttural noises.

Jeff took another step back, uncertain what to do next.

"What's going on?"

Jeff turned at the voice behind him. "I don't know, Helga. All of a sudden he got real agitated. I guess he doesn't want to go to bed."

150

"Ouu. Ouu." Ed began pummeling his head with fisted hands.

Helga stepped between the two men. "Shoe. He's saying 'shoe.'"

Jeff moved to the side. "How do you know that?"

"I've worked with him enough to know that's what 'ouu' means." She arched her neck to get a look at the chair by the closet. "You've got his shoes on the wrong side of that chair. They were supposed to be between the chair and the dresser, not next to the outside leg."

She stepped out of Ed's way.

The young man, his face like a single avid eye, bolted toward his shoes.

Kneeling, he grabbed them and put them between the dresser and chair and began spinning them in a circle.

Jeff watched as Ed ritualistically repositioned the shoes, setting them down and carefully straightening the shoelaces each time. "You said, 'Fold his pants and put them on the chair next to the dresser, hang his shirt on the back of it, and put the shoes by the chair leg.'"

"Guess I should have been clearer." Helga stepped past Jeff and put her hand on Ed's back. "Come on, Ed, it's time to get in bed."

Smoothing the laces a final time, he rose.

Helga guided him back to the bed, then turned off the light. She and Jeff stepped into the hall, and she quietly closed the door behind them as Jeff followed her to the living room.

"Sorry. I missed that detail in his routine."

Helga shrugged. "He'll get over it."

151

Jeff heard the indifference in her voice. "I know, but still, it really upset him."

"You'll get over it too." She dismissed his concern with a wave of her hand. "After you've worked here awhile, it's no big deal. He's been here for the two years we've been open, and I don't think he's ever had visitors. Nobody's going to say anything." She gave him an easy grin. "Go finish up in the kitchen. I have to make some calls."

As Jeff wiped down the counters and swept the floor, he couldn't stop thinking about what had happened. He'd seen Ed become agitated before, but there was something about his reaction to such a trivial detail that magnified how tragic the young man's situation really was. And worse, Jeff knew it was his lack of attention to the routine he'd been shown on previous nights that had caused the episode.

He put the broom and dustpan away, then stepped into the hall. He hesitated.

Peeking into the living room, he saw Helga was on the phone. He turned and walked silently back to Ed's room.

As he opened the bedroom door, he slipped through it, then closed it quietly behind him.

For a moment his eyes adjusted to the filtered moonlight, then he moved to Ed's bedside and squatted next to him. The young man was uncovered, lying on his back.

"*Ouu. Ouu.*" Ed's desperate, panicked voice replayed in Jeff's mind. His eyes misted. "I'm sorry," he whispered.

He dropped his gaze to the floor, his heart filling with compassion . . . *I don't think he's ever had visitors.*

Without warning, a spear of conviction shot through Jeff as he realized that in the week he'd been at Haven House he'd never thought about any of the clients as other than "a job." A way out of his financial problems, possible only because he had deceived Betty during his interview.

He turned his eyes to Ed . . . *the least of these* . . . That's what Jesus had said. The hungry, the poor, the hopeless, they were the least in this world. *Inasmuch as you did it to one of the least of these . . . you did it to Me.*

Jeff closed his eyes. *Oh, Lord God, forgive me.*

He rose. Bending over the bed, he lifted the covers and pulled them over Ed's shoulders. Then he stood, gazing at the young man. Ed's eyes were closed, mouth open, gawking blindly into the darkness . . . into his future.

Jeff blinked rapidly. Had anyone ever prayed with Ed, or told him about Jesus?

Jeff bowed his head. *You know Ed, Lord. You understand every sound he makes, You know everything about him, and You know his purpose here.*

Jeff felt goose bumps rise on his arms, and an overwhelming sense of love surged through him. He didn't know what Ed knew, or could even understand. But Jeff did know that as long as he worked at Haven House, he would show Ed God's love. He would tell Helga that now that he knew Ed's routine he would take care of putting him to bed. And he wouldn't do it carelessly. He would do it as unto the Lord.

Convicted of his own callousness, Jeff turned and left the room. One of God's purposes for Ed's life was suddenly quite clear.

Walking down the hall toward the living room, he heard Helga talking on the phone. ". . . You know how undependable Piglet is. She won't be coming back."

As Jeff took a chair across from her, she flipped the phone shut. He turned to her. "Have I met, um, Piglet?"

Helga dropped the phone into her shirt pocket. "No."

Jeff hesitated. "Why do you call her Piglet?"

"If you knew about her, you'd probably call her worse than that. Besides, she's fat."

Jeff winced at the harsh words. "Oh."

He glanced at his watch and rose. "Looks like we've got some downtime." He stepped toward the front door and lifted his backpack from one of the hooks on the short wall next to it. "I think I'll study in the kitchen."

"That's cool with me." Helga picked up the remote and turned on the television. "And keep that confidential about Piglet—she doesn't know anything about it."

Piglet. He'd heard that name before. "Does she work graveyard?"

Helga threw the remote onto the coffee table. "She worked this shift. But she's always missing work, always got something wrong with her. If it's not her car, it's something else. This time it's her leg or something." Helga settled back in her chair, eyes on the television. "She's the one you're replacing. I don't think they're going to give her notice, though, for another couple of weeks. They're short-staffed right now and want to make sure the new hires are going to stay long term."

Jeff's heart began to pound, and heat rushed to his cheeks.

Helga was talking about Jessica.

Jeff sat in his car in the parking lot of the apartment complex, staring at the front door of their unit. He had to tell her.

He knew he'd heard that name Piglet and he'd finally placed it. That's who he'd overheard Gina and some man talking about the night he'd sneaked out of Jessica's room. They'd said there was a rumor she'd be fired. Apparently it was a topic of gossip even then.

He continued to filter through his memory. "Piglet." He'd heard that name in a phone conversation . . . when he was talking to Jessica . . . a long time ago. Yes, the pieces fell into place. She'd said it was just someone who worked at Haven House. He dropped his eyes. She hadn't wanted him to know it was her. His eyes drifted back to the front door. One more slap in the face, one more putdown. Suddenly, there was nothing he wanted more than to hold her in his arms.

He opened the car door and got out. As he walked across the lot and up the stairs, he realized that Jessica's losing her job had been in the works before they ever rented the apartment. Their dreams of two incomes and replacing his savings had been doomed before they started. And just yesterday they had decided to get a credit card to buy things they really needed. If only Gina had warned Jessica, if only Betty had mentioned something. He sighed. If only he'd been honest at his interview, maybe none of this would have happened.

He tried the door. Finding it locked, he took out his key, slipped it into the knob, and quietly turned the handle.

Peeking into the apartment, he saw Jessica had fallen asleep on the couch, a pillow clutched to her chest, her dark auburn hair hiding her face.

He stepped inside the door. The apartment was neat and clean, the scent of lemon oil in the air.

He smiled. He'd teased her about oiling his beat-up old furniture, but it had touched him deeply to watch her maneuvering as best she could on her cast to reach the top of his bookshelves with a cleaning rag, then lining up his books, tall ones on the right, short ones on the left. He'd repeatedly reminded her she was supposed to stay off her leg, but every day when he came home from work or school, more unpacking was done, and little by little the apartment had become their home.

He tiptoed to the kitchen and opened the refrigerator. Next to a carton of milk, a paper plate held a sandwich in a baggie with a sticky note attached. He tilted his head to read it. "Love U."

How was he going to tell her? Grabbing the milk with one hand and the plate with the other, he kneed the door shut. He chugged some milk from the carton and unwrapped the sandwich.

"Jeff?"

"Hey. You're awake." His stomach knotted as he took a bite of his sandwich and walked to the living room.

Jessica sat up and leaned against the wall. "How was work?" She stifled a yawn.

"Okay." He took another bite of his sandwich and climbed onto the couch next to her.

"Something good happened." Her blue eyes smiled at

him. "I called around to the banks today and found out how to get a credit card."

Jeff swallowed.

"Your bank had the best deal. They said they have a special program for students. If your credit is good, you can get a card with a limit as high as a thousand dollars."

Ignoring his sandwich, she leaned forward and laced her arms around his neck.

"Jeff, I love you so much." She kissed him lightly on the lips, then leaned back against the wall. "The first thing we need to do is get some things for the kitchen. A microwave for sure."

"Jessie, maybe we should wait a little bit, until we can put some money back into the savings." He took another bite of his sandwich, chewing it slowly, then swallowed.

"There're some things we can't wait on. We don't even have dishes."

"I don't mind using paper plates." He put the last of his sandwich into his mouth.

"What about a coffeepot? I'm the one who's been camping here all week." Her eyes weren't smiling. "We've got to get a few things. And why wouldn't we? In another day or so you'll be finished with your training and you'll start making more money. Credit cards are the perfect way to get us through the next few months. By then I'll be back to work and we'll have two good incomes."

"I'm just saying we should go slow. You never know. Things happen."

Her face sobered. "Like what?"

He searched his mind desperately for something he

could use to lead into talking about her job. "Sometimes things just don't work out."

She stared at him a moment, then her eyes misted. "What are you trying to say?"

How could he tell her she was going to be fired and everyone she worked with knew about it? He felt his own eyes tearing up. He dropped his gaze and took a deep breath.

"Jessie." His eyes returned to her face. "Jessie . . . I . . ."

Her lower lip began to quiver. "What?"

"Uh." He reached for her hand.

She pulled it back. "What are you trying to say? That this isn't working out?" Her voice rose. "That you wish we hadn't moved in together?"

Jeff grabbed her hand. "No. No, nothing like that." He could feel her trembling.

Her face contorted. "Then what?"

He heard distance in her voice. He couldn't tell her like this. He should have thought it through more.

Her nostrils dilated, and her mouth quivered in an ugly quirk as she fought to keep her composure.

She dropped her hands to her sides, palms down on the mattress, stiffening her arms, her eyes on his in a focused, unblinking stare. Hardened, she waited for him to speak.

Something stirred in Jeff's heart, and for a moment the woman before him faded behind a misty veil. In her place he saw a wounded, frightened child cowering, bruised and broken. And as clearly as if she had spoken, he knew everything about her suffering and her fear.

158

No one had ever loved her.

Jeff reached out and pulled Jessica to him, pressing her head into his chest. "Jessie, I'm not going to leave you, now or ever." He should have asked her to marry him before they ever moved in together.

As he stroked her hair, he felt her tears through his shirt. "Shhh, shhh. Please don't cry." Squeezing his eyes shut, he fought tears of his own.

Gradually, her breathing steadied and she raised her head. "If you don't want to leave, what is it then?"

He gently pushed her hair back from her face. Her eyes were red and her face blotched. Suddenly, he knew what he wanted to do. "It's just that we need to be real careful with our money and . . ." He kissed her forehead. "And I want to get married."

"Married?" She struggled against him, pushing herself up, her face a mixture of confusion and excitement. "Married?"

Jeff turned toward her, pulling his knees up under him and sitting back on his heels. He took her hands in his. "Will you marry me?"

Jessica wiped her tears away with her hands, sniffling and laughing at the same time. "Yes. Yes. I will."

He pulled her to him and kissed her.

She wiggled away from him. "We'll get married next year. In the summer. I've always dreamed of a summer wedding." Her eyes sought his. "Okay?"

"Umm. I thought maybe we'd get married right away. How about *this* summer?"

"Oh, Jeff, it's already May. That's way too early. Besides, I want to have an engagement ring and be officially engaged." She stretched her left hand out in front of her and admired her ring finger. "A diamond set in real gold."

Jeff pulled his legs out from under him and sat cross-legged, facing her. "Jessie, we can't afford that right now."

Jessica let her hand drop into her lap. "I know, but we can save. It's worth waiting for." Her eyes pleaded with him. "I've dreamed all my life of being engaged."

Jeff drew a deep breath. He loved her. And the truth was, there wasn't much he could give her. But he could give her this. He could give her *her* dream.

He lowered his eyes. He'd had dreams about marriage too.

He raised his head. "If that's what makes you happy, that's what I want to do."

Jessica squealed. "I love, love, love you, Jeff Scott." She clasped her hands to her chest. "We can start looking at rings right away. Of course, we'll have to wait for the credit card. But then there'll be plenty of money to get the ring and things for the apartment too." She hardly took a breath. "And you know what?" She didn't wait for him to answer. "As soon as I get the place fixed up, I want to invite your mom over."

Her words brought reality front and center. "My mom?"

Jessica nodded her head decisively. "She's going to be my mother-in-law, isn't she?"

Jessica was right. This was the perfect way to start mending their relationship.

"Yes, she is." Jeff took Jessica's hands in his and squeezed them. "And the grandmother of our children."

12

Jessica tiptoed from the bedroom and closed the door behind her. She stopped on her way to the kitchen and raised the blinds on the front window. The morning sunlight streamed into the room. Raising her face to it, she closed her eyes for a moment. This was the first day of the rest of her life.

She held her left hand in front of her and angled it back and forth in the light, trying to make her diamond sparkle. It rewarded her with a tiny pirouette.

Jeff had wanted to wait until they could pay for the ring in full, but she'd finally been able to make him see there was really no difference between making monthly twenty-dollar payments to a savings account and making them to Discount Jewelers' Outlet. Besides, getting the store credit card gave them another 10 percent off. Even the salesman had said they were two responsible young people with good jobs, and there was no reason she shouldn't wear the ring out of the store. So they'd done the paperwork and last night she'd become officially engaged.

Jessica spun in a circle, her hand still in front of her.

I'm engaged. He loves me. We'll make a life together, until death do us part. She spun in a circle again, admiring her ring. In love with the idea of being in love.

She walked to the kitchen, making sure her steps were even. She'd favored her injured foot since the cast had come off two days ago, and her back was starting to ache. Pulling the coffeemaker next to the sink, she filled the pot with water. It was so nice not to have to drink instant coffee anymore. She'd wanted to stock the kitchen with everything they needed, but Jeff had insisted they buy only the bare necessities until she went back to work. He hadn't considered the coffeemaker a necessity, but after she'd agreed to give up an electric can opener, a blender, and lots of other appliances that every home should have, he'd finally relented. She pressed the start button on the coffeemaker and pushed it to the back of the counter.

She slid a loaf of bread from the top of the refrigerator, took two slices, and dropped them into the toaster. Moving to the cabinet next to the sink, she took out a cup and plate.

Winter white. She grinned. That's what the sign had said on the card table set up in the driveway. Beneath it: Place settings for five—$5. That the saucers were missing didn't bother her a bit. The cups looked like mugs anyway. She smoothed the face of the plate with her hand. They were beautiful.

When the toast popped up, she buttered it, then took the plate and a cup of coffee and sat at the dining room table. As she ate, she surveyed the apartment. They managed to find all the furniture they really needed at bargain prices. She was proud of all they'd accomplished over the past few weeks, and she knew Jeff was too. Especially since his mother would be coming to dinner.

Jessica rose, washed her dishes, and put them away, all the while going over and over the day's to-do list in her mind. The first time the three of them had dinner together it had ended badly. Jeff had moved out soon after that and had spoken to his mother only a few times since. This time Jessica wanted things to be different.

The lasagna was in the refrigerator and ready to be popped into the oven. The house was clean and needed just a little of her attention to bring it to the standard that was reserved for a fiancé's mother.

Jessica had spent the week getting things ready so she could spend today on herself. She huffed a sigh. Jeff had driven her crazy, bugging her every day about calling work and telling them she was getting her cast off and could come back. She'd finally called late last night when she was pretty sure Betty would be gone. She hadn't wanted to take a chance that Betty might ask her to come in this weekend so she'd left her a message on her voice mail saying she'd be in the office Monday to get her work schedule.

She considered Betty a good friend. The woman had hired her when Haven House first opened and had always been wonderful to her. Jessica winced, thinking of all the work she'd missed over the past few months. Still, she hadn't been able to help it. Her diabetes had become more of a problem, there were days the prickly pain in her legs slowed her down, and she never knew when the car was going to keep her from getting to work on time. But things were going to be better from now on. For the first time in her life she was optimistic about the future. That was another reason she didn't want to talk to Betty until Monday. Betty had hinted several times that she was disappointed in Jessica's chronic tardiness and absenteeism, so Jessica wanted to reassure her, face-to-face, that that was all in the past.

Jessica walked to the bathroom. Standing in front of the sink, she leaned toward the mirror. Her hair was a disaster. Its thick, natural curl frizzing out in all directions was flecked with flakes of dandruff. She'd have to do an oil treatment. As she reached into the cabinet under the sink for a tube of conditioner, she saw Jeff pad past the bathroom door.

"Good morning," she called after him.

"Morning." His voice drifted across the living room.

She stuck her head around the doorjamb, listening to him moving around the kitchen. Turning back to the sink, she crouched, reaching under the sink again, feeling behind the towels stacked against the back of the cabinet. Her fingers touched the slippery skin of the baggie she'd hidden there.

She straightened and faced the mirror. "What time do you have to be at Sears?"

"I'm on at ten. I'm not sure when I'm getting off."

"I was hoping I could have the car while you're at work. I wanted to get my nails done. I've got an appointment with Lucy."

"Sure." His voice came closer. "Don't worry about me, I'll get someone to bring me home." He stopped at the bathroom door. "What time is Mom coming?"

164

"Six."

"Did you call Haven House?"

"I left Betty a message last night. Will you stop bugging me about that? It's like you can't wait for me to get back to work."

Something flashed in his dark brown eyes.

She frowned at him. "What?"

His gaze met hers. "Nothing, Jessie. It's just that we really need money, and the sooner you have a job the better."

She tossed her head. "I have a job. Betty loves me and I've been there longer than anybody." She put her hands on her hips. "What are you going to tell your mom about your grades?" That should get his mind off her job.

"I'm going to tell her I passed all my classes, which is the truth."

"Well, let's hope she doesn't ask you by how much."

Jeff took a step back from her, put his hands on his hips, threw out his chest, and tossed his head exactly the way she did when she was mad. "Are you trying to start a fight?"

She set her lips in a firm line, stifling a giggle. It was a tactic he always used to defuse an argument. And it always worked. She burst out laughing. "No, I just feel like you're pressuring me about going back to work." She dropped her hands and turned to the mirror. "Like I could help it I had to have my leg in a cast."

He stepped toward her and put his arms around her. "It isn't that, and you know it. Now stop it." He kissed the top of her head.

She reached up and rested her hand on his arm. "Sorry. I'm just nervous about your mom coming."

He pressed his cheek against her head. "The house looks beautiful and I saw that lasagna in the refrigerator. She's going to be so impressed."

Jessica turned and faced him. "Do you really think so?"

He kissed her lightly. "I know so." He stepped away from her. "You'd better hurry up if you're going to take me to work."

Jessica picked up the bottle of conditioner. "Would you bring me a chair from the kitchen? My legs are killing me."

Jeff brought it to her and she sat as she conditioned her hair. The prickly pain had gotten worse since the cast had come off. She'd considered calling the doctor to get pain pills, but they didn't really have the money for the co-pay.

She thought about the baggie under the sink.

No. She'd promised Jeff she'd quit smoking pot. And even though she'd sneaked it a time or two since they'd lived together, things were different now. She was engaged, and that's what she was going to tell Lucy. The girl had been her connection for weed long before she met Jeff. Doing nails was a secondary business at the nail salon, and today Jessica was going to sell the marijuana back to her.

By the time she finished with her hair and makeup, she found herself rushing to get dressed in time to take Jeff to work.

"Why don't you go down and start the car?" she shouted

into the living room over the noise of the television set. "I'll be right there."

She listened for Jeff to shut the door.

Giving her sweater a final tug over her hips, she slipped her feet into her shoes, then grabbed her purse. She rushed to the front door and opened it a crack. Jeff was pulling the car up next to the sidewalk. She hurried to the bathroom, reached under the sink, and pulled out the baggie, then she pushed it to the bottom of her purse. As she straightened she caught a glimpse of herself in the mirror. She stood for a moment smiling at her reflection. She looked good.

With a firm grip on her purse, she dashed to the car.

It was 9:58 when they pulled into the parking lot at Sears. "Told you we'd make it in time if you let me drive."

Jeff leaned across the front seat and kissed her cheek. "Love you."

"Love you too," she called out as the car door slammed shut.

She watched him walk into the building, then drove to the far side of the lot and put the car in park. Sharp pains had started shooting through her legs while she was driving to Sears, and it made it hard for her to feel the pedals beneath her feet. When this had happened from time to time in the past, the doctors always told her she needed to get her diabetes under control. She needed to lose weight and exercise. Only they never explained how she was supposed to exercise when she couldn't walk. She'd finally decided the doctors weren't good for much except a pain pill prescription.

A memory flashed through her mind . . . Jeff wanting to take her to Urgent Care the night she'd become sick at the restaurant. She'd lied and told him she couldn't go because she owed them money, that she hadn't been able to pay them because her money had gone to fix her car. But the truth was, she owed them money because she'd gone there repeatedly with all kinds of stories, some true, some made up, but all for the purpose of getting drugs. In the beginning it *had* been to escape the pain in her legs. Later it had just been to escape.

She glanced at her watch. She needed to get to her nail appointment. She backed out of the parking space and turned onto the main road. If the pains got worse, she'd call the doctor who'd seen her at Community Hospital. He didn't know anything about her past with Urgent Care. But by the time she arrived at the nail salon, the pains had subsided.

"Haven't seen you in ages." Lucy motioned Jessica to the chair across from her small worktable.

Jessica smoothed her hand over her stomach, pulling her sweater back down over her hips, then quickly dropped into the chair and put her purse next to her feet. Placing her hands on the table, she spread her fingers.

"Hey, what's that?" Lucy pointed at her engagement ring.

Jessica straightened in the chair and wiggled her ring finger. "I'm getting married." She wiggled her finger again. "Doesn't it have a nice sparkle?"

Lucy leaned closer to the ring. "Uh. Yeah it does." She sat back in her chair. "How much did you want to spend today?"

Jessica put her left hand in her lap.

Code words. An invitation for Jessica to say, "Forty dollars," or whatever amount she wanted to spend on pot. Or she could respond with, "I don't know, what do you think?" letting Lucy know she was selling. But suddenly Jessica wasn't so sure she wanted to let go of the baggie. The pains in her legs were too fresh and thoughts of Leigh coming to dinner crowded into her mind. She fingered the edge of her sweater.

"I just want a manicure. My future mother-in-law is coming to dinner." She raised her hand and rested it back on the table. "For the first time."

"Has she seen you before?" Lucy picked up Jessica's hand and began to file her nails. "I mean, has she met you before?"

Why had she come here? Lucy had always been like this, putting her down with little digs. Jessica knew exactly what Lucy meant. She was referring to Jessica's weight. She was probably just mad because Jessica didn't want to make a buy.

"Yes, she's met me before, and she's totally excited about the wedding."

By the time Jessica's manicure was finished, she'd told Lucy all about Jeff's wonderful mother and the beautiful wedding she was helping Jessica plan.

Jessica rose and handed Lucy two ten-dollar bills. Lucy made change out of her drawer and handed it to Jessica.

"It was great seeing you again. I'll be watching for a wedding invitation. Can't wait to meet Jeff and your future mother-in-law."

169

Leigh checked to make sure her doors were locked as she turned onto Fourteenth Street. She began scanning the old houses for an address. Spotting Jeff's car, she pulled into the parking lot, parked next to it, and turned off the ignition. A glance at the clock on the dash confirmed she was a few minutes early. She dropped the keys in her purse and picked up the scrap of paper next to her. "2D."

Settling back in her seat, she scanned the doors of the apartment building until she found the address. She stared at the closed door and drew a deep breath. Everything about this was hard.

Leigh had prayed repeatedly that God would intervene and bring Jeff back to his senses, even asking the prayer chain at church to pray for him. And recently she'd discussed it with John. She felt the knot in her stomach loosen. It was wonderful having him in her life again. He had an unshakable faith that God was in control. His prayers for Jeff were always about God's will being done. And somehow, with John's counsel, she'd found her own prayers changing. Now, instead of directing God to make Jeff and Jessica see the error of their ways, she was asking God to help her stop judging them and to open her heart to Jessica.

There was something mysterious and wonderful about John's faith, yet she couldn't put her finger on it. She'd pressed him about his personal relationship with Jesus, but he always turned the conversation to something that had been mentioned in the Sunday sermon, or some basic tenet of the Bible. She sighed. She wanted what he had.

She closed her eyes a moment. *Lord, I'm here because I love my son. You know I want to learn to love Jessica too. Please help me see her as You see her.* Leigh opened the door, stepped out of the car, and locked it.

As she walked up the stairs to the apartment, she couldn't shake the feeling that this was the same as giving up ground. Somehow her coming to dinner was like saying what they were doing was okay. She pushed the feelings down, quickly reviewing her position. She was going to love and accept them, but that didn't mean she loved or accepted what they were doing. If the opportunity arose, she wanted to tell them that. She knocked on the door.

Jeff opened the door. "Mom, come in." Stepping toward her, he hugged her, then stepped aside, making a dramatic sweep of his hand.

It had been over a month since she'd seen him, and he looked wonderful. He was smiling.

She suddenly felt emotional, his sweet smile spiraling through her memory, linking scene after scene from their shared past. Stirring her heart, resurrecting all the dreams she'd had for him. The numbing, the distancing she'd done in the past weeks, vanished.

Jessica rose from the couch and walked toward her. Leigh reached out, and the women embraced. Then Leigh stepped back. "I like your hair."

Jessica fingered a spiral curl by her ear self-consciously. "I put it up myself. Well, actually Jeff helped me." She flashed him a coy smile.

171

"Here, Mom, sit down." Jeff pointed to the couch. "Dinner'll be ready in a few minutes. Can I get you something to drink? We made orange cinnamon tea. It should be cool by now."

"I'd love some."

Jessica followed Jeff to the kitchen. As soon as they disappeared around the corner, Leigh looked around the apartment. Clearly Jessica had been more prepared to start a home than Leigh had thought. A little smile tugged at her lips. She leaned forward and looked toward the back of the apartment and got a clear view of the bathroom. Two more rooms were on each side of it.

Turning her attention to the kitchen, she heard Jessica and Jeff talking about getting the ice out of the freezer. She quickly rose, took a few steps, and got a good look at the bathroom. Neat as a pin, and everything matched. Shower curtain, bath mat, soap dish, and toothbrush holder. The theme was butterflies. Apparently their two incomes *were* enough for them to live on. She stepped back to the couch and sat down, suddenly relieved . . . and impressed. The apartment was as cute as it could be. Not only were they making it financially but Jessica was making a nice home for Jeff.

"Here you go." Jeff handed her a tall glass of iced tea. "Jessica's getting the salad ready." He straightened, holding his arms stiffly at his sides. "Um, come with me."

Leigh set down the tea and followed him into one of the rooms next to the bathroom. She recognized his desk and bookshelves.

"I wanted to talk to you a second." He shut the door behind him.

172

Leigh turned and faced him. *What now?*

"Um. I've asked Jessica to marry me. We're engaged." His face was a mixture of resolve and concern. "We got the ring last night."

Leigh almost felt relieved. During the first weeks Jeff had been gone, she'd hoped he would wake up and come back home, but eventually she'd come to realize that this was undoubtedly going to happen. And, to her surprise, actually hearing it wasn't as upsetting as she'd thought it would be.

"Jeff, if you're positive this is what you want, and Jessica is the girl for you, I won't oppose it. But I still don't think you should be living together."

He dropped his gaze. "I know, Mom." He raised his eyes and looked into hers. "It's what I want. Thanks for understanding."

He opened the door, and they stepped back into the living room. Leigh seated herself on the couch.

"Jessie, come here a sec."

Jessica walked with odd, deliberate steps across the living room.

Leigh looked at Jessica's feet. She wasn't wearing any shoes. "What's wrong?"

Jeff took Jessica's hand in his. "She hurt her foot and just got the cast off."

Leigh raised her eyebrows. "Must have been hard getting up and down those stairs every day with a cast on."

"The doctor told me to stay off it. So, except for shopping, I had to stay here."

"How'd you get to work?"

Jessica shrugged. "Oh, I've been off work the last month, but I'll be going back next week."

A wave of uneasiness swept through Leigh.

"Mom, Jessica and I want to tell you something."

Jessica looked at Jeff, face flushed and clearly anxious for him to continue.

Leigh folded her hands in her lap, suddenly very glad he'd taken the time to prepare her.

"We're getting married."

Jessica pushed her left hand in front of Leigh's face.

Leaning back, Leigh looked at the ring, a thin gold setting with the tiniest diamond she'd ever seen, hardly visible beneath the little prongs that held it. "That's lovely."

Jessica pulled her hand back.

"Have you set a date?"

Jessica smiled. "I told Jeff I—"

"No, we haven't set a date yet. Jessica, is dinner ready?"

Jessica stared at him a moment, then replied, "Almost."

Her answer had an edge to it.

"Can I help you finish?" Leigh rose and picked up her glass of tea.

"No, Mom. Just go ahead and sit at the table. I'll help Jessica with the plates."

After they were seated, Jeff said grace.

"This looks wonderful." Leigh put her napkin in her lap.

Jessica scooped some salad onto her plate. "Well, this is the first time I've really cooked anything here. We didn't have a thing for the kitchen. Not even plates until a few days ago."

Leigh took a bite of the lasagna and chewed slowly.

"But last week we finally got the credit card Jeff applied for."

Leigh swallowed.

Jessica turned to Jeff. "We got some more applications in the mail today." She turned back to Leigh. "It must be his good credit. Everybody wants to give us a credit card." She looked delighted at the idea. "But Jeff says the three we have are enough."

Leigh raised her eyebrows. "Three?"

"I had the gas card." Jeff set his fork down. "And then we had to get another card because we needed to get the place set up, and—"

"I'm the one who found out we could save on my ring by getting a card to buy it."

Well, aren't you a clever girl. Leigh swallowed another bite of food, but her appetite was vanishing. "I haven't seen you two at church lately. Did you find one close by?"

Jeff carefully cut his lasagna. "We're going to. But it's been kind of busy. Maybe we can go tomorrow, now that Jessica has her cast off."

"I imagine getting finished with school was a relief. How'd you do on your finals?"

"With school out I applied for more hours at Sears. So now I have two full-time jobs. We're planning to save over the summer, and I can cut back when school starts again."

Leigh watched her son as he spoke. She knew him well,

175

and his dodging her question told her all she needed to know about his grades. It was a technique he'd devised long ago to avoid telling her something she didn't want to hear.

As the meal continued, the conversation dwindled.

Leigh tilted her head. "What's that noise?"

"Oh. My cell phone." Jessica pushed herself away from the table and hobbled to the couch. "Hello?"

She returned to her chair, still talking on the phone. "Um. Could I call you back in a little bit?" Jessica nodded absently as she listened. "Bye."

Jeff put his fork down. "Who was that?"

"Betty."

"What'd she say?"

Leigh picked up a definite change in Jeff's manner. "Who's Betty?"

Jeff turned to her. "Betty's our boss at Haven House."

Jessica laid the phone on the table. "She was returning my call about going back to work next week."

Leigh wiped her mouth and laid her napkin on the table. "Does she usually call people on Saturday night?"

Jessica shrugged. "Haven House runs twenty-four hours a day. She's probably trying to get the schedule set for Monday."

Leigh picked up her plate. "Can I help you with the dishes?"

"No, Mom. We'll do it later. Don't you want some dessert? We have ice cream."

"Jeff said praline is your favorite, so we got some. I'd never heard of it before so I tried some at lunchtime. It's really good."

Ice cream for lunch. Lasagna for dinner.

"That was so thoughtful of you. But I'd better pass." Leigh patted her stomach. "I have to watch my weight." She rose. "You sure I can't help?"

"Don't worry about it." Jeff took the plate from her hand. "How about some coffee?"

Jessica's eyes cut to Leigh. "Yeah, that doesn't have any calories."

Leigh held Jessica's gaze for a moment. Maybe she *should* stay and have coffee and sit them down and explain to them they needed to be more disciplined about their spending, their morals . . . and their eating.

Suddenly, Leigh found herself anxious to get out of the tiny, drab apartment . . . and away from the girl who was ruining her son's life. "Uh, no. I should be getting home."

A shadow of sadness passed over Jeff's face. "Sure, Mom."

He put his arm around her shoulder and walked her to the door.

"Don't forget this." Jessica walked in deliberate, awkward steps to the couch and picked up Leigh's purse.

Leigh took it from Jessica's outstretched hand. "Thank you both again." Forcing a smile, she left the apartment. At the bottom of the stairs she turned and waved.

"Good night," Jeff called out, then shut the door.

Leigh clutched her purse, scanning the parking lot as she hurried to her car. If only it were a good night. Jeff and Jessica were headed for disaster. The only glimmer of hope was that Jessica would be returning to work on Monday.

177

Jessica waited for the final click of the front door closing, then crossed her arms. "Why'd she have to make a point about telling me she has to watch her weight?"

Jeff set the deadbolt. "She's always watching her weight. She didn't mean anything by it."

Jessica narrowed her eyes. "Yeah, right."

"You did a great job on the dinner and the lasagna was delicious. She probably thought she ate too much." Jeff smiled at her. "Why don't you call Betty back? I'll go clean up the kitchen."

As Jeff started clearing off the table, Jessica took her cell phone to the couch and dialed the Haven House office.

"Hello?"

Jessica recognized Betty's voice. "Hi, it's Jessica. I just wanted you to know that I can work Monday."

"I don't think we'll need you Monday."

Jessica frowned. "Why?"

"The schedule is already full. When I didn't hear from you by Thursday, I went ahead and filled it."

"Oh." Her voice trailed away.

"I'm sorry." Betty's voice was hesitant.

"I understand. Then I guess I'll be starting the next Monday."

"Jessica, I need to explain something."

Jessica's heart began to pound as her boss's voice took on a serious tone.

Betty continued. "I've talked to you before about all your absences and the complaints we've had from other

178

employees that you don't do your fair share of the work with the clients."

"They're lying. You know that's not true. I've been with you since the day Haven House opened. You and I worked together for months in the beginning. You know I'm a hard worker."

Jeff appeared beside her and sat next to her, his face filled with concern.

"That's true. But recently it does seem like you've slacked off."

"It's just that stuff has happened I couldn't help. I can't help it if I had to have my foot in a cast."

"I understand that. I'm not talking about this time. It's all the times over the previous months. You've been absent or late twelve times in the last three months."

Jessica began to cry. "Don't do this to me. I need my job, I need my insurance. If you do this to me, I'll be on the street."

She felt Jeff's hand slip across her back as he pulled her to him.

"I'm sorry, Jessica. I've agonized over this too."

She pulled back from Jeff. "I'm begging you. Please don't take my job away. Our clients are like my family. I bet they've been asking about me."

Betty was silent.

This couldn't be happening. "When I first started working for you, I confided in you. I trusted you. You know more about me than anybody. And you said you would help me. You even gave me money until I got a paycheck." Jessica began sobbing. "I shouldn't have believed you cared about me."

"I do care about you, but this is a business decision."

"Then don't do this. I'm more than a piece of business. I need your help now more than ever. I haven't had any income for a month. I didn't apply for unemployment because I thought I had a job to come back to."

"Jessica, I just don't know." Betty's voice trembled.

"Please. Please." Her words trailed away into sobs.

"Okay." She heard tears in Betty's voice. "I'll give you one more chance, Jessica. But you're going to have to work graveyards. You'll work alone and you'll have to float to whichever residence needs you from week to week."

"I can do that. I won't be late either. You won't be sorry."

"Plan to start graveyards a week from Monday. Come in early, and the schedule will be in your box."

"Thank you. Thank you." Jessica closed her phone.

Jeff pulled her to his chest.

Jeff. The only person she could trust.

The only person who would never deceive her.

∞

Family. That's what Betty had said. *"We're family."*

And it had felt like that.

Jessica stared at the ceiling, listening for the pattern of Jeff's breathing.

Outsiders wouldn't understand how at Haven House they worked together helping people with their most basic needs. Many of the clients couldn't bathe themselves, or use the toilet without help. Over time, schedules overlapped, and everyone worked with everyone else, side by side, performing the most intimate tasks imaginable as they cared for people who needed them.

Just like family.

Biting her lip, she pressed the damp edge of the sheet against her eyes. But Betty had decided to fire her.

Jeff's breathing deepened.

Jessica wiped her eyes one last time with the edge of the sheet. Moving as quietly as she could, she pulled the covers back and rose from the bed. She glanced at Jeff, listening again for his breathing. Reassured he was still asleep, she slipped through the bedroom door, closing it behind her.

She waited a moment to be sure she hadn't awakened him, then took a few steps to the second bedroom. There she opened the closet door, pulled her coat from a hanger, and shrugged it on. Taking measured, careful steps, she went into the living room.

In the dim light from the front window she could see her purse on the floor at the end of the couch. She picked it up, tiptoed to the front door, and let herself out. As she started down the steps, the tears began to flow.

Stupid fat pig. No one wants you in their family.

The words assaulted her, fighting for her attention. A foster father's husky voice, a woman's shrill shriek. She began to run to the carport, limping badly.

She felt in her purse, pulled out her car keys, unlocked her car door, and got in.

Clutching her purse in her hands, she stared straight ahead and took slow, deliberate breaths. Her chest ached. She clenched her jaw to kill the pain, but the voices continued from the deep well that was her past.

She opened her purse, felt her way to the bottom, and pulled out the baggie. Then she leaned across the car seat and opened the glove compartment. Straining to reach to the back of it, she wrapped her fingers around a pipe and pulled it out.

She wasn't going to let people hurt her anymore. She didn't have to. She stuffed the pipe with the dried leaves. Reaching back into the glove compartment, she found her lighter. The leaves smoldered and she took a drag.

She was engaged, and next summer she would be married. She held her left hand toward the windshield, trying to catch the moonlight.

The hazy smoke began to fill the car.

She closed her eyes. Leigh hadn't fooled her one bit. Leigh didn't think she was good enough for Jeff. Fine. She and Jeff would make a life together. Without her. A smile curved Jessica's lips. It took only two to make a family.

The ache in her chest began to ease. It was going to be just like she'd always imagined. She was going to have a family of her own.

And it wouldn't include Leigh.

13

Leigh watched John as he loaded the fishing tackle into the back of his pickup. It had been a perfect day. They'd been dating steadily for over a month and somehow had come to an unspoken agreement that regardless of what the rest of the week held, they would reserve Sunday afternoons for each other.

This Sunday they'd dropped her car off at his house after church, and then they'd driven north, deep into the mountains to go fishing. "We're actually in Montana," he'd announced when they'd parked. "That's the Two Forks River." They'd walked a short distance and finally reached a wide stream.

The fish hadn't been biting, and John had used that as an excuse to help her practice casting her line, wrapping his arms around her each time, and putting his hands on hers as they snapped the pole.

She felt heat in her cheeks. His perpetual smile and easygoing manner made him a pleasure to be with. But it was his sweet kiss, thanking her for the picnic lunch, that had kept her hoping the fish wouldn't bite for the rest of the afternoon.

Johnny, I could fall in love with you again.

He turned and looked at her, as though he knew what she was thinking.

She started. "Uh. I was just thinking how beautiful it is here."

He shut the tailgate and slowly walked to the driver's door. "It sure is. But it's time to go." He winked at her. "My sweetheart will be missing me."

As Leigh got into the cab of the truck, John started the engine. Pulling off the shoulder and onto the pavement, he settled back in his seat. "You know you haven't said a word about the dinner at Jeff's last night."

She turned to him. "What a mess."

"Want to talk about it?" He reached across the seat and took her hand in his.

"The fact they're living together is bad enough." She hesitated. "I still can't believe Jeff chose to do that. It's against everything he ever believed in."

John didn't take his eyes from the road. "Sometimes when a young guy loves a girl, he does what he has to, to be with her."

"How he could be in love with her is beyond me. I don't even know how he respects her. As far as I can tell, she's done nothing with her life, and if she has, she has nothing to show for it."

John glanced at her. "It doesn't mean she never will."

Pulling her hand from his, Leigh folded her arms across her chest. "And now that she's got a hook in him, she's using him to get credit cards so she can spend money they don't have."

John gave Leigh a sideways glance. "Let me get this

straight. You're convinced she's wrong for him, she'll never amount to anything, and that Jeff shouldn't love her." He paused a moment.

Leigh turned toward him, waiting for him to continue.

He shrugged. "Maybe you could break them up."

"It's too late for that. I talked until I was blue in the face before Jeff moved out. I did everything in my power to stop this from happening."

John tapped his fingers on the steering wheel. "Well, now that he's gone maybe you could write him a letter and tell him what you think."

Leigh dropped her hands into her lap. "At this point, I think I've said all there is to say."

John turned to her for a moment, his kind, dark eyes observing her, his expression one of expectation.

She returned his gaze, then her mouth dropped open. "Are you insinuating that this is like what my father did?" Anger edged into her words. "This is absolutely nothing like that. Jessica really does have nothing to offer Jeff. And besides that, I'd never do anything as cruel as what my father did to you."

John didn't speak.

In the silence she found herself sitting at the little dining table in Jeff and Jessica's apartment. *I have to watch my weight . . . Well, aren't you a clever girl.* Retribution pouring from her tongue and judgment pouring from her heart. Tears stung her eyes.

Still focused on the road ahead, John laid his hand, palm up, on the seat between them.

She slipped her hand into his, and he tightened his

grip. Heat emanated from his fingers where they pressed her flesh.

Don't marry her, Jeff. I can accept a lot. But don't marry her.

The words she'd spat at Jeff before he moved out rang in her ears. She'd said that, knowing he was going to move in with Jessica. Effectively telling her son that right and wrong depended on the circumstances.

Suddenly, a blade of conviction cut through her, stripping away pretense and revealing the moral equivalency of what she was doing to Jessica and what her father had done to John. As though a veil were lifting, she saw herself. A cold and unloving woman, in a turf battle for her son. Even when Jeff had told her he was officially engaged, she hadn't encouraged him to go ahead and get married right away and do what was morally right.

They rode in silence until they reached the main road, then Leigh turned toward John. "You're right. It's true."

"Leigh, it's the Holy Spirit who reveals truth."

She slowly shook her head. "I can't believe how caught up in this I've been." Her shoulders slumped as the full weight of her actions settled on her. "I owe them both an apology."

Turning her face to the window, she took in the clear blue sky shining behind the pine-covered mountains, the breathtaking beauty of the area somehow comforting her. By the time they reached the highway, she'd decided she'd call Jessica one day next week and ask her to lunch. Maybe if she quit fighting the girl, she could find common ground with her.

"Johnny, Jeff's all I have." Leigh straightened. "I guess

if I'm going to have a family, it's going to include Jessica."

"Sounds right to me." He squeezed her hand.

As the miles slipped by, they sat in comfortable silence. Leigh's thoughts returned to John's words about the Holy Spirit.

"Johnny, can I ask you something?"

"Sure."

"What you said about the Holy Spirit revealing truth."

He nodded.

"I believe that. In fact, I've thought a lot about it lately." She hesitated. "Remember me telling you about Paramount Publishers saying they would look at a book proposal from me?"

He nodded again.

"Right before that happened I'd started praying that God would show me the Holy Spirit working in my life."

John glanced at her, waiting for her to continue.

"Then, out of the blue, Paramount called my agent and told her they were interested in having me submit."

"Not only does God hear our prayers"—he turned to her and smiled—"He answers them."

"Right before I started going to your church, the pastor at Grace Bible Church was preaching from the book of Acts. I've read from Acts many times, but as he got into it, I really began to understand how the Holy Spirit is God's messenger." She looked at him, waiting for a response.

"Leigh, the Holy Spirit's equal in power, but the Bible says He won't speak on His own authority. Instead, whatever He hears He will speak." He glanced at her. "He's always drawing people to God."

"Equal in power." She took a deep breath and let it out. "Wow. And just think, the Holy Spirit dwells in us. Can you imagine really having the power of God?"

He turned to her, a blank half smile on his face.

"Can you imagine writing a book written with the power of the Holy Spirit? That's a book that could change people's hearts."

"It sure could."

She remembered the bookcase in his living room. "I noticed you have quite a few books on the subject of the Spirit."

"I do." He shifted in his seat.

"Could you recommend a book . . . for a beginner?"

He grinned at her. "You've already got the best book on the subject. The Bible."

"I know what you're saying, but I'm talking about for today. I'm fascinated by the things I hear about in church. People who actually have the gifts of prophecy, words of knowledge, healing. I want that. The Gift. I want to be used by Him. That way, but if not, then through my books."

He turned to her, his eyes looking directly into hers, suddenly serious. "Do you have a regular prayer time when you meet with the Lord?"

"Pretty much every morning."

"Ask Him about your book the next time you meet."

"I have been. But every idea that comes to me falls flat. I don't have any sense of divine inspiration."

"Leigh, seek His face and not His hands." John's voice

became firm. "As you get to know Him personally, I think you'll find He and the Spirit are one."

She did know God and the Spirit were one. Part of the Trinity. The tone of his voice made her feel like he was talking down to her.

Anger winged across her shoulders, straightening her back. She'd take his advice and spend more time in the Word. Then she'd bring the subject up again. If they were going to have a relationship, which the time they'd spent together this afternoon had certainly encouraged, they had to be able to discuss their faith.

She felt the car slowing. They were still in the mountains and there wasn't a building or another vehicle in sight. "What's up?"

"There's a gas station just around that next curve. I'm going to stop and fill up."

Leigh glanced at the gas gauge. It registered over half a tank.

As they rounded the next curve, Leigh saw a run-down building with two old pumps in front of it.

John pulled the truck next to the first pump, turned off the engine, and jumped out of the cab. She heard him take off the gas cap and put the hose nozzle in the tank. As she pulled down the visor to check her lipstick, a movement outside her window caught her attention. She turned just in time to see John move away from the front door of the building and stride around the corner toward the back. She craned her neck trying to see exactly where he was going. But he disappeared behind some old cars.

Leigh pushed up the visor and rolled down the window, listening. The only sound she heard was the pump shutting off. Her eyes returned to the building. There was no sign of anyone.

Opening her door, she got out. After waiting a few moments, she moved to the side of the truck, removed the nozzle from the tank, hooked it back into the pump, and replaced the gas cap. Then she walked to the door where she'd seen John.

It was locked.

She put her hands on her hips. The place looked deserted.

Turning, she took a few steps toward the corner of the building. Maybe John had gone to look for the attendant. As she neared the corner, she could hear a man's voice, low and urgent.

Someone was crying. She stopped, listening, torn between a desire to help and the feeling she should mind her own business. Slowly tilting her head, she managed to get a clear view of the side of the structure. There was nothing but the old cars.

Curious concern moved her feet. She began to pick her way toward the voices. When she reached the back of the building, she stood on her toes behind a stack of old tires. Stretching up as far as she could, she was able to see John sitting on a slab of cement next to another man with black spiky hair. Their backs were to her. She held her breath, trying to catch their words. The sounds became fragments of sentences. ". . . God . . . Jesus loves . . . care . . ."

John had his arm around the man's shaking shoulders, and his head was bowed. She dropped back on her heels, suddenly feeling like an intruder. Retracing her steps, she returned to the truck and jumped in.

⨳

He'd felt it as soon as he'd seen the curve in the road. God was calling him.

It always happened the same way. First a vision of the place to which he was being called, then a sense of urgency, and finally an image. The image always appeared in front of a veil of silvery mist. And at some visceral level John understood that beyond the veil was where God operated. Beyond the veil he was a vessel and nothing more. Nothing more.

John rounded the corner at the back of the building. "Anybody here?" No answer.

A door. He had to find a door.

Quickly surveying the area, he saw a run-down house in the trees, about thirty yards ahead of him.

He bolted toward it, bounding up the front steps and pounding on the door. No answer.

He stood, listening. The air was still as death.

"Jesus."

He spoke the Word that had changed the world, into the barren silence.

Turning on his heel, he ran down the steps and toward the back of the house. A detached, narrow garage came into view. He felt a rush of adrenaline.

Sprinting across the yard, he grabbed the garage door handle, and with one powerful, sweeping motion, pulled the garage door up.

191

Light flooded into the building. Revealing a man hanging from a rope. A noose around his neck.

John rushed to him. Putting his shoulder under the man's torso and pushing up, he circled his left arm around the man's legs. Then he reached for the chair lying·on the floor. Pulling it to himself, he righted it, then climbed up onto it. Working the noose loose, he freed the man, letting the body fall across his shoulder.

He ran with quick, deliberate steps to the clearing behind the gas station and laid the man down on the ground.

As John felt for a pulse, he noticed the man was hardly more than a boy. Perhaps seventeen or eighteen. His face was bruised.

For a moment, John thought he felt a heartbeat, then lost it.

He squeezed his eyes shut. "Please, Jesus."

The presence of love and the fragrance of roses immediately permeated the air.

"You brought me here, at this time, to this place, for Your purposes. I don't believe the lie of the Enemy that this boy is dead." He lay down beside the young man.

Then, with the faith of Elisha, as he had done only once before in the twenty-five years he'd walked with Jesus, he rolled on top of the boy, covering him like a blanket.

"All things are subservient to you. Even death."

Suddenly he was surrounded by a silvery mist. He closed his eyes and prayed.

"Your will be done, on earth as it is in heaven."

After a few moments, he felt a release and moved to

the boy's side. Kneeling, he pulled the young man's upper body into his lap. Cradling him like a child.

The young man murmured. "Momma?"

John gently shook him. "No, I'm a friend."

The boy opened his eyes, looking around him. His hand went to his neck.

John could see angry welts beneath the young man's fingers.

John rose, then pulled the boy to his feet. "Come with me." He put his arm around the young man's shoulder, guiding him to a large cement block. They sat on it. "What's your name, son?"

"Tito."

John put his arms around Tito's shoulders. "God sent me here to tell you Jesus Christ loves you." He moved closer to the boy. "Did you know that?"

The boy hung his head, a sob escaped his lips. "There ain't nobody loves me. My mom's dead and my old man's a drunk." His hand touched his bruised cheek.

John looked toward the house. "Is he home?"

"No, he's in jail." The boy wiped his nose with the back of his hand. "Some woman that's been livin' with him called the cops last night. Cops took 'em both to jail."

The boy turned to him, face contorting. "I got fired from my job this morning. They said there was money missing. I didn't take no money from them or nobody." He dropped his head. "Why'd you have to come here? You shoulda' left me alone. You had no business comin' here."

John put his forefinger under the boy's chin. "Look at me."

Tito lifted his eyes.

193

"It's no coincidence I came here today. Somebody does care if you live or die. Me, for one."

Tito's focus sharpened.

"And there's somebody else. Someone who has a plan for your life. Someone who knew you before you were born, and knows you now. His name is Jesus."

The boy dropped his gaze.

John felt a quickening in his heart. He discerned that the boy had been told of Jesus before, and had rejected him. His heart was hard.

And John discerned something else. The boy's mother had prayed for him, asking God to take care of him when she was gone.

"Your mom was sick a long time, wasn't she?"

Tito looked up, suspicion in his eyes. "Yeah."

"And she died about a month ago?"

The boy's lower lip trembled and he jerked his head in a nod. "What do you know about it?"

John continued. "I know she's not suffering anymore. God called her and she answered."

"She left me." Tito drew back, his face etched in pain. "She left me and I hate her."

He squeezed his eyes shut. A sob tore from his lips. "I hate her."

John grabbed Tito as the boy slid from the cement block toward the ground. He pulled Tito to his chest.

The boy went limp against him. "Momma, come back. Please come back."

John stroked the boy's head. *Jesus, I am Your willing vessel.* There was only one thing that could change the heart of man.

Instantly, John felt the love of Christ flow through him.

The boy's body shook as the balm of Gilead poured over a lifetime of wounds. Working its way down to the deep, hidden places. Restoring hope to the heart and light to the soul.

John whispered to the boy, "You're going to be all right. It's going to work out."

Gradually, Tito's breathing evened and the trembling stopped. He slowly pulled back from John's arms.

"How old are you, son?"

The boy wiped his face on his shirtsleeve. "Eighteen."

"You got a car?"

Tito nodded.

"There's a church called His Place in Ridgeline. Go there and ask for the pastor. Tell him John sent you. He'll find you a place to stay and help you get a new job."

The boy's face filled with emotion as a flicker of hope passed through his eyes. "You think so?"

"I know so." John smiled.

With shy awkwardness, Tito reached toward John and hugged him.

John received the embrace, recognizing it for what it was. An act of faith by a child wounded so deeply he'd chosen death instead of life.

He felt a quickening in his spirit. God had a call on Tito's life. That's what this was about—the Enemy trying to steal from the kingdom's treasures. God was going to use the boy mightily.

❧

Leigh kept checking her watch. She felt like she'd been waiting in the car for well over an hour. But every time she looked at her watch, only a minute or so had passed. She frowned. Leaning toward the windshield, she craned her neck, trying to catch the angle of the sun.

She checked her watch again, and huffed a sigh. However long it had been, it had been long enough.

Just as she started to get out of the truck, John reappeared. He went to the locked gas station door, took out his wallet, and stuck some money between the door and the jamb. Then he returned to the truck, slipped behind the wheel, and started it.

Leigh cleared her throat. "Um. You were gone kind of a long time."

"Oh, I visited with Tito a little while." John pulled away from the pump. "Thanks for being so patient."

"Tito?"

"Yeah, he's the child of a friend of mine. Been going through some hard times lately."

She was dying to ask him what had happened. "Um. How much did you pay him for the gas?"

John raised his eyebrows. "What do you mean?"

"You didn't even look at the pump."

John chewed his lower lip. "Let's just say I left enough money and didn't worry about the change."

She studied John's face, the whole episode beginning to make sense. John probably decided to stop and check on the boy when he'd realized he was passing by the gas station, and he hadn't felt like he should tell her about the young man's personal problems. The boy had clearly been upset when she'd seen him. She smiled to herself.

196

John had used the excuse of buying gas to give the young man money.

She lowered her eyes. John was a good man. She wanted this relationship to continue. "John, you know I haven't told my parents about us."

"When we talked it over, you said you wanted to wait until your dad recovered from his last round of chemo."

That was true. She'd thought a lot about the conversation she had to have with her father since she'd learned the truth. Telling him she knew what he'd done, and that she'd reconnected with John, was going to dredge up painful issues that had lain buried for twenty-five years. The whole situation was deeply disturbing and just thinking about bringing up the past with him put her stomach in knots. But it was more than that. She knew she had to forgive him.

"He's finished, and went in for his nine-month checkup last week. His prognosis is very good." She rested her hand on John's thigh. "It's something I want to do soon. I don't like the fact that I can't talk openly about seeing you, and I want to get this behind us. All of us."

He took her hand in his and squeezed it. "Is there anything I can do to make it easier?"

"Just pray for God's will."

⬥⬥⬥

"Dad, I need to talk to you." Leigh cleared her throat. "Dad, there's something I want to talk to you about."

She glanced through her windshield at the front door of her parents' home. Her mother was liable to open the door any minute if she'd heard Leigh's car pull into the driveway.

On the way back from John's house she'd decided she wasn't going to wait any longer to talk to her father about what had happened. She hadn't gone to see her parents since after work on Thursday, and now was as good a time as any.

This afternoon with John, in his arms by the stream, had been heaven. They both knew why he kept insisting he needed to help her cast her line "one more time." And when he'd held her close, she'd closed her eyes for a moment, feeling the heat from his body, the roughness of his cheek against hers, the strength of his hands around her fingers. And it had felt right, and good, and she wanted to be there forever.

The reality of what could have been returned to her . . . then slipped away.

The more she thought about it, the angrier she became. Her father had set out to destroy her relationship with John. And he had. Then, for all these years he'd led her to believe John had just faded from her life, keeping the subject taboo, fostering the idea that he had been right about the Indian.

"Don't want to see that Indian coming around here." The terse words shouted to her from a bitter scene at their dinner table.

"Someone said they saw you with that half-breed after school today." The smoky voice snaked across her childhood bedroom.

Fiery eyes, dark with concern. "He's not coming back, Leigh. Forget about him."

She opened the car door and slammed it shut behind her. What he had done was wrong and had changed the course of two people's lives.

She stormed up the walkway with hard, deliberate steps and rang the doorbell. Then without waiting for someone to answer it, she opened the front door and walked in.

The sound of voices came from the family room.

"It's me," she called out.

Her mother was rising from the couch as she walked in. Her father was talking on the phone.

Her mother put her forefinger to her lips, then whispered, "It's your brother."

From the look on her parents' faces, it was clear R.J. was having some kind of a crisis. He probably needed money. Whether it was money, a plane ticket, clothes, or praise, she was sure her father would be more than happy to give him whatever he wanted. The perfect son who could do no wrong.

"Do you want to say hi to your brother?" Her father's voice cut into her thoughts.

No, she didn't. Right now she wanted to be heard. "Tell him I'll call him back." Her mouth quirked. "*If* he has a phone number."

"He just gave me his number. I have it right here." Her father held up a scrap of paper. "She'll call you later."

Well, that was a first. She set her mouth in a firm line. She hadn't meant her words to sound so harsh.

Her father said good-bye and hung up the phone. "You're certainly wound tight tonight."

Her mother perched on the edge of the couch, hands knotted in her lap, face pale. Clearly, R.J. had upset her.

For a moment Leigh started to lose her resolve.

She swallowed. No. For once in her life she wasn't going to take a backseat to R.J.

"Sit down, honey." Her mother patted the couch.

Leigh walked between her parents to the fireplace and sat on the hearth, facing her father, feet planted in front of her, fisted hands resting on her thighs. "I just left John Higheagle's house."

Her father's eyes narrowed. Then widened. "John Higheagle! The Indian?"

"Yes. The Indian. The one you made it your business to cut out of my life. He told me what you did. You knew where he was and that he was trying to stay in touch with me." She could feel herself shaking. She'd never spoken to her father like this, but now, somehow every word ignited another, and she couldn't stop.

"You ruined my life and I hate you for it."

She heard her mother catch her breath. Tears sprang to her father's eyes.

The words continued to pour out without conscious thought of forming them. "You never loved me. You always favored R.J." She felt tears on her cheeks. "Just like now, him calling, wanting something."

"He didn't ask for anything."

Leigh's eyes flashed to her mother.

"He's so excited about this movie he's in." Her mother's voice came out a whisper. "We're so glad he did call. It gave us a chance to tell him." Her mother dropped her head.

Leigh turned to her father. Her hateful words still in the air, making his voice distant.

"The cancer is back."

200

John shut the door behind him, switched on a light, and threw his keys on the coffee table in front of the couch. "Hey, Sweetheart, I'm home."

The familiar clickety-clack on the hardwood floors greeted him.

He knelt down for a snooty kiss, then scratched Sweetheart between her front legs. Her tail went straight up as if to say, "Ohh, don't stop. Don't stop."

Chuckling, John rose, walked into the kitchen, and opened the glass slider. She scrambled to the backyard. He closed the door, turned on the back light, and watched for a moment as she made a beeline to her feeding area.

Turning on his heel, he walked back to the living room and flopped on the couch. What a day. After Leigh had left, he'd driven to the church to see if Tito had taken his advice. He had. The boy was waiting for the pastor to take him to the home of one of the church families. "God, pour Your blessings out on that boy."

He leaned his head against the cushion back. *Leigh.*

Being with her today had been heaven. God had made him wait twenty-five years, but it had only made it all the sweeter now. A smile tugged at his lips.

His eyes drifted to the bookshelf. *"Could you recommend a book . . . for a beginner?"*

He scanned the shelf. He knew every book well. He'd studied them for years.

Leaning forward, he rested his forearms on his thighs. There was a real good Bible study on Acts he'd used. He rose, took the few steps to the bookcase, and squatted.

Locating the guide, he reached for it. As soon as his hand touched the spine of the book, goose bumps rose on his arms.

He pulled the book out and returned to the couch. He thumbed through it. As he glanced through the chapters, he began to get a strong impression that God was speaking to him.

He laid the book on the coffee table and bowed his head, hoping for some further revelation.

Snippets of conversations he'd had with Leigh played back to him. How she'd asked him about the Holy Spirit the first time she'd come to the house. How she'd mentioned it off and on over the past month or so as they dated. And then again today she'd brought it up. Suddenly, it all took on more importance.

He got a second chill.

As clearly as if he'd heard a spoken word, he knew the Lord was going to use him in Leigh's life as she pursued her writing career. And he knew something more. The Lord was going to give her the book of His heart.

His heart soared. Surely this was a confirmation for what he'd been thinking about ever since he'd kissed her by the stream.

The low rumble of a summer storm sounded in the distance.

He rose from the couch and walked to the living room window. A flash of lightning drew his eyes to the night sky.

God had allowed Leigh into his life, knowing how he felt about her, knowing how she felt about him, knowing where she was in her spiritual walk. The timing was perfect in so many ways. And now this word from the Lord. A clear sign, a clear direction.

He was going to do it.

Another clap of thunder sounded overhead.

He was going to ask Leigh to marry him.

14

Leigh hadn't been able to sleep all night, or concentrate at work all day. The scene with her father had devastated them both.

She'd stayed at her parents' house until long past midnight, trying to pick up the pieces of their lives. Trying to retrieve the words that had judged and condemned. Trying to distance herself from her own pain while drowning in her father's. But it had done no good. Their relationship was shattered. The only thing they had in common now was their suffering.

By the time she returned home, she'd decided two things: she wanted her father's forgiveness, and that meant she would have to put her relationship with Johnny on hold. When Johnny had called her at work and asked her to dinner, she'd accepted. It felt like God was opening a door for her.

The doorbell rang. She glanced at the clock by her bed. 7:00 p.m.

Stopping for a moment, she tried to gather her thoughts. *Lord God, give me the words I need so Johnny will understand that this isn't the right time for us. I don't want to hurt him. I want him in my life. But right now we can't be more than friends.*

She stiffened, holding her tears in check. She loved Johnny, but she loved her dad too. And she'd made up her mind to use whatever time her father had left to try to make peace with him. She hoped and prayed he'd let her.

Yet, she didn't want to cut Johnny off. Not after finally finding him and realizing that they still had feelings for each other . . . deep feelings.

She walked slowly down the stairs. The doorbell rang again just as she reached the front door. Pulling it open, she saw John standing behind a big bouquet of flowers.

She paused, suddenly conflicted. Why tonight, of all nights, would he decide to bring her flowers? He hadn't done that since they'd started dating.

"Come in." With as much enthusiasm as she could muster, she took the bouquet from him. "They're just beautiful. Thank you so much." She pressed them to her face and inhaled deeply.

The sweet scent of the flowers sparked a memory. They were standing in the trees behind the high school, meeting secretly, as they did every day after classes. Johnny had brought her wildflowers he'd picked. She remembered how nervous he'd been, finally asking her to be his girl.

That day she'd eagerly said yes.

She pushed the memory from her mind. "Let me put these in water."

He followed her into the kitchen, helping her get a vase from the cabinet.

After she filled the vase with water and set the bouquet in it, he took her elbow. "Let's put them in the family room."

He guided her to the couch, then took the vase from her and put it on the coffee table. "Could we talk a minute?" He sat on the couch and patted the cushion next to him.

As a strong sense of uneasiness washed through her, she took a step back and sat, leaving some distance between them.

He turned and faced her, then reached for her hands. "Leigh, I love you."

Her heart lurched.

"I know this might seem sudden," he said, grinning from ear to ear. Then, slipping from the sofa to one knee, he released her hands and reached into his shirt pocket.

"Will you marry me?" He snapped open a velvet box, revealing a simple princess cut solitaire.

Leigh's hand flew to her lips.

He began to chuckle. "You can't be too surprised. I'm crazy about you, and you know it. I just thank God that He brought us together."

Leigh felt acid pouring into her stomach. "Johnny." Dead silence. "I'm so flattered."

His smile froze.

"But—" Her mind raced. Was trying to mend the relationship with her father going to end her relationship with Johnny? "We have to talk."

"Talk?" He settled back on his heel, hand still extended. His brow creased. "We don't have to get married right away." He flashed her a boyish smile. "I just want you to be my steady girl."

The mock innocence on his face and the use of the same words he'd used in high school magnified the terrible feeling of helplessness that had started in her stomach and now floundered in her throat. "Please. Sit." She gestured to the sofa.

All pretense left his face as he shifted clumsily onto the edge of the couch. The ring box, still open, now clutched in his fingers, his hand stiff in his lap.

He turned to her, eyes concerned, face attentive. Waiting.

God, help me. "Johnny, last night I went to see my parents and I confronted my dad about the letters." She dropped her head, suddenly not sure what she wanted to say. "It didn't go very well." She clenched her fists, trying to hang on to her resolve. "I don't know what happened. I just lost it. I said terrible things." She raised her head. "I told my father I hated him." Her voice wavered. "And that's not the worst of it."

The concern on John's face deepened.

"His cancer is back."

"I'm sorry." His voice came out a whisper.

"This isn't the right time for us, Johnny." She saw him stiffen. "I'm not saying we can't see each other. I'm just saying this isn't the time to announce our engagement. I've got to work through this with my father. Not just for his sake, but for mine."

John's shoulders slumped. He sat for a moment, not moving, then closed the ring box, and put it back in his pocket. "Where do we go from here?" His voice was flat.

Suddenly, the reality that she could lose Johnny again

207

hit her. Was she going to end up estranged from all three of the men in her life? First Jeff, then her father, and now . . . Panic rose in her chest.

Since they'd been reunited, John had been a rock to lean on. And more than that, she felt drawn to him spiritually . . .

The book.

The thought came to her so strongly she felt as though the words had been spoken.

They could work on the book together. He'd been excited about her ideas. Now he could be a part of them. "Johnny. The book."

His eyes narrowed slightly.

"The book. You know. Writing the book of God's heart is my dream." She leaned toward him. "In time, the rest of this will sort itself out. I know it will. But for now we can work on the book together." She watched his face for some reaction. "Maybe that's part of the reason God brought us together."

His cheeks paled, and a sorrow so deep it brought tears to her eyes filled his face.

Her throat constricted, knowing she'd hurt him. "I love you, Johnny. It's going to work out."

He shuddered, his eyes distant.

Suddenly, he rose from the couch and walked out of the room, his footsteps echoing in the hall.

"Johnny." Leigh rose, running after him. "Johnny." She felt a cold rush of night air as the front door opened.

Her voice tore from her lips. "Johnny! Come back!"

⟨∞⟩

God had betrayed him.

Lungs burning, John pressed on as dead branches grabbed his ankles and thorny boughs slapped him.

The drive from Leigh's had been a blur. When he'd reached his driveway, he'd stopped the truck and jumped out. Then, cutting across the field behind his house, he'd bypassed the well-worn trail to the clearing at the top of the ridge, taking the shorter, steeper way up the mountain.

Gasping for air, he burst through the final stretch of trees into the clearing. Unfettered by the dense brush, he stumbled forward a few more yards, finally collapsing, facedown, to the earth.

He pounded the ground with clenched fists.

Angling his face awkwardly toward the sky, his voice traveled through the night on deep, ragged breaths. "Why, Lord? Why?"

He dropped his head back into the soil. Tears and spit grinding dirt into his face.

Turning his face to the side, he squeezed his eyes shut, only to find Leigh, on the couch facing him, lips moving, speaking a silent curse. *"But for now we can work on the book together."*

That's when it had happened . . . as it always happened—the image and the veil.

John had seen a book clearly as Leigh faded behind a veil of silvery mist. And he'd understood that God was showing him his purpose in her life. Why He had brought them together.

It was about her books . . . her writing . . . not about Leigh.

Beyond the veil was where God operated. Beyond the veil John was a vessel and nothing more.

Nothing more.

Hot with anger, he railed against a lifetime of walking with God. What possible importance could Leigh's desire to write books have? How could book signings at Borders or little write-ups in the local papers matter, compared to his life and future?

But God remained silent.

John rose to his knees. Facing the night sky, he began to bargain with God. Promising all he and Leigh together would do for Him. How they would minister, and touch and change lives. How, if they were married, Leigh could write full-time, and her books would bring glory to His name.

But the black canopy above him, with its thousand blinking eyes, only stared silently at him.

Raising his fist, he recounted all he had done for God, all he had sacrificed for God, and how little he had asked of Him.

Only this one thing. Nothing more . . . ever.

Still, God didn't answer.

Dropping his head back, he screamed into the heavens, "I sacrificed my life for You. I asked nothing in return."

The moment the words left his lips, the enigmatic truth they held reached his ears.

"I sacrificed my life for you. I asked nothing in return."

His eyes widened. Suddenly seeing himself. Self-righteous, demanding, arrogant. Separated from God.

He dropped his head to his knees, now strangely aware of the physical world around him. As though he were cut off from all things spiritual, except for the one Truth, present and palpable.

In that moment, John recognized in a way he never had before that the choice was his. He had free will to serve God . . . or himself.

Bowed and broken, he spoke.

"Your will, not mine, Lord."

⁓

Jessica pushed her purse into the basket of clean clothes, then dropped the basket next to the bottom step of the stairs that led to the apartment. She glanced toward the street. It was past eight o'clock, and Jeff should be pulling in any minute.

She hoped he hadn't forgotten to stop at Al's Auto Repair. Now that they were going to be working different shifts, they needed both cars. She and Jeff had decided if Al would let them make payments, they'd get her car fixed.

Jessica looked up the long row of steps that led to the apartment. With her cast off, she could drive again, and she'd made up her mind to find a doctor who would give her pain medication. She was plagued by the prickly pain in her legs, and lately sometimes her feet were numb. When that happened, it made her feel off balance. To walk up the stairs, she had to keep one hand firmly on the railing.

She released a deep sigh. Going to the doctor would mean tests, which would mean bills, which would mean more debts they couldn't pay. She sat on the bottom step of the stairs. Just before she'd met Jeff she'd talked to a doctor about it, and he'd told her it could be caused by her diabetes, though he thought it unlikely because, at the time, she'd had diabetes for only a little over a year. Maybe if she waited a little longer the pain would just go away like it had then.

The sound of her cell phone broke into her thoughts. She reached into the basket, pulled it out of her purse, and flipped it open. Seeing the number on the screen, she swore.

Leigh . . . again.

Jessica flipped the phone shut and threw it on top of the clothes.

Leigh had called once this morning, once a few hours ago, and again now. She'd left messages on the voice mail saying she wanted to get together for lunch. Well, forget it. How stupid did she think Jessica was? After Leigh's snide remarks at dinner Saturday night, Jessica had made up her mind she'd never give Leigh an opportunity like that again. The woman was a hypocrite. A big talker about Christianity and God's love, when she was nothing but a judgmental witch.

Too bad Jeff couldn't see it. He was always defending her, refusing to say a bad thing about his mother. They'd even had a fight about it Sunday, and Jessica had finally told him maybe he should make a choice. That had hurt him.

Jessica lowered her eyes. She felt bad about that, but she'd known people like Leigh all her life. People with agendas, people who thought everyone should be like them, people who thought she was nothing more than white trash.

Jessica folded her arms across her chest and stuck out her chin. Bring it on.

Jeff's car pulled into the parking lot. She could see him smiling through the driver's door window. She dropped her arms. Maybe he had good news about her car.

He parked and stepped out of the car. "Hey, Jessie." He jogged to her, kissing her as soon as he reached her.

Stooping over, he picked up the clothes basket and hoisted it onto his shoulder. "Let me help you."

Jessica stepped to the side so he'd go up the steps first, then walked behind him, holding onto the railing.

When they got into the apartment, Jeff put the clothes basket on the floor by the couch and sat down.

"Did you stop at Al's?" Jessica seated herself in a chair opposite him, the loneliness of the day vanishing.

"Yeah, I just left there. It was lucky he happened to be working late. He said if we'd pay for the parts he has to buy, we could make payments on the labor."

"When can he take it?"

Jeff raised his eyebrows. "As soon as we have the money for the parts."

"Jeff, I've got to have my car next week for work." Her words sounded sharper than she'd intended.

"I was thinking, Jessie. You come to work when my shift is over. I could just drive the car home and then come and pick you up when you get off."

"That won't work. I'm going to be working in a different house. If I pick you up, it'll make me late."

Jeff nodded. "I thought of that too. None of those houses are more than a mile apart. I can just walk to wherever you're working."

Jessica reached down, rubbing her calf. "Jeff, we need two cars. Your hours at Sears are always changing, and

I have things I need to do during the day." She leaned back in her chair. "Could you borrow the money from someone at Sears? Just for a couple of weeks?"

"Jessica, I'm not borrowing any more money."

She recognized from his tone that pursuing the idea probably wouldn't get her what she wanted.

A thought occurred to her. "Why don't we get a payday loan? That's not really borrowing. That's getting an advance on money that's coming."

"I've never done that. How does it work?"

"It's easy, I've done it lots of times." She scooted to the edge of the chair. "You just take in a pay stub and a blank check from your checking account. Then you write your check for up to half the amount on the pay stub. Then, on your next payday you cash your paycheck and take them the cash, and they give you your check back."

"That's all?"

"That's it. Uh, they charge a fee, but it's not much. Like fifteen dollars."

Jeff frowned. "For how much money?"

"I've usually gotten a hundred dollars."

"Fifteen dollars to use their hundred dollars for two weeks?"

"Told you it was a good deal."

"That's 15 percent interest for two weeks." He drew back. "Do you realize that's 30 percent a month?"

Why was he creating a problem where there wasn't one? "It's not interest. They explained that it's a flat fee. Anyway, what difference does it make? It's worth fifteen dollars to get the car fixed."

"I don't know, Jess. It seems like we could manage

until I get paid. And you'll be getting a paycheck on the thirtieth."

"That's just the point. We're both working now. There won't be any problem paying it back." She stretched forward, pulled the clothes basket to her, picked up her cell phone and tossed it into her purse.

Jeff pointed at her. "Oh, my mom called me today. Said she'd been trying to reach you."

Jessica shrugged. "I've had my phone with me all day."

"She wants to take you to lunch."

He was clearly delighted with the idea. He was acting like the argument they'd had Sunday never happened.

"Jeff, I told you. I don't need your mother in my life. I've never had a mother and I'm not looking for one now. And if she calls you again, you can tell her I said so."

Jeff's smile faded. "I'm not going to disrespect my mother, Jessica."

"Fine. If she calls you again, tell her she'll have to talk to me." Jessica felt tears sting her eyes. She stood, grabbed the clothes basket, and dragged it to the dining room table.

Jessica stood with her back to Jeff folding a pair of his pants. He had a mother . . . and he loved her. So what. It didn't matter to Jessica at all. She was getting along just fine.

A tear rolled down her cheek.

She bent down and reached into her purse, feeling her way to the bottom.

The baggie was still there.

When her car got fixed, life would be so much easier.

215

15

Leigh pulled out of the parking lot of the Cedar Ridge post office. *Second Chance* was on its way to the publisher. "Whoo hoo, Lord. Thank You for that."

Trying to get a day's worth of errands run before ten o'clock in the morning had been a challenge. She should have made a list, but there hadn't even been time for that. She glanced at her watch. Still, it looked like she was going to make it. She turned onto the road that would take her to her parents' house.

The last few months had been an emotional roller coaster. Every effort she'd made to become part of Jeff and Jessica's lives was rebuffed by Jessica. Whether Leigh invited them to dinner, the movies, or just a Sunday afternoon at the house, Jessica always bowed out at the last minute, leaving Jeff to come alone.

The first few times he'd offered excuses. Eventually it had become, "Give her time, Mom." Now when he showed up alone he said nothing at all, which told Leigh more than any words he could have spoken. It told her she'd been right about Jessica from the beginning. The girl was trouble. The only bright spot was that Jeff had returned to college at the end of August.

But as stressful as all of this had been, she'd found it had drawn her closer to God. Her prayer list had become a prayer journal. She prayed faithfully for her father's healing and salvation. In fact, today's plans had sprung from that prayer time.

She also continually requested that God would open Jeff's eyes. And as Leigh looked for His answer, she'd found God opening doors. She'd turned Jessica cutting her off into an opportunity to spend time alone with her son. It had helped her build a bridge to Jeff, letting him know that should things change in his life, he was always welcome at home.

And she journaled, asking God to somehow reconcile Johnny and her father. She'd tried to bring up the subject of Johnny with her father several times. But the minute he saw where she was going, he would change the subject. And she had to admit, in the context of her relationship with her dad, Johnny's name did resurrect painful memories of her childhood, or even worse, brought the recent past front and center.

Since the blowup with her father, she'd come to know Johnny in a different way. If it hadn't been for him, she most certainly would have been forced to make a choice between the two men. But unexpectedly, John had patiently stayed in the background, settling for seeing her on Sundays. And over the months, Sunday had become a lifeline. No matter what crazy or upsetting things happened during the week, Leigh knew that Sunday she would find sanity and support at Johnny's church and home.

Best of all, he'd taken a real interest in her writing. She'd fallen into the habit of emailing him the chapters of *Second Chance* as she finished them. It turned out he had an amazing knack for seeing possible plot twists and had rejoiced with her when the book was finished.

With that behind her, now she could work full-time on the proposal for Paramount. She and her agent had talked about a couple of storylines but none of them was outstanding enough. Riva had stressed Paramount wanting something new and different. Something with a strong spiritual message and a broad appeal.

As Leigh pulled into her parents' driveway, a slight movement of the curtain covering the front window caught her eye. When the drape fell back into place, she realized her father had been watching for her.

She turned off the car and sat for a moment, giving him time to get back to his chair. He wouldn't want her to think he didn't have things to do, important things that were expected of a man, like working in his yard, or repairing something in his shop. He'd had to set aside time to go on a drive with her. He told her so when she'd asked him if he'd like to visit Two Forks River. But each time she stopped by to visit since then, the last thing he said before she left was, "Now you said you'll be by at ten on Saturday, right?"

She blinked rapidly. Yes, it was at ten on Saturday when life for him would be worth living again, when he would be able to visit the northern Idaho mountains where he'd fished and hunted before the cancer. When the future was about living and not dying.

How many more outings would there be, how many

more Saturdays did he have left in his life . . . how many more would she have with him? She climbed out of the car.

Ringing the doorbell as she opened the door, she called to him, "Dad, it's me. You ready?" She continued down the hall to the family room.

Steadying himself with the arm of the chair, he rose. "Is it ten already?"

"Yes, a little past. I had a lot to do this morning. But it's a beautiful day and we're going to have a nice drive and a picnic." She hadn't suggested that they bring fishing poles because she knew how quickly he tired, and watching him straighten slowly, she was glad she hadn't. "It's a perfect day to sit by the stream."

He glanced at her, and as their eyes met, she knew that he too was thinking about what they would not be doing at Two Forks. She looked away.

Leigh followed her father down the hall. He stopped at the coat closet by the front door and took out his old fishing hat. He pushed it onto his head, then turned to her. "Now I'm ready." He straightened and moved toward the door with renewed energy, defiance in his step.

She wanted to reach out to him, wrap her arms around his neck, and hug him. But at some level she knew it would make him uncomfortable. He'd never been demonstrative about his feelings, always keeping people at arm's length. But more than that, for her to suddenly ignore the rules he'd laid down all his life would be like acknowledging how drastically his life had changed, at a time when the mundane things, the pulse of an ordinary life, were what he yearned for. Today he was going to the

219

mountains as he'd done a thousand other times. Today the rules would be observed. She gave him a sharp half nod. "I'm right behind you."

As they wound their way through the mountains, her father's eyes began to brighten and a little color rose in his cheeks. He rolled down the window, resting his head against the back of the seat, breathing deeply of the fresh air. "Jeff was over yesterday."

Leigh tried to hide her surprise. "Oh?"

"Your mom invited him and his girl for dinner."

She waited for him to continue.

"Jessica couldn't come. Had to work or something. I was glad he came anyway. Haven't seen him in quite a while." He hesitated. "We gave him some money." Her father glanced at her. "I thought you should know."

Leigh tightened her grip on the steering wheel.

"He told us that he works full-time nights."

That wasn't what Jeff had told her when she'd had dinner at his house. He'd said when school started he would drop his full-time job.

"And I guess his girlfriend's had some health problems."

"Again?" Leigh's stomach turned. "What now?"

"He didn't say and we didn't ask. He's a grown man, and it's none of our business."

"If he was a grown man, he wouldn't be asking you for money."

Her father looked at her. "I didn't say he asked for money, I said we gave him some."

His words startled her. Her parents were on a fixed income, and her father's health problems had been a drain over the past year. Her mother had even made a few veiled comments about having to cut back . . . Leigh's heart lurched. Had Jeff said enough that her father had become concerned about the college loan?

"He's got to stay in school, Leigh, and graduate next June."

Icy fingers of fear crawled up her back. "He will, Dad."

There was no conviction in her words. And they both knew it.

"Where exactly is this place we're going?" Her father straightened in his seat. "I've never been to Two Forks and I thought R.J. and I knew every good fishing spot in northern Idaho."

"That's why I wanted to take you. It's kind of hidden. There was nobody there when we visited."

"We?"

"Uh." She hadn't purposely avoided telling her father how she'd learned of Two Forks; it just hadn't come up. Until now.

"John Higheagle brought me here once."

Her father raised his eyebrows. "Oh?" He hesitated. "Recently?"

"This past summer." She felt like she was walking through a minefield. This was the closest her father had come to permitting any conversation about the man who in many ways had defined their relationship.

Her father sat silently for a moment, then spoke. "Well, it's way the heck out here."

"It is. But that's part of what makes it so special. You feel like you've found a little piece of heaven on earth."

Leigh glanced at the gauges on the dash. "Oh no. No!" Her voice rose.

"What?" Her father grabbed the ledge of the open window.

"I can't believe it. I forgot to fill up this morning."

He leaned toward her, tilting his head to see the gauges, then clucked his tongue. "How far are we from town?"

Leigh looked around, trying to get her bearings. "We're way out of town." She took her foot off the gas, slowly pulling to the side of the road. "I can't believe I did that."

She stopped the car. "Dad, could you hand me my purse? It's by your feet."

He handed her the purse, and she retrieved her cell phone. Flipping it open, she saw there was no reception. She closed it and dropped it back in her purse.

"Leigh, we're not out of gas yet. Maybe there's a gas station ahead."

"There's no gas station for mi—" She startled. "Wait, there is. Johnny stopped at one. We hadn't driven that far . . ." Closing her eyes, she filtered through her memory, trying to retrace their route.

She turned to the window and looked up and down the road. "I'm almost positive we haven't passed that gas station yet. But it was kind of set back in the trees."

Pressing the accelerator, she pulled onto the pavement. "It almost looked abandoned." She continued along the winding road. "It'll be on our left." *Please, Lord. Where is that gas station?*

She watched the gauges as she drove, the mileage going up, the gas going down. Panic began to rise in her chest. "Dad, what if we run out of gas? No one will ever find us out here."

"Leigh, it's Saturday. I bet there will be other people coming up here to fish and picnic."

She wanted to believe that. But when she'd been here with Johnny, they hadn't seen anyone the whole afternoon. "I don't know, Dad."

The car rounded a curve and suddenly Leigh knew exactly where she was. The place she and John had parked his truck was immediately ahead of her. "I guess we did pass that gas station." She looked at her father and shrugged. "We're here."

She pulled the car onto the shoulder of the road and turned it off. "Sorry, Dad. This kind of puts a damper on things." Her hand rested on the keys. "Do you think we should go back and get gas first?"

Her father looked at her intently, his eyes resting on hers.

She found herself wanting to look away, suddenly realizing that they seldom made eye contact. A snapshot flashed in her mind. *Were you off with that Indian? The young girl dropped her gaze to her father's feet.* She blinked away the image.

"Leigh, I think you should show me this special place you found. Running out of gas . . . and other things . . . just don't upset me like they used to."

His words took her by surprise. "Then let's go. I'll get the lunch out of the trunk." She opened her door and climbed out.

As they walked, he reached out and gripped the handle of the cooler. The rough edge of his hand brushed hers.

223

In a strange way, she felt like her father was taking her to the stream.

They found a clear spot next to the water's edge.

"Oh, I forgot the blanket."

Leigh ran back to the car and got the old quilt she'd thrown in the backseat. When she returned, she found her father making a little pile of twigs. She shook out the quilt and let it waft to the ground. "What are you doing?"

"I wanted to make a fire. It's something R.J. and I always used to do when we went camping."

For some reason, the mention of her brother's name didn't have its usual sting. And as she watched her father perform the practiced ritual, she understood that for him it wasn't about the fire or R.J. It was about touching the reassuring, familiar past.

As the kindling caught fire, her father sat next to it, arching his neck to catch the smoke-scented air.

Leigh opened the cooler and began lifting out the sandwiches. "Hungry, Dad?"

When he didn't answer, she looked up.

He was standing, his face turned away from her, toward the mountains. She busied herself with setting out the lunch.

Before long he came and sat beside her. "That looks real good." His voice was loud and overexpressive, trying to draw attention away from his reddened eyes.

Leigh graciously obliged him, taking a plate and filling it slowly.

"Look, Leigh."

Her father was pointing across the river, where the pines edged the water. She set the plate down.

A huge buck emerged from the trees. The big animal lifted its head, watching them for a moment, and then moved toward the stream. He stopped directly across from them, lowering his head to drink.

Suddenly a breeze picked up, and as it moved through the trees it made a soft sound. Almost a call. In a moment a rabbit appeared near the buck. It sat on its haunches watching him drink. And soon a bird landed nearby, dipping its beak into the water.

Leigh felt her father's hand on hers.

She turned her head to catch his eye. But his gaze was fixed on the scene before him.

Suddenly, she became keenly aware of everything around her. The scent of the pine, the sound of the water, the angle of the sun. Her father's profile, the old hat resting on his head, his lips slightly parted. Though she could not say why, she recognized that they were sharing something God-given and uniquely for them.

She lowered her eyes. *Thank You, Lord.*

"Wasn't that something?" Her father turned to her, tears glistening in his eyes.

She looked back across the river. The animals were gone.

"You say John Higheagle brought you here." His words came out a statement rather than a question.

She nodded. "He says this is the land of his people."

Understanding flickered in her father's eyes. "I can't argue with that."

He took off his hat, running his hand around the brim, watching the rough edge curl beneath his fingers. Rolling the rules back into place.

He raised his head, looking past her.

"I just wanted the best for you."

❧

Leigh pulled into the gas station and up to the pumps. "I knew it wasn't far." Glancing at the gas gauge, she gave an exaggerated sigh of relief. "And it's a good thing it wasn't."

Looking around her father, out his window toward the station's office, she frowned. "Doesn't look like anybody's in there." She put her hand on the door handle. "Wait here, Dad. This is the same thing that happened last time."

Before going to the office, she stopped at the pump, took the lid off the gas tank, and shoved the nozzle into it. She pulled the lever and waited for the welcome hum of gas running through the hose.

Silence.

She frowned, clasping the lever in the handle harder.

Nothing.

She turned around, staring at the pump, looking for some button to push or lever to lift.

Finally she hooked the nozzle back into the pump, closed up her tank, and walked the short distance to the office. After trying the door and finding it locked, she called out.

No one answered.

She heard her father open his door. "What's up?"

"Nothing, Dad. I'm going to walk around back. Last time the guy was back there."

Leigh made her way through the old cars and junk

226

and, reaching the back of the station, called out again. "Anybody here?"

She continued to walk around the building until she'd made the full circle and was in front of the office again. She knocked on the dirty office window.

Her father was out of the car, leaning back against the hood. "The pumps are shut off, Leigh. Looks to me like this place is closed."

"I can't believe that." Leigh jogged to the car and got her cell phone from her purse.

She opened it and held it out in front of her, walking out of the trees, toward the road. "Well, there's some reception here at least. But trying to explain where we are isn't going to be easy." Closing the phone, she walked back to the car. "Guess I'll call Triple A." She dug her wallet from her purse and pulled out the white and blue card. "Dad, there's a bench by that front door. Why don't you go sit down while we wait? It's nice and cool there in the shade."

After searching for the best reception, Leigh stopped and turned over the Triple A card, then dialed the number printed on it. The phone rang and rang.

Finally a woman answered. Leigh explained the situation.

"It'll be a couple of hours. There's a big accident on Highway 95 and all our trucks have gone out there."

"Two hours!" Leigh scanned the desolate station. Maybe her mom or Jeff could bring out some gas. "I'll call you back." She closed the phone. Her gaze drifted to her father, then back to the pumps.

Johnny.

He knew the station's location.

The possibilities of the situation suddenly became obvious. John could bring them gas and meet her father. It would be a way of bringing the two men together.

As she thought about it, the idea blossomed. What were the chances that she would run out of gas on an outing with her father? And on the very day that her father had, in a very veiled way, inferred he'd been wrong about Johnny.

What a coincidence. The more she thought about it, the more it seemed like a God thing.

She stole a glance at her father. He was sitting quietly on the bench.

A wave of uneasiness washed through her. What would he say?

What *could* he say? They needed gas. She tapped the phone on her chin. What if she told him AAA was busy and that they'd had to call someone else? That was almost the truth. The only difference was that she was making the call. The fact was, Triple A might have called Dan's Automotive in Ridgeline if she'd pressed them. She thought for a moment. Wasn't the most important thing to bring the two men together? What possible difference could it make if she or Triple A made the call to Johnny?

She opened her phone and dialed.

The call didn't go through.

She looked at the phone's screen. The signal strength icon showed two bars. Just what it had been when she made the first call.

Holding the phone at arm's length, she began to walk

in a big circle, hoping to catch a stronger signal. The two bars held.

She stopped and pressed Send again.

Nothing.

She closed the phone, then opened it again, glaring at the screen.

"Dad."

He looked toward her.

"Would you walk around the building and see if there's any way to get into it? My phone won't work. Maybe there's one in there."

As he walked around the building, Leigh continued to try to connect to John's cell phone. At one point the signal strength jumped to three bars. But even though she immediately pushed Redial, the call didn't go through.

"Leigh."

Her father was waving at her from the open office door. "There's a phone in here, and it still works."

She jogged toward him. "How'd you get in?"

"The side door was unlocked. Actually, it doesn't even close completely. There's a house back there too, but nobody's home." He waved his hand in the direction he'd just come from. "I saw a bathroom back there." He turned and walked out of the office.

Leigh listened for the sound of his footsteps fading, then rushed to the phone and dialed John's cell number.

"Hello?"

"Johnny, it's me. We're out of gas. You've got to bring us some. We're here at that gas station by Two Forks."

"Speak up, Leigh. I can hardly hear you. Is something wrong?"

She froze. She hadn't thought this through. Should she tell Johnny about her plan? Her toes curled in her shoes.

"Leigh?"

"I brought my dad up to Two Forks for a picnic, and we ran out of gas. I'm at that gas station you and I stopped in, but the pumps don't work."

"Where's your dad?"

"He's here." She glanced over her shoulder.

"Why are you whispering?"

"I'm not. Will you stop asking so many questions and bring me some gas?"

There was a pause. "Leigh, does your dad know you're calling me?"

"He knows I'm calling for help. Are you going to bring that gas?"

She could hear him breathing.

"Leigh, I don't like the sound of this. I don't like the idea of just showing up there. Why didn't you call Triple A?"

Men could be so annoying. "I did. But they're tied up with some accident on Highway 95."

"In fact, that's where I am now. I couldn't get up there to you for at least another hour or so."

"That's okay." She glanced over her shoulder again. "We'll wait."

His words were clipped. "I still don't like the sound of it." He paused. "Just sit tight, I'll take care of it."

Her father's voice came from behind her. "Leigh? Did you get them? Are they coming?"

Hanging up the phone, she turned to him. "Help is on the way."

She and her father walked out to the front of the station and sat on the bench.

As the hour passed, she began to have second thoughts. Maybe she should tell her father the truth.

She glanced at him, searching her mind for a way to start such a conversation. What if he got mad? By the stream he'd seemed willing to talk about Johnny. But that was then. It was different there somehow. She clasped her hands in her lap. Still, this seemed like such a great way for the men to start over. Nobody would feel on the spot. John was just doing his job.

Every time she had herself convinced that the end justified the means, something stirred in her stomach and the anxiety started all over again.

The sound of a vehicle interrupted her thoughts.

Her father stood.

It was Johnny's truck, pulling up behind her car.

As her father walked toward it, the driver's door opened.

Her eyes widened. It wasn't Johnny. It was a young man with spiky hair. Her stomach clenched. Had her phone call made matters worse with Johnny?

The young man went around to the truck bed and pulled out a gas can. He nodded in her father's direction. Leigh hurried toward them.

The boy wiped his hand on his pants leg and extended his arm. "Hi. I'm Tito. John said you needed gas."

Her father shook the boy's hand. "John who?"

The young man moved to Leigh's car and opened the gas tank. "John Higheagle. He said you called."

231

Her father slowly turned to Leigh with knitted brows. "I thought you called Triple A."

"I did."

Tito's gaze traveled between the two of them. "John said Triple A is tied up with that big accident on 95."

God bless you, Tito. Leigh shrugged. "Well, what's important is that you came with the gas."

"How does John Higheagle know what Triple A is doing?"

Tito put the gas can nozzle into the car's tank. "He's out there too. He called me at the shop."

"What shop?"

"Dan's Automotive in Ridgeline. I work there." Tito grinned. "Thanks to John. He gave me a job."

Leigh balanced up on her tiptoes. "Isn't he a great guy?"

"He sure is. I met him last summer." Tito glanced at the building. "Right here."

Reminded, Leigh settled back down into her heels, suddenly recalling how she and John had stopped there . . . she'd waited in the car . . . the spiky black hair. . . . Leigh looked at the building, then back to the boy. Tito . . . this was the same boy.

"Things were really going bad for me back then. He just showed up out of nowhere. Spent an afternoon talking to me." Tito dropped his head, intent for a moment on putting the gas cap back on the tank. "Saved my life."

Leigh's heart swelled. John must have come back to see Tito after they'd stopped.

Tito looked up at them. "I'd never met him before in

232

my life, and he was there for me when my family wasn't. Got me a job and a place to live." The boy slowly shook his head. "He's a guy who really lives his faith."

Her father cleared his throat.

Leigh stiffened. Why was the boy saying he'd never met John before that day? And she and John hadn't spent the afternoon at the gas station, they'd stayed only a few minutes. Besides that, she was sure John had said Tito was the child of a friend.

"You're all set." Tito walked back to the truck and put the can in the bed.

Leigh struggled with the desire to question Tito about what he'd said. But it was awkward with her father there. "How much do I owe you?"

Tito opened the truck door and got behind the wheel. "John said to tell you to enjoy the rest of your day. No charge."

Her father took out his wallet. "No need for that."

"Dad." Leigh put her hand on his arm.

He held her gaze a moment, then put his wallet back in his pocket. He looked at Tito, and with the slightest inflection of one who stands corrected, he said, "Thank you for your help."

A broad smile spread across Tito's face. "Glad to do it." He shut the door and pulled away.

Leigh watched the truck disappear down the road, snatches of conversations niggling at her mind . . . *all afternoon . . . never met him before in my life . . . he's the child of a friend of mine.* The whole thing just didn't add up. But John had never lied to her in the past. There had to be an explanation.

"Let's get going." Her father's voice brought her back to the present.

"Sure, Dad." Leigh slipped behind the wheel. As she started the car, she remembered how that day last summer she'd had the sense of sitting in the car for a long time, but her watch indicated she'd waited only a few minutes. It didn't make sense.

And she was going to find out why.

16

Leigh knocked on John's front door. She wanted to talk to him face-to-face about what Tito had said. And she hadn't called to let him know she was coming. She wanted to observe his initial reaction when she brought it up.

The door swung open.

"Leigh. Hey. Come in." John waited for her to step into the room, then closed the door behind her.

Leigh saw Sweetheart peeking around the corner from the kitchen. "Hi, Sweetheart." She stooped down, clapping her hands together softly.

Sweetheart stared at her a moment, then gave a huffy grunt and abruptly turned around and walked off.

Giving Leigh a sheepish grin, John turned his palms up. "What can I say? My sweetheart wants to be number one with me." Then he pulled Leigh into his arms and gave her a light kiss. "What she doesn't know won't hurt her."

Leigh slipped from his grasp and took a seat on the couch. "John, I want to ask you about something."

His face sobered as he took a seat beside her. "Sure."

"It's about today."

He nodded, waiting for her to continue.

"You sent Tito with the gas and—"

"I couldn't come right then. And . . ." He hesitated. "And it just didn't seem right to come unannounced like that. It didn't seem like the right way to start over with your dad."

"That's not what's bothering me."

His eyes narrowed.

"It's what Tito said."

John's brow creased. "Was he rude?"

"No. Nothing like that. He told us how you met."

John's face remained attentive.

"Was that afternoon we stopped there the first time you met him?"

He held her gaze. "Yes."

"Why did you say he was the child of a friend of yours?"

John seemed to consider his answer. "Because he is."

"What's your friend's name?"

He rested his forearms on his thighs and clasped his hands. "Leigh, what's this about?"

"I feel like you weren't honest with me about that afternoon. Nothing Tito said made sense. He said he'd never met you before in his life, and he also said you were there for hours. We weren't there more than fifteen minutes. I must have looked at my watch ten times."

John looked at his hands.

As the moments passed and he didn't speak, a knot began to form in Leigh's chest. He didn't want to tell her his friend's name, or apparently anything else. Was

236

he hiding something that had happened in his past? Something he was ashamed of?

She chose her words carefully. "Johnny, I don't have any idea what this is about. But if we're going to continue to see each other, we can't have secrets."

He rose and walked across the room to the window. He rubbed his forehead, then shoved his hands in his pockets. Everything about his stance spoke of indecision.

Pushing up, she turned to him. "Maybe I'd better go home."

He didn't respond.

Leigh took a few steps toward the door. "Johnny, this is scaring me. I thought I knew you." She could hear her voice rising. "What else don't I know about you?" She waited for a response. "You can't even look at me."

He slowly turned to her, his face etched in pain. "I love you. Can't you see? I love you." Suddenly he was in front of her, his arms closing around her. "The only thing I haven't been honest about is how it's tearing me apart to see you one day a week. How I get up every morning and my first thought is how many more days, how many more hours."

She could feel him trembling, raw emotion coursing through him.

He kissed her hair, then pressed her head into his shoulder. "I never want to lose you again. Never."

The strong, familiar arms, the words stripped bare of pretense, the urgent intimacy of the moment, turned her anger to concern. "Tell me what's going on. What's this about?"

He slowly released her. Taking her hand, he walked her to the couch, then sat down, pulling her beside him. "I'm going to start at the beginning. You deserve that."

He began to talk of how he'd tried to take his life when he'd received the package of letters from her father. How the chaplain on the ship had led him to Christ and how his relationship with his Savior had deepened over time. He told her of his failed marriage and how he'd come to realize that no one would ever take Leigh's place. That it would be only through the hand of God that he would ever be reunited with her.

The selfless purity of his love touched her deeply, and the restraint he'd placed on himself over the past months humbled her. As he continued, tears rolled down her cheeks.

He paused. Several minutes passed.

Leigh squeezed his hand, encouraging him to continue.

"Leigh, I want to be as close to you as a man can be to a woman. And you're right. We can't have secrets."

When he didn't continue, she raised her face to his. His eyes were squeezed shut and deep emotion etched his face, the external evidence of some internal struggle. Helpless, she averted her eyes.

"I'm going to tell you something I've never told anyone."

Her stomach clenched.

"You know how you've asked me about the Holy Spirit?"

She glanced toward the bookcase. "Yes."

"There are times God calls to me. He speaks to my spirit."

She lifted her eyes to his. The warm, gentle gaze that she always found there was gone. Instead his eyes held the distant look of memory.

"That's what happened that day at the gas station."

She could hardly grasp what he was saying as he told her how the Holy Spirit had shown him the gas station in his mind's eye as they drove down the road, and then led him to the garage where he'd found Tito. How the Holy Spirit had revealed to him details of the boy's past, and drawn the boy to Jesus as John told him about the Savior's love for him, that he was a child of God.

His gaze connected to hers. "Do you see now that Tito is the child of a friend of mine?"

She nodded absently, her mind reeling. "But why did Tito say you were there all afternoon?"

John stroked her hair away from her face. "I've learned the Holy Spirit doesn't operate within the constraints of our physical world. Seconds, minutes, and hours don't measure time for Him. He operates in the time of eternity."

Her thoughts flew back to the front seat of the car, craning her neck to see the angle of the sun, a sense of time passing yet no evidence of it.

She sat stunned as the full impact of what he was telling her began to register. It seemed far beyond the things she'd heard at her church. "Why did you keep it from me?"

"It's something I've always considered holy. Something between me and God."

She pulled away from him, turning so she faced him.

239

"Johnny, do you realize what a testimony you have? Look how you changed Tito's life."

"I didn't do anything. The Holy Spirit did it all."

His voice seemed too firm, his denial too strong. It was almost as if he wanted to close the conversation.

"What other things have happened? How do you get the power, the Gift?"

"Leigh, it doesn't work like that."

"Was that what happened when you saved those two women in the wreck?"

Suddenly guarded, his eyes searched her face. "That's not the point. The point is, I love you. I never want you to think I'd lie to you or deceive you."

In a matter of minutes, things had changed. She felt like she was being thrown a lifeline. This wasn't the Johnny of her past. This was a man of many dimensions, a man who knew God in a way that she yearned to. A partner, someone who could pray for her and with her. Thoughts of Jeff and Jessica, her father's illness, the constant pressure of the Paramount proposal, the heavy yoke of her life, became palpable. She reached for his hand.

"All afternoon I was wondering whether I even knew you. This feels like answered prayer on so many levels. I became a Christian over ten years ago, but somehow I feel like I don't have the personal relationship with Jesus that so many talk about. I accepted Him as my Savior, but that feels like it should be only the beginning. I want the presence of the Holy Spirit."

His face softened, and his expression made her feel like a little girl. "Leigh, you've already received the Holy

240

Spirit. When you accepted Christ, you received forgiveness from sin, and His Spirit came to dwell in you."

"But not like you're talking about. I want that. You're talking about spiritual gifts. Will you pray that for me?"

He hesitated, as though weighing his words. "Should we pray right now?"

She nodded.

He took her hands in his and bowed his head. "Lord, I ask that You give Leigh the greatest of Your gifts."

Leigh's heartbeat quickened. This was a man whom God talked to. Surely God would hear his prayer and take control of her life. She wanted to be used by God. Especially as she pursued her writing.

Suddenly a thought quickened in her mind. She caught her breath. This really was answered prayer. She turned her eyes to his.

"I love you, Johnny."

❧

"Move, Max."

Leigh picked up the big cat and set him on the floor, then turned off the lamp on her nightstand and climbed into bed. It was after eleven o'clock and she was supposed to meet Johnny for breakfast before church in the morning.

She lay staring at the ceiling, her mind unable to let go of the story idea for the Paramount proposal that Johnny had inspired. It would be about Johnny and the gifts of the Spirit.

It had come to her in its entirety as she listened to Johnny

241

talking. The novel would be about a woman of great faith whom God uses mightily. She would fictionalize what she'd learned from Johnny and the experiences of the people in her church to show how believers could touch and change the lives of others. She'd already emailed her agent with a brief summary of her thoughts. Riva had emailed her right back, saying the idea was unique and different.

Leigh smiled. It was answered prayer. What perfect timing.

She felt Max jump back on her bed, his loud purr announcing his intentions. As he did every night, he walked in a circle on the pillow next to hers, where he wasn't allowed, and then lay down. Leigh turned on her side and petted him.

"Max, I'm in love with Johnny. He's the best thing that ever happened to me."

Max's purr grew louder.

"And you know what's best of all? He loves me. He really loves *me*. I don't have to be a better daughter or a better wife or a better person. No one has ever loved me like that." She turned onto her back. "And he's an awesome Christian. I want what he has. I want God to use me."

The vibration of a door closing somewhere in the house startled her. She raised her head slightly, listening.

Footsteps?

Max's purring stopped.

Her heart began to pound.

Suddenly, Max jumped from the bed.

Leigh quietly pulled back the covers and swung her feet to the floor. Keeping her eye on her open bedroom door, she slowly rose.

Footsteps!

The unmistakable long, low creak of the bottom stair step sent a bolt of fear through her. Her breath quickened, as her heart hammered in her chest.

Instinctively, she crouched down. Someone was coming to her room. Her knees buckled. Her mind ordered her to reach for the phone by her bed, but her body wouldn't respond.

The groaning steps shouted their warning as something flew at her from the bedroom door.

She screamed.

"Mom?"

Light flooded the bedroom as Max, having made a perfect landing, calmly walked to the pillow.

"Jeff? What on earth are you doing here? You scared me to death."

Jeff, eyes wide and face drained of color, stared at her. "I thought maybe you weren't asleep yet. If you were, I wasn't going to wake you, but then you screamed."

Using the edge of the mattress, Leigh pushed herself up and dropped onto the bed, pressing her hand to her chest. "What's happened? Why are you here?"

Jeff crossed the room and sat beside her, his face filled with concern. "I'm sorry, Mom. I just wanted to talk to you."

His gentle voice and repentant face reminded her of a little boy. Her anger dissolved. "About what? What's wrong?"

His expression grew pensive and lines formed on his brow.

Leigh scooted back on the bed. Leaning against the

headboard, she pulled the blanket up over her legs. As she waited for him to begin, she noticed how much he had changed over the months he'd been gone—his hair was over his ears, and he had dark circles under his eyes. The last time she'd seen him, his shirt wasn't ironed and his pants were dirty. That hadn't changed.

"We've been evicted."

The three simple words hung in the air, gathering momentum, then slammed into her stomach.

"Evicted?" The word escaped as a gasp.

His gaze wandered to the bed stand, then across the bed, finally coming to rest on Max. "I've been living in the car since last Wednesday." He glanced at her.

"Where's Jessica?" she asked, not wanting an answer.

"Betty's letting her stay in the basement at one of the Haven House residences. Jessica works graveyards now so she's there at night anyway."

I told you so. I told you getting involved with her was a mistake. "Where are your things?"

"My clothes are in my trunk. The rest of our stuff is in one of the garages at Haven House."

Leigh's heart lurched. "You're still in school, aren't you?"

He nodded. "But it's been real hard. Not much time to study."

Leigh didn't want to know the details.

"Mom, I need a place to stay."

At least he had the decency not to ask her to take in Jessica. "Jeff, there's a lot more to this than just a place to stay."

He raised his eyes to hers. "I understand that."

It was all she could do to hold her tongue. Jessica had waltzed into her home, seduced her son, and then proceeded to ruin his life. "What's going to happen to you and Jessica?"

"I don't know." His gaze returned to Max. "We've done a lot of talking lately. There're some things she hasn't been willing to change in her life."

Leigh knew her son so well. He would never speak ill of anyone, much less a girl he thought he loved. But the expression on his face told her that Jessica had hurt him. Leigh could only imagine what the girl had done. She stopped herself from letting her mind wander. That was in the past. This was an opportunity to salvage Jeff's future.

"You know you're welcome here. I'll do everything I can to help you. But you've got to make some hard decisions."

He raised his head and took a deep breath. "I understand. I've had a lot of time to think these past few nights in the backseat of my car." He gave her a weak smile.

"I think some time apart right now is a very good idea."

"It's not the way I want it, Mom. But that's the way it is . . . for now."

Jeff was telling her in his own way that he wasn't through with Jessica. Leigh clenched her jaw. Was he blind? Couldn't he see the mess Jessica had gotten them into? What hold did Jessica have on him?

Leigh kept her thoughts to herself. "We'll talk more about it in the morning."

He stood. "I have to be at Sears at eight o'clock."

245

"Then you'd better get to bed." She waved her thumb down the hall. "Want to sleep in the guest room?"

"Is my sleeping bag still in the basement?"

Leigh nodded.

"I think I'll throw that on the floor of my old room." He stepped toward her and hugged her. "I love you, Mom. Thanks."

"I love you too, honey." She watched him as he walked across the room. "Jeff?"

He turned toward her.

"I'm glad you're home, Son."

She listened as his footsteps faded down the stairs, then she turned off the light and slid under the covers.

God had brought Jeff home. The Lord was giving him a chance to take his life back.

Thank You.

As she turned her face to her pillow, she resolved in her heart to do everything in her power to help God accomplish His purposes.

❧

John set his mug on the coffee table and leaned back against the couch. Closing his eyes, he summoned her voice again . . . "I love you, Johnny."

Tonight was the first time Leigh had spoken the words he'd waited prayerfully for twenty-five years to hear. But it wasn't answered prayer. His stomach churned. Though he willed that it were so, it wasn't.

Stretching forward, he picked up his open Bible from the table and set it on his lap. When she'd spoken, he'd felt a caution in his spirit and at that same moment realized Leigh wasn't responding to him. She was responding to the story he'd shared with her about the powerful workings of the Holy Spirit. She might love him at some level, but the sudden display of emotion had been sparked by Tito's story. He'd felt it.

Until tonight, he'd never told anyone of his gifting. It was something he'd kept between him and the Lord. Though there was nothing scriptural instructing that one hide their gifting, there was something else. And it troubled him deeply.

The uneasiness he'd felt earlier returned to him as he scanned the page of Luke that was before him. *"Nevertheless do not rejoice in this, that the spirits are subject to you, but rather rejoice because your names are written in heaven."*

This was the reason he never told those he helped of the call the Lord had on his life. God had led him to the verse years ago, and he took it as a caution from the Lord. They were to worship the Giver, not the gift. They were to rejoice because the presence of the Holy Spirit reveals Christ. Its appearance proof that Jesus had risen from the dead and returned to the Father. That was the unfathomable phenomena that should awe the mind of man. That God's great love for humankind had provided a way for eternal life with Him and that great love was still at work today. God's gift to humankind. The manifestations were but the ordinary workings of the Spirit of God.

His shoulders slumped under the weight of uncertainty. For the first time in years he felt he was out of God's will. For the tenth time, he thought back over all that had happened. God had allowed Leigh to come into his life. Yet He had spoken to John clearly that night on the mountain that this was not His timing for John's relationship with Leigh. That instead, her books were the reason for them meeting now. At least that's what it had seemed like. And so he'd faithfully read her chapters and offered ideas until she completed her manuscript for *Second Chance*, all the while wondering what purpose it could possibly serve. And he'd continued to encourage her about writing the proposal for Paramount by praying for her, and reminding her to pray and seek God's will for the book.

Restless, he rose and walked out to the front porch. Leaning on the railing he gazed into the dark, again recounting the events of the day. It had all started when Leigh had called, wanting him to show up unannounced at the gas station as a way of meeting with her father. He'd immediately felt a check in his spirit, and even sending Tito had been against his better judgment, but he'd felt he had no choice. Leigh's intentions were good, but he knew it would take the hand of God to heal the deep rift between the two of them. And God would never use a deception to do it.

"Lord, if what I did today was out of Your will, please forgive me."

A blade of conviction cut through him. The truth was, he knew he was out of God's will. Not only had the Lord cautioned him that man's eyes were to be on the Giver, but the Lord had clearly shown him that this was not His timing for the relationship with Leigh that John wanted so badly. It was out of fear of losing her again that he'd told her about God's call on his life.

He dropped his chin to his chest, as deep remorse filled him. "Forgive me."

He immediately felt the peaceful presence of the Holy Spirit drawing him to his knees.

Kneeling on the hard boards of the porch, he silently worshiped the loving, forgiving Father.

After a time, he rose, finally feeling released from transgressing God's will. More determined than ever to be sensitive to the Spirit.

He looked at his watch. It was past midnight. He'd better get to bed, he was meeting Leigh in the morning. He couldn't take his words back, but he could tell her what he'd shared with her was confidential.

Not to be repeated to anyone.

17

Jeff sat silently in his car outside the residence where Jessica was living. They'd barely spoken since he'd moved back home. He'd waited a full week, hoping she'd call or stop him when their paths crossed at work, or do something to let him know she was hurting as much as he was. But she hadn't. And he'd finally called her.

She'd told him he had to make a choice and, until then, there was nothing to talk about. He slowly shook his head. She didn't mean it. It was her way of telling him that she was afraid he was going to leave her. Afraid what she feared the most was true. That she would never have the life others had been born to, that she would never find love and a family . . . and worth. He lowered his eyes. Beneath the anger and pain was a little girl who cautiously observed him from behind hardened blue eyes, and unconsciously sought refuge in his arms from the nightmares that tormented her sleep.

The months they'd lived together had only deepened his resolve to make Jessica his wife. He loved her. But the days they'd been apart had revealed to him that she was right, there was a choice to be made. And it was hers.

He eased the Starbucks latte that he'd brought for her from his lap, then opened the car door and climbed out. The October chill in the early evening air quickened his steps as he made his way across the yard. Entering the residence through the side door of the garage, he went through the utility room and then down the stairs to the basement where Jessica was staying.

As he knocked on her bedroom door, he heard muted sounds of movement.

"It's me. Jeff."

A distant voice answered him, highlighting the telltale delay. "I'm coming."

A moment later, the door opened a crack.

He was struck again by how blue her eyes were. "Hey." He lifted the cup he was holding. "I brought you something."

The door slowly opened. She took the cup and walked toward the head of the bed, leaving Jeff standing in the hallway.

"Jessica." He glanced around the room. There were no pictures on the walls, nothing on the bed stand but a lamp, and the only thing on the top of the dresser was her purse.

She dropped down onto the edge of the mattress and turned toward him.

He took the few steps across the room and sat next to her. "We need to talk."

Lacing her fingers around the cup, she held it firmly between them. "Is there anything to talk about?" Her tone dared him to continue.

"I think so."

Raising the cup, she took a slow, deliberate sip of the coffee. Then slowly lowered it to her lap and lifted her eyes to his.

"I've been thinking a lot since I went back home." Jeff cleared his throat. "I realize that the way we were living is wrong. I just can't live my life not answering my phone because it might be a bill collector, or making excuses to the landlord, or pretending our lives are on track."

Jessica stiffened. "It was only like that because we got behind when I couldn't work."

"No. It was like that because we spent money we didn't have, bought things we couldn't afford, and worst of all, we were living outside of God's will."

"Your mother never liked me. She's tried to break us up since the day she met me. She just wants to contr—"

"Stop, Jessica." He raised his palm toward her. "This isn't about my mother. This is about us and what we did wrong. As far as my mother goes, she tried to tell me this wouldn't work for lots of reasons. And she was right."

A frightened, hostile girl glared at him from behind the blue wall. "Your mom got to you." She set the coffee cup on the bed stand and placed her arms across her chest.

"No, it wasn't my mom that got to me. It was my conscience. I can't go through life lying to myself about the way I'm living."

"Lose the holier-than-thou attitude. So we've had some hard times. You used to believe in us."

"I still do, Jessie. But things have to change."

Jessica tossed her head. "Like what?"

He braced himself. "Like no drugs."

"Why is it always about me? Why am I the one always being judged?" Her voice rose. "Why is it I'm the one who has to change?"

"Because, Jessica, I did the changing last time. And it didn't work."

Suddenly she pushed up, lashing out. "You're just like everybody else. I could never count on anyone in my life and you're no different." She stormed out of the bedroom. "I hate you." The sound of her voice faded with her footsteps and then a door slammed.

Resisting the urge to run after her, he clenched his jaw. He'd made up his mind before he'd come. He had to stand firm. He wanted to give her the life she dreamed of, but that could never happen if things didn't change.

He rose, his knee bumping the nightstand, sending the Starbucks cup tumbling to the floor. Coffee poured onto the carpet as the lid rolled to the side.

"The perfect end to a perfect evening."

Jeff dashed into the bathroom, grabbed a towel, and threw it onto the spilled coffee. Squatting down, he pressed the towel into the carpet. As it absorbed the liquid, he continued to press on the towel. Following the wet track under the bed, his fingers brushed something. He lifted the bed skirt.

A Bible.

He carefully lifted the book from the floor.

His Bible. His mother had given it to him the day he'd graduated from high school. It was open to Matthew 7.

He rose and dropped onto the bed, his eyes skimming the page. The heading of the chapter was Do Not Judge.

He read the first verse. *Judge not, that you be not judged.* Is this why Jessica had mentioned judging?

His mouth quirked. Of all the chapters in the Bible for her to start reading, why did it have to be this one? One she could twist around and use as a weapon against him.

During their months together he'd come to realize that Jessica believed Jesus Christ was the Son of God and had died on the cross for the sins of the world. But somehow she didn't understand He'd died for her. She didn't know Him and how He loved her. Her heavenly Father seemed to be as suspect as her earthly fathers had been.

He let the Bible drop into his lap. He paused a moment, recalling how many times he'd prayed the Holy Spirit would draw her to God's Word, how many times he'd encouraged her to read the Scripture, how many times he'd read them to her.

Slowly, the sweet truth of a faithful God spread through him. Humbled, he bent over and carefully slid the Bible back where he'd found it.

He rose, and after stepping on the towel a few times, he picked it up and rinsed it in the bathtub. He hung it over the edge of the tub, turned out all the lights, and headed to his car. Slipping behind the wheel, he started the car and pulled out onto the street.

God was working. Jeff stepped on the gas, firmly gripping the wheel. It didn't matter that they were homeless and Jessie said she hated him. She could use all the weapons she wanted. He turned onto the main street. How many times in his life had God shown him an open heart when he least expected it . . . walking through an alley behind a homeless shelter . . . picking up a hitch-hiker on a snowy night . . . sitting in Starbucks working on homework. And now, Jessie was reading the Bible.

He blinked rapidly as the full realization of what God was doing settled over him. He drove faster, making a hard right, then a left. He pulled into the parking lot of Grace Bible Church, near the side door that was always open.

He strode through the building with conviction and purpose to the front of the sanctuary and fell to his knees on the altar. God had heard his prayers for Jessie. Even though he had turned his back on God's teaching, stopped going to church, lived in sin, and disrespected his mother, God had given him mercy . . . and then reached out to Jessie. He had failed God, but God had not failed him.

Kneeling at the altar, Jeff recommitted his life to his Savior. And as he prayed for forgiveness, he felt the all-consuming love of Jesus Christ fill his heart. A faith-inspiring love that lifted him up in the knowledge that all things were possible with God. Broken lives, broken relationships, and broken hearts were the business of God.

As clearly as if he'd heard a spoken word, he knew. Jessie could continue to fight, but she couldn't win. No matter what lay ahead, God was fighting for her soul. God wanted *her*.

And love was the weapon God would use.

Jessica moved out from behind the hedge where she'd been standing and watched Jeff drive away. She didn't hate him. She'd missed him desperately the week they'd been apart. Alone in her room, day after day, she'd realized how good he'd been to her. Rubbing her legs when they cramped, always telling her how pretty she was, always telling her he loved her. Her eyes drifted to the empty street. The last few months had been the best months of her life. She turned and limped back to her room.

That's why she'd gone to the garage where they'd stored their things and dug through the boxes, looking for the pillow he'd slept on when they lived together, knowing it still held his scent. A Bible had been just beneath it, sparking memories of them sitting on the couch together, Jeff reading it while she rested in his arms. She'd taken that too.

Tonight was the first night she'd actually opened the Bible since she'd brought it to her room. She'd reread the inscription Leigh had written, and had just found the verse in Matthew when she'd heard Jeff knocking.

She shut the bedroom door behind her and walked to the bed. Stooping over, she pulled the Bible out. The carpet felt damp. Glancing at the bed stand, she realized that Jeff must have spilled the coffee. She smoothed the pages of the Bible. Luckily it hadn't seeped under the bed. With the book in hand, she scooted up and across the bed, until she was leaning against the headboard.

Running her finger down the page she found the verse. *Ask, and it will be given to you; seek, and you will find; knock, and it will be opened to you.* The words were in red. She read them again, thinking about the fact that Jesus himself had said them.

She lifted her head. It wasn't true. It might be true for everyone else, but it wasn't true for her. God had never given her anything. Jeff and every other Christian she'd met in her life told her God loved her. But she'd never felt it or seen any evidence of it. No one had ever loved her . . . except Jeff. And tonight even he had told her that if she didn't change, it was over.

She tossed the Bible aside and slid to the edge of the bed. She pulled her right leg up and took off her shoe and sock. Turning her foot, she could see the angry red patch where a blister was forming again. She let her leg drop back to the floor. If she'd had the co-pay, she would have gone back to the doctor. She'd pawned her engagement ring a few days before to get grocery money and a little weed. And now that was gone. She glanced around the sparse room, her gaze coming back to rest in front of her. She looked through the open bathroom door at her reflection in the mirror. Hair uncombed, blouse gapping over her stomach, she was heavier than she'd ever been. She felt tears sting her eyes. *Ugly, slob. Who would want you?*

A hard pit formed in her throat and she tried to swallow it. But it only grew harder, choking her. Jerking her head away from the mirror, she reached for Jeff's pillow at the head of the bed and pulled it into her lap. Burying her face in it, she breathed deeply.

She began to tremble as a sob formed deep in her gut. Rising, pushing, gathering strength from years of horrific memories that she kept hidden there. *We keep you because we have to. We need the money.* Eyes squeezed shut, straining, she tried to stuff the pain. *Never tell. No one will believe you.* But she couldn't. She couldn't do it anymore.

A cry tore from her lips . . . then another . . . and another. Waves of hatred washed over her, spewed from open mouths of faceless tormentors who screamed obscenities from the black hole that was her past.

Between choking sobs, she tried to breathe in. Seeking his scent. Each gulping breath was life. "I need you."

She recoiled at the words linked to a lifetime of pain. A razor of fear cut through her, warning her away.

She could feel his arms drawing her. His love encircling her. *Jeff.*

"I need you so much."

She stumbled to her feet. If she could find him, she could tell him she would change. She needed him. She wanted to be with him. He was the only good thing that had ever happened to her in her life.

She grabbed her purse, and heavily favoring the side of her right foot, she made her way to her car.

Out of breath, she dropped into the driver's seat. Now that her cell phone service had been shut off, she'd have to go looking for Jeff if she wanted to talk to him. She wiped her eyes with the back of her hand, started the car, and took off to Leigh's house.

Weaving through the streets, she began to have second thoughts. What if Jeff rejected her? He'd let her walk away earlier in the evening. What if Leigh had convinced him he could do better, find a perfect Christian girl? She lifted her foot from the gas pedal. What if when she'd walked away earlier he'd decided it was over between them? The car continued to slow.

Finally, Jessica pulled over to the curb, the turn to Leigh's house just ahead. The vague, questioning thoughts had begun to harden into certainty. Jeff was through with the relationship. He'd as much as said so.

For the first time in a long time, an idea occurred to her. Weeping as she listened to the smoky voice from her past, the words grew louder. *There is a way out*.

She could take her life.

She stole a glance at herself in the mirror. An ugly girl with red eyes and smeared makeup looked back at her. *Pig. No one would care*.

Eyeing the road ahead of her, going to Leigh's house suddenly seemed risky. She looked at the clock on the dash. It wasn't that late. What if Leigh was home and told her to leave?

There is a way out.

Angry tears stung her eyes. Why was it always like this? Why hadn't her mother wanted her, why had her foster families used her and thrown her away, why was she so worthless? Didn't she deserve a mother . . . a family . . . a husband? Was it too much to ask?

Ask.

A misty wisp. *Ask*. A still, small voice.

Ask, and it will be given to you.

"Liar." She hadn't asked anything from God since she'd left her last foster family at seventeen. God didn't care about *her*.

Ask. The red words whispered. *Ask, and it will be given*

to you; seek, and you will find . . . A hushed taunt that magnified the fact she had never had what others had.

Yet somewhere deep in her heart, she desperately wanted the words to be true. She wanted to believe.

Ask.

She would dare Him.

"Give me a reason to live, Jesus." Her words were defiant. "I'm asking, just like you said. Give me a reason." Her voice broke. She couldn't fight anymore. Her face contorted with despair and grief as she slumped against the seat. "Please, please, I'm begging you." Her voice trailed off. "Help me."

The minutes passed as she continued to struggle with the thought that Jeff might have already made up his mind about her. He might have finally realized how worthless she was and decided to move on. The thought of facing his rejection paralyzed her with fear, but the truth that there was only one other way out frightened her even more. She grabbed the steering wheel and stepped on the gas.

As she neared the house, she could see there were lights on, but Jeff's car wasn't in the driveway. Unsure what to do, she cruised past the house and made a U-turn at the end of the block.

Approaching the house for the second time, she saw a car turn onto the street toward her, then into Leigh's driveway. It was Jeff. Stepping on the gas, she sped down the street and pulled in behind him.

He stepped out of his car and turned toward her. Even in the dim light, she could see his smile.

"Jeff," she cried out. Her hands shaking, she fumbled

with the door handle. "I'm sorry." Finally, getting the door open, she climbed out of the car.

His arms were around her. His voice soothing her. "Don't cry, Jessie. I'm right here."

Blinded by tears, she spoke into his shoulder. "I want to change. I want to do it your way."

He stroked her hair. "I know you do."

She took a shaky breath. "Do you still love me?"

He stepped away from her, put his forefinger under her chin, tilted her face to his, and kissed her. "More than ever." He cradled her in his arms.

"I feel like the luckiest man in the world."

—

Headlights flashed across the bedroom wall. Leigh casually glanced toward the window that overlooked the driveway. "Is that Jeff, Max?"

Turning back to the computer, she began rereading the last paragraph of her manuscript.

A second set of headlights fanned across her wall. She looked toward the bedroom window, waiting for them to disappear. But they didn't.

She rose and crossed the room. "What's going on out there?"

Max began to purr. Leigh stroked his head as she leaned into the window. She caught her breath. "Jessica."

Jeff was kissing her.

How could this be happening? They'd talked and talked since Jeff had been home. The boy who'd moved out had returned a grown man. He'd told her how he realized the mistakes he'd made. How he'd been outside of God's will. How he would never let himself get in that position again. And now this?

Jerking her head away from the window, Leigh turned her back on them. What was he thinking? Jessica was trouble. She'd proved herself to be selfish, lazy, and irresponsible.

Who would want her?

18

Leigh watched the screen saver take over her computer screen for the third time.

Pushing her chair away from the desk, she rose. There was no use trying to work on the proposal for Paramount. Jeff and Jessica would be arriving any minute for a meeting . . . at Jessica's request. Anxiety spurted through Leigh's stomach. She hoped it wouldn't get confrontational. She was looking out for Jeff's best interests, and nothing could be said that would change that.

It had been only last weekend, but it seemed like a year ago that she'd looked out the window and seen Jeff kissing Jessica. The days that followed had been a nightmare. A clear example of the spiritual warfare she had been reading about. Jeff was convinced that Jessica had really changed . . . this time. He'd managed to get her to meet with Pastor Jim at Grace Bible Church, and she'd convinced the pastor that somehow during the days she and Jeff had been apart, she'd encountered God, and it had changed her. Jeff was more committed than ever to the idea that this was the girl God had chosen for him. How could he be so blind?

As Leigh turned and started down the stairs, her conscience pricked her. Maybe she shouldn't be so skeptical. God did touch and change lives. That's what becoming a Christian meant. Being reborn. The message was clear throughout the New Testament.

That was one good thing that had come out of the whole mess. Leigh had found herself spending more time with the Lord, praying for Jeff's future. And it seemed that all she had recently learned about gifting and the Holy Spirit were meant for a situation just like this. She found herself calling on the Holy Spirit to work in Jeff's life and show him God's plan for him.

Jeff had told her he and Jessica had talked about premarital counseling when they'd visited the pastor. She sighed. She wasn't going to give up. She was going to trust the Holy Spirit for a miracle. God could change people's hearts. As she approached the kitchen, she heard voices in the back hall.

"Mom?" Jeff rounded the corner, Jessica right behind him.

Leigh forced a smile. "Hi, you two."

Jessica smiled back at her. "Hi, Leigh."

"Let's sit in the family room." Leigh gestured to her right.

As she followed them, she quickly eyed Jessica from head to toe. The girl looked different somehow. Her hair was pulled back in a shiny, full ponytail. She was wearing a clean, pressed skirt and top. Leigh realized she'd never seen Jessica in a skirt before. Pulling her bottom lip between her teeth, she tilted her head . . . something was different.

264

Jessica and Jeff sat on the couch and Leigh took a chair across from them. As they settled into their seats, the silence grew louder.

Finally, when every last adjustment to hands, feet, and posture had been made, they sat looking at each other.

"Well, here we are." Leigh volleyed to the couch. "You look nice today, Jessica." Leigh immediately wondered if her words sounded like Jessica had never looked nice on any other day.

The silence lengthened between them.

"Uh." Jeff turned to Jessica. "Jessica wants to say something."

As Jessica looked at her hands and laced her fingers together, Leigh observed her. Jessica's once defiant face was uncertain, her hardened eyes lowered in humility, her breathing ragged, as she began to blink rapidly, trying to keep her emotions in check.

As gentle as the touch of an angel's wing, compassion swept through Leigh's heart.

The glistening blue eyes turned to her.

"I'm sorry for everything that happened." Jessica stopped for a moment, first pressing her lips together, then taking a deep, measured breath.

Jeff reached out and rested his hand on hers.

Jessica raised her chin and closed her eyes a moment. "I promised myself I wasn't going to cry."

She turned, facing Leigh, her body rigid, her face now a mask, but her voice contrite. "Can you forgive me?"

Leigh found herself trying to speak through a myriad of emotions. Suspicion, caution, and common sense struggled to frame her answer. Finally, a sense of Christian duty parted her lips. "Yes."

A tear slipped down Jessica's cheek. "I'd like to start over."

Leigh shifted in her chair. What did Jessica mean exactly? Start over as if nothing had ever happened? Pretend Jeff still had his credit and his abstinence? Ignore the fact that Jessica's past would haunt her forever, tainting her marriage, her children, and every other relationship she would ever have? Beyond that, had Jessica *really* changed?

It wasn't that simple. Leigh felt trapped. "I'd like to start over too."

A smile broke across Jeff's face, and he pulled Jessica's hand into his lap. "We want to get married soon. But we want to do it right this time." He and Jessica exchanged glances. "We were thinking." He paused. "We were thinking, maybe Jessie could take that extra bedroom upstairs for the next couple of months while we save up. We thought maybe we'd get married on my semester break in December."

Leigh felt herself tense. Jeff was talking so fast she'd hardly understood anything after "Jessie could take that extra bedroom."

"I don't know, Jeff." She looked toward Jessica.

"Leigh, I understand how you feel. But I have nowhere to go. When Betty let me stay in the basement at Haven House, she told me it was only because it was an emergency and it was only temporary." Her tone was matter-of-fact. "I need to find something else, but as you know, I have no money. I'd like to work out something that you feel okay about."

266

The girl was looking her right in the eye and not making excuses. Leigh glanced at Jeff. His gentle brown eyes searched hers.

"Give us a chance, Mom. We want to get our lives straightened out."

This will never work.

"Jeff, could I talk to you alone for a few minutes?"

Jeff hesitated. "Do you mind, Jessie?"

A tense silence enveloped the room, then Jessica rose. "I don't think we should have to beg." An edge crept into her voice.

Leigh leaned forward. "I don't think you should either. But this has taken me completely by surprise, and I feel like I'm entitled to ask some questions."

Jessica's hands knotted. "I understand that. But don't you think it would be better for the three of us to talk together?"

Leigh considered Jessica's words. She hated to admit it, but Jessica was right. If they were ever going to get past what had happened, they were going to have to talk about it. "Why are things going to be any different this time than they were last time?"

Jeff patted the cushion next to him, and Jessica slowly lowered herself to the couch. He took her hand. "Because this time we're going to do things God's way. Jessica and I have talked this over. We know it's not going to be easy. We went to a credit counselor Tuesday. They worked out a plan for us, and we're going to pay off our debts. And I already told you we've started premarital counseling with Pastor Jim."

Leigh turned her eyes to Jessica.

267

Jessica made a quick half nod. Her expression firm, but not haughty.

Jeff gave Jessica an almost imperceptible nudge, then a questioning glance.

Jessica hesitated, blinking, her brow creased. She bit her lower lip.

Slowly, she raised her eyes to Leigh's. "I'd like to ask you something."

Fresh concern rose in Leigh's chest. What more could be asked? Jessica had already asked to live with her, as if everyone should conveniently forget how she'd waltzed in and wreaked havoc with Leigh's life and relationship with Jeff.

Leigh tried to keep her voice neutral. "What is that?"

"Would you call me Renelle?"

"Renelle?" Leigh filtered through her memory, trying to make sense of the request.

"It's my middle name."

Leigh nodded slowly. "I see."

Jessica cleared her throat. "I kind of feel like Jessica is who I used to be. I really want to start new. I've always loved my middle name and, well . . . " She lowered her gaze, fighting to control her emotions.

Leigh could see tears edging Jessica's eyes. Just then, Jeff lifted his hand, gently smoothing Jessica's hair, as though she were a child. The tender, caring gesture touched Leigh.

Jeff loved Jessica.

It was as clear to Leigh as if he'd spoken the words. Despite the financial problems, health problems, and even homelessness that life with Jessica had brought, he still loved her. Suddenly, Leigh felt ashamed.

"Of course, I think that makes sense . . . Renelle."

Jessica raised her head, the young woman's eyes hopeful, her trembling lips slightly parted. Jeff leaned his forehead against her cheek.

Leigh heard his whisper. "I told you things would work out. My mom is awesome."

Leigh felt heat in her cheeks. It wasn't about being awesome. It was about seeing things for what they were and realizing there were no other options. How could Jeff think these arrangements were "things working out"? Things weren't working out at all. Jeff was heading for more of what he'd just been through.

"Mom?" Jeff's voice broke into her thoughts. "Could I move our stuff out of that garage at Haven House and into the basement?"

Leigh exhaled through grim lips. "I suppose." She rose. "I need to get back to work on my book." She turned and left the room.

"Mom."

Jeff was at the foot of the stairs. She stopped at her bedroom door and faced him.

He covered the distance between them two steps at a time. "Thank you so much. I know this isn't the best situation, but it's just for a few months." He smiled. "And it will give you a chance to really get to know Jessica." He grimaced. "I mean, Renelle." He lowered his voice. "That seems to be really important to her, so please try to remember to call her that.

"She told me she can't explain it, but she feels like

God gave her that name the day she was born. Somehow saving it until now. She said she felt like she never had a father until the night she met God. And now she understands He's her Father. I prayed with her that night, Mom. And she said that she heard God call her name. Her middle name. Renelle."

The excitement on Jeff's face was evident, and if believing it made it so, it was true. Leigh wished she could be as sure as he was. "I hope so, Jeff. I've been praying God will show you the plan He has for your life."

Jeff kissed her cheek. "Thanks. That's my prayer too." He turned and bounded down the stairs.

Leigh crossed her bedroom and pulled out her desk chair, dropping into it with a resigned sigh. *Renelle.* She'd never even heard the name before.

She wiggled her mouse, pulling up the proposal for Paramount.

Synopsis—*The Gift*, appeared on the screen.

She was almost ready to start writing the first of the three chapters that were required for the book proposal. Johnny had taken a real interest in the book, and at first she'd thought they could work on it together. But she'd soon realized he was extremely modest about the way God had blessed him, actually telling her not to repeat what he'd told her about Tito. She'd let the subject drop. God had given her the idea and she was sure Johnny would come around if Paramount actually contracted for the book. Then he'd see this was something people were interested in. A way to reach people for God.

She'd given it a lot of thought since it first occurred to her to make the power of spiritual gifts the topic of her book. Everything she'd read in her Bible and from other resources had only confirmed the idea to her. The manifestation of signs and wonders seemed to be increasing everywhere. In a very real way, the book had become her own journey. More and more, her prayers were that God would favor her with a gifting like John's.

Renelle. The name replayed in her mind. Jessica had said she'd heard God's voice. Leigh quirked her mouth.

Jessica Renelle Braun.

Suddenly, Leigh moved her mouse and pointed the cursor at the Favorites icon on her toolbar.

The list appeared on the side of her screen. She scrolled down to Names, a site she always used when she was naming her characters. It had the meanings of thousands of names. She clicked on the link.

When the site came up, she typed "Renelle" into the Search field, then pressed Enter.

The results popped up. She caught her breath as she read the definition in strong black letters on the screen . . .

Reborn

⚬⚬⚬

John Higheagle sat in his car, parked across the street from Leigh's parents' house, his eye on the front door. The sense of uneasiness that had begun the night he'd told Leigh about Tito had returned the very next day. And though he'd prayed and fasted, he'd been unable to get any clarity as to why his spirit was unsettled. Conscious of God's leading that he was to help Leigh with her book,

271

he'd tried to talk to her about *The Gift*, but she'd put him off, saying she was still working on her ideas. She didn't need help with the book. At least he'd been able to dissuade her from the idea that somehow the Holy Spirit was a divine power given to Christians at their request.

He'd finally decided that the rift with her father must be the reason he could find no peace. Leigh's effort to throw them together had brought the issue front and center. It was unfinished business from his life before he became a believer, and he needed to clean it up. He'd decided to go to her father and apologize.

It didn't matter that he had never done anything to the man, that his only sin was being born half Indian, that Bob Williams had singled him out and made his teenage years hell. It didn't matter, because Jesus said to forgive men their trespasses.

John shifted in his seat. When he'd left the house, he'd planned to knock on the door and introduce himself. He'd tell Bob that he was sorry for all that had happened. And if he saw that Bob was receptive, he'd share his faith with him. God willing, there would be a chance to pray with him.

John's eyes drifted over the yard. For some reason, when he'd actually arrived at the Williams's home, he hadn't been able to follow through. He glanced at the clock on the dash. He'd been sitting in the car for over fifteen minutes, as if some invisible hand were holding him in his seat.

Suddenly the front door of the house opened. John watched as an older man walked unsteadily toward the curb.

Bob Williams. Eyes intent on the ground in front of him, he single-mindedly headed to the mailbox. It was the first time John had laid eyes on the man in over twenty-five years. But it took only the familiar profile, the arrogant tilt of his head, and the stubborn determination of his steps to turn back the clock and resurrect the long-buried feelings of anger, hatred, and betrayal that memorialized John's youth. John clenched his jaw. The answer was suddenly clear. He hadn't been able to get out of the car because deep in his heart, he still hated Leigh's father.

The truth struck him like a two-by-four across his chest, leaving him gasping for breath as a cacophony of images and smoky voices exploded in his head. Memories that had been banished for years reappeared with the same clarity as the day they'd happened. The condemnation, the accusations, and the rejection seized him, squeezing the air from his lungs.

He stared at the figure. Silently watching until Bob Williams disappeared back into the house.

Shaking his head to clear it, John started the car and slammed his foot on the accelerator. He sped through the stop sign at the end of the street, then wove blindly in and out of traffic as he made his way back to Ridgeline. By the time he turned onto the country road that would take him to his house, he'd managed to reclaim his senses. Shaken to the core, he pulled into his driveway and turned off the engine.

He sat for a moment, trying to make sense out of the deeply troubling emotions that still gripped him.

Finally, opening the door, he climbed out of his truck. For a moment he stood, looking north to the clearing on

273

the ridge. The place he'd gone so many times in his life to find the certainty of a God-driven world.

As a chill coursed through him, he stiffened. Not today. Not now. What Bob Williams had done to him was brutal. It had not only robbed him of his childhood and his future, it had almost taken his life. There was nothing that could justify it, nothing that could minimize it. It was . . .

He started toward the house.

. . . Unforgivable.

19

Leigh watched from the back of the church as Renelle took pictures of the altar. She grinned as the young woman adjusted a vase of flowers, then stepped back and took yet another shot. Late last night, when they'd finished decorating for the wedding, Renelle had joked that she might spend the night in the church just so she could wake up in the morning and be sure she wasn't dreaming.

"Oh, I didn't see you come in." Renelle waved her forward. "Here, stand by the arch so I can get your picture."

"I'm a mess." Leigh stamped the snow off her boots and brushed her hands over the front of her wool pants. "Besides, I was in a lot of the pictures you took last night."

Renelle's shoulders relaxed and a smile spread across her face. "I know." She hesitated, then dropped down on a front pew. "Come here a second. I want to talk to you about something."

Over the two months that Renelle and Jeff had lived with her, Leigh had come to know her future daughter-

275

in-law. At least to the extent that Renelle permitted it. One thing that had become clear to Leigh was how desperately the young woman longed for a family. Renelle hadn't told her with words. Instead, she revealed it in the sweet smile that appeared when she let her hand rest for a moment on freshly folded towels, or the way she hummed as she wiped the kitchen table after dinner, polishing it until it shone.

But those moments had given Leigh only a glimpse of the woman her son was marrying. Leigh knew there would always be a part of Renelle that would remain closed to her. Shrugging out of her fleece jacket, she sat on the pew beside Renelle. "I'm listening."

Renelle set the camera down, folded her hands in her lap, and took a deep breath. As she turned to Leigh, tears edged her eyes. "I want to thank you for all you've done for us."

Leigh reached out and patted Renelle's arm. "I'm glad I could help."

"There's something I want to ask." Renelle quickly brushed her fingertips under her eyes. "I asked Jeff about it and he thought it was okay." The words rushed out, then were followed by silence.

Leigh studied the girl's face. High spots of color on her full cheeks, lashes damp, her expression eager, yet anxious. She squeezed Renelle's arm lightly.

"Could I . . . Could I . . . Could I call you . . . Mom?"

The request took Leigh by surprise. "How sweet of you. Of course."

"Hey, ladies." Jeff's voice came from behind.

Renelle jumped up. "Oh, you're already dressed." She

grinned at him. "And you're here just in time. Would you take a picture of me and Mom?"

A broad smile made its way across Jeff's face as he strode down the aisle and took the camera from her hand. "Come on, Mom."

Leigh rose. As she stepped next to Renelle, Renelle put her arm around Leigh's waist.

"Smile." Jeff pointed the digital camera at them and clicked.

"What time is it?" Renelle's manner was suddenly brisk. Whatever the moment had meant to her was now hidden.

Jeff glanced at his watch. "About noon."

"We'd better get ready, Renelle." Leigh rose quickly, raising her hand to her chest. "I thought I'd dress here with you since I still had some last-minute running around to get done before I came here. Our clothes are in the car."

Leigh glanced toward the back of the church. "In fact, Jeff, why don't you wait here for the cake? It should arrive any minute. Have them put it in the center of that long table with the green tablecloth on the right, by the doors."

Renelle clasped her hands together. "I can't wait. Everything looks so beautiful." She turned to Leigh. "And thank the Lord we decided to have the reception right here. It's snowing."

Jeff nodded. "There's still a winter storm warning."

"I'd better get those dresses." Leigh slipped into her coat and started for the door.

Jeff was at her heels. "Mom, let me do it."

277

"Jeff, there's no reason for you to mess up your clothes, and besides, we don't want you to see her dress."

He chuckled. "I'll close my eyes then." His voice sobered. "It's really icy out there, Mom. Let me get them?"

Leigh pulled open the front door of the church and was hit with a freezing, wet blast of air. She looked at Jeff. "Where's your coat?"

He retrieved it from a back pew and headed out the door.

"Make sure the plastic is pulled all the way down," Leigh called after him. "And don't drag them on the ground. Oh, and bring that big tote from the backseat."

As soon as Jeff brought the dresses in, Leigh and Renelle hurried to two rooms adjoining the sanctuary, leaving Jeff to wait for the cake and his grandparents.

Leigh's mother couldn't have been more excited about the wedding if Renelle had been her daughter. But her father had had only a surface interest . . . until he learned R.J. was coming. Leigh laid her pants and top across a chair.

She hadn't realized Jeff had sent his uncle an invitation until R.J. had called to accept his nephew's request to be his best man. R.J. had arrived the day before and was staying at a hotel. She hadn't been surprised at his refusal to stay at her parents' house. It was just more of the same aloof behavior that had begun shortly after he left home, and it had only grown worse as he grew older. Over time, he had become increasingly vague about his addresses and phone numbers. Leigh stepped into her dress.

When she'd learned he was coming, she'd decided to

make a point of sitting down and talking to him about their father's health and financial issues before he left. His decision to stay at the hotel had worked in her favor. She was going to catch up with him there later tonight. He wouldn't be able to put her off like he usually did whenever she tried to bring the subject up. Apparently, he felt if he could stay out of the loop, he didn't have to get involved. She dug in the tote for her shoes, slipped them on, then grabbed the bag and left for Renelle's room.

"Renelle, you look just beautiful." Leigh dropped the tote on the floor and closed the door behind her.

Renelle turned her back to Leigh, then put her hands on her hips, squeezing her ample waist. "Could you zip me?"

Leigh stepped toward her and slid the zipper up. Nearing the neckline, she stopped. "What's that?" She touched the edge of a large clear patch near Renelle's shoulder blade.

"Oh, nothing. Just something the doctor gave me." Renelle's dismissive tone closed the subject.

A sense of uneasiness washed through Leigh. Over the months, she'd struggled to build a relationship of trust with Renelle. Yet, there was a certain secretiveness that seemed to underlie the way Renelle lived her life. She went places without ever saying where, she got phone calls that caused her to drop her voice and leave the room, and she seemed to sleep a lot. It all left Leigh with the feeling that Renelle's jaded past was never far away. She'd tried to talk to Jeff about it, but he didn't seem to be concerned. He just made excuses for Renelle, keeping whatever he knew to himself. Leigh locked the zipper in place.

279

"Renelle, your shoes are in the tote. I need to go to the sanctuary and make sure the guest book is out and everything else is ready. When John gets here, I'll send him this way."

Since the night that John had confided in her about how God had used him in Tito's life, they had grown close again. He'd been more than supportive of her writing, the kids, and the wedding. He'd even suggested he walk Renelle down the aisle, which had delighted the young woman. But the issue between John and her father had remained unresolved. No matter how she'd tried over the past two months to get the two men together, it never seemed to work out. Either John was too busy or her father was too ill. She had noted all of it in her prayer journal because the healing of the relationship between the two men would clearly take the work of the Holy Spirit. Not so much on John's side. He was so close to the Lord he would welcome the healing of the broken relationship, but for her father to accept John, it would take God changing her father's heart.

Last night at the rehearsal the men had finally met, but after a tense introduction, they'd avoided each other. Her father's behavior hadn't surprised her, but she'd been mystified when John had left the church afterward without saying good-bye.

Renelle twirled across the room, then stopped, looking at Leigh. "This is the happiest day of my life." Her eyes filled with tears and she started fanning her face. She giggled. "I can't cry now." Then her face sobered. "Thank you so much for everything."

"You're very welcome." Leigh smiled through conflicting

emotions. Renelle's obvious open appreciation, at odds with the dismissive, secretive tone of moments before.

Leigh left the room and made her way to the sanctuary, trying to dismiss the subtle reminder of Renelle's past behavior. After a lot of thought and prayer, Leigh had gone out on a limb and convinced one of the agents in the office to rent a duplex unit to the young couple despite their bad credit. The two months they'd lived with her they had managed their money, paid their bills, and really seemed to have committed to rebuilding their lives. *Please, Lord. Don't let me down. I'm trusting You to work in their lives and prosper their finances.*

In a way, she felt like she was living a parallel life with the heroine of the book proposal she'd written. She'd finished the synopsis and three chapters and her agent had submitted them to Paramount. It was the story of a woman's spiritual journey. How the woman had received the Gift through the outpouring of the Holy Spirit in her life. Her heroine was a woman of purpose, with the power of God behind her.

Leigh had decided to wait until she found out whether Paramount was going to buy the rights before sharing anything about it with Johnny. It was her hope that when he saw how fiction could be used to reveal to many that the awesome gifting of the Holy Spirit was available to all believers, he would be willing to share more of his experiences with her, and help her with the book. And perhaps by then, God would have given her a testimony of her own. She'd faithfully journaled her prayer requests. Everything from God giving favor to her book proposal, to the healing of Renelle's deep wounding, to the healing of her father's cancer. All of it was in God's power to do. And she wanted to be His woman of purpose.

Leigh entered the sanctuary through a side door and was greeted with the hum of activity. She spotted her mother at the entry with a young girl she didn't recognize, who was taking people's coats and pointing them to the guest book. Her father was seated in the front pew that had been reserved for family. Several of Jeff's friends from church were guiding guests down the aisles. The church wasn't divided into "his" and "her" sides. People were simply allowed to choose where they wanted to sit.

"You look lovely."

Leigh turned to the voice at her elbow. "Johnny."

He kissed her lightly on the cheek.

She leaned into his chest, and he put his arm around her. "I can't believe Jeff is getting married." His arm tightened in a quick squeeze. She patted his hand. "Why don't you go say 'hi' to my dad?"

"I thought I'd go talk to Jeff and see if he'd like me to pray with him before the ceremony starts. He's in Pastor Jim's study waiting to come out and take his place."

"That sounds like a good idea, but do speak to my dad first."

John stepped away from her, and she watched him cross the room and shake hands with her father. Even though he smiled, he seemed stiff and reserved. They'd hardly exchanged two sentences when Johnny tipped his head and walked away. At first she felt a twinge of anger that John wasn't putting forth more effort. But the feeling passed. It *was* awkward. It would take time. At least the two men were speaking.

Moments later, R.J. arrived. Ruggedly handsome, looking like the movie star he wished he were. Her father lit up as soon as he spotted him, waving him over, putting his arm around R.J.'s shoulders. Within minutes several of the single college girls, who were friends of the church more than friends of the couple, found seats directly behind him. Leigh raised her eyebrows and rolled her eyes.

"What's wrong, honey?"

Leigh started. "Uh. Nothing, Mom." She felt heat in her cheeks. "Guess we'd better sit down; the pianist has started playing."

Within moments Jeff was at the front of the church. R.J. slipped from the pew and stood behind him, grinning broadly and patting his pocket. A friend of Renelle's, whom she'd introduced to them at the rehearsal, stood across from the men.

Leigh scanned the church. The kids had insisted on planning the wedding themselves. Renelle had chosen red and green in keeping with the Christmas season. Considering their limited funds, it looked beautiful. She'd proven to be quite resourceful, with a good eye for decorating while working on a shoestring. Leigh had been especially pleased with their decision to buy simple silver wedding bands. As far as she knew, they'd managed to pay cash for everything. It was what had finally convinced her to vouch for them on the rental. She felt herself relaxing. It was all going to work out. The entrance music for Renelle rang out.

As everyone stood, Renelle walked down the aisle, Johnny at her side. Leigh stole a glance at her father. His eyes were on R.J.

She turned her attention back to the bride. Johnny caught her eye and gave her a quick wink, then returned his gaze to the front of the church. She grinned.

Just beyond him Leigh could see through the church window. The snow was beginning to swirl, and ice was sheeting on the glass. It seemed darker than it should be for early afternoon. As Renelle took her place and Leigh took her seat, Leigh glimpsed the windowsills at the side of the sanctuary.

The grin faded from her face. Water was seeping in, driven by the high winds. Apparently the storm warning had been justified.

She forced a smile. There was something unsettling about the darkening skies and the biting, icy winter storm that raged just beyond the church doors.

. . . As if the storm were waiting to greet the newlyweds the moment they stepped outside to begin their new life.

∽∾

Leigh pulled into the parking lot of the Kopper Kettle Inn, found an open space, parked. She grabbed her purse, and hurried through powdery snow to the lobby.

As she approached the counter a young woman turned toward her. Her name tag read Becky. "Checking in?"

Leigh smiled. "No, I'm here to see Robert Williams. Could you call his room and tell him his sister's here?"

The woman consulted a file, then picked up the phone. After a moment, she hung up. "They're not answering."

Leigh tilted her head. "I think you called the wrong room. He's here by himself."

Becky pulled out a sheet of paper from a file. "Robert Williams?"

Leigh nodded.

"I can't give you any information." She hesitated. "But I did call the right room."

Leigh chewed her lower lip. So R.J. had come with a girl. She should have been suspicious when he was so adamant about not wanting to stay at her parents' house. She frowned. But why hide the girl? Their parents wouldn't have said anything if he'd said he was staying with his girlfriend in a hotel. "Thank you."

Becky turned back to her work, and Leigh walked across the lobby to the sunken seating area. Spotting a fireplace blazing at the far end of the room, she wove her way through the empty chairs and seated herself on the large hearth. She closed her eyes a moment, enjoying the heat from the logs. A grin crept across her face. That rascal. He just didn't want to face their mother.

Suddenly her heart lurched. Maybe the woman was married. It would be just like R.J. to get involved with a married woman.

Leigh pursed her lips and raised her eyebrows. So what would her father think about the more-than-perfect R.J. if he knew?

She glanced out the windows. The snow hadn't let up. She should probably get home before it got any worse. Yet she hated to give up this rare chance to speak to her brother face-to-face.

She folded her hands in her lap, then looked at her watch. The wedding and reception had been over hours ago. They'd all said their goodbyes at the church. R.J. excusing himself, saying he had an early flight.

The sound of low voices drifted from the open lobby. Leigh leaned forward, looked across the room and the entry, and craned her neck to see if it happened to be R.J.

It was a couple with their back to her, leaning over the counter talking to Becky. Holding hands beneath the counter's edge.

It *was* R.J.

Leigh rose quietly and took silent steps, trying to get closer without being seen. The woman appeared to have short silver hair peeking out from under a knitted cap. Oh, boy, was that the big secret? He'd met an interesting older woman? Leigh quirked her mouth. A rich one, no doubt.

As she moved closer, her heart started to pound. She stopped and grabbed the back of a chair, her knees suddenly weak.

It *was* R.J.

And another man.

She ducked behind the chair. There had to be an explanation. She watched as the two men walked through the lobby toward the elevators . . . hands to themselves.

She stared after them. They looked like two ordinary men, probably just friends. She straightened. Maybe it had only looked like they were holding hands. They'd been standing close together. She continued to watch from a distance as they entered the elevator.

When the doors closed, she covered the distance as the lighted indicator above the doors marked the floors.

It stopped on 3. She pushed the button showing an up arrow.

As soon as the elevator returned to her, she stepped into it and pushed 3. Tapping her foot, she watched the numbers slowly creep across the bar above the door. When the doors finally opened, she walked out into a small area.

She listened. Hearing voices, she tilted her head around the corner and looked up and down the hall. R.J. and his friend were to her right, unlocking the door of a hotel room. She stepped back into the elevator lobby.

Her mind was racing. Should she leave? Confront him? Maybe it was just a big misunderstanding.

She set her lips in a firm line. That had to be it. She'd been a distance away. There had been hardly any light other than the fireplace. Maybe the man was an old friend.

Leigh felt the knot in her stomach loosen. Of course. That was it. This was probably someone R.J. had known when he'd lived in Cedar Ridge, and he'd wanted to visit with him before he left in the morning. A wave of relief washed over her. They hadn't been holding hands. How could she have thought such a thing? She put her fingertips to her lips. Wouldn't he die if he knew?

She straightened. Once again revisiting the moment she'd seen the two men at the counter. She felt a twinge in her chest . . . they'd been standing so close together . . . still . . . how ridiculous.

She was mistaken. She clutched her purse under her arm and started down the hall. When she reached the door where she'd seen them go in, she knocked.

From behind the door she heard an unfamiliar voice say, "That can't be room service already."

The door opened.

"Leigh!" R.J.'s eyes grew wide.

The silver-haired man peered from behind him. "Who is it?"

R.J. stepped to the side. "It's my sister."

Leigh could see past the men to a king-size bed with their coats thrown on it.

When she looked back to R.J., she saw he'd followed her gaze. There was hot color in his cheeks. He lowered his eyes.

The older man stepped forward, his hand extended. "Hello. You must be Leigh. Your brother speaks of you often. I'm Sydney."

Leigh shook his hand, then turned her eyes to her brother.

The two men exchanged a silent glance.

"Leigh," R.J. spoke slowly, "Sydney is the director of that movie I told you about."

The two men exchanged glances again.

R.J. tapped her elbow. "Why don't you come in?"

Leigh crossed the room and took a chair at a small table.

R.J. sat opposite her as Sydney vanished into the bathroom and closed the door.

Leigh searched her brother's face, waiting for him to speak. Hoping he would. Hoping he wouldn't.

Finally, he did. "I'm sorry, this isn't the way we planned it."

He rested his hand on her arm.

"Sydney is my partner."

20

It was their anniversary.

Humming as she worked, Renelle put the finishing touches on the cake, then set it in the middle of the small dining room table. She stepped back, admiring it. They'd been married one whole month. And married life was everything she'd dreamed it would be.

Jeff loved her, and told her so often. She smiled to herself. She'd been told she was loved more times in the past month than she had her entire life. And just as awesome, though in a different way, she felt like Leigh really had become a mom to her.

She glanced around the apartment. Leigh had given them so many things for their home. She'd told them they could have whatever they wanted from the bedroom where she'd stored furniture she'd kept from when she'd been married in Montana. Renelle bent over, straightening the fringe on the edge of the area rug that defined the living room. Pains shot up her legs.

She crossed the room and sat in the wooden rocker by the couch. Leigh had said she'd rocked Jeff in it when he was baby. Renelle pressed her lips together. That's when she'd told Leigh they couldn't have children. Renelle slid back into the chair and began to rock. Leigh had hidden her disappointment well. That's how real moms acted. Leigh didn't lord over her the fact she was a failure because she couldn't give Jeff children. Instead Leigh had simply said, "God is in control," and never mentioned it again.

Renelle stopped the chair from rocking. If God was in control, why had He allowed her foster father to abuse her, kill the unborn child, and then make sure she never had children? *That'll never happen again.* A man's voice echoed in her mind. A wave of nausea passed through her stomach.

Ignoring the pain in her legs, she rose. Jeff would be home soon to take her to work. Lately, the bottom of her feet had been numb, and she'd been unable to feel the pedals when she drove. If Betty hadn't agreed to let Jeff get off twenty minutes early from his shift every night, Renelle would have lost her job.

She pushed the thought away. If either one of them lost their job, not only would they lose the income, they'd lose their insurance. With Jeff's Straterra and her pain medication, just the co-pays kept them broke. She limped to the bedroom.

Renelle took clean pants and a top out of her chest of drawers and dressed. She glanced at her watch, then walked to her side of the bed. Sitting on the edge of the mattress, she picked up the photo album on her bed stand. She smoothed the front of it with her hand, then traced the gold script letters on the cover with her finger.

My Family Album

One by one she went through the wedding pictures she kept there. There were a few of her and Jeff, but mostly they were of her family: Uncle Johnny walking her down the aisle . . . Grandma pouring punch . . . Grandpa laughing with R.J.

Her eyes rested on a picture of her and Jeff standing behind the wedding cake, Jeff's hand covering hers as they held the knife to cut the first piece. Leigh was in the background, partly cut off, unaware she was in the camera's range. She was looking at Renelle, her expression wistful.

Renelle closed her eyes a moment. Leigh still didn't trust her.

Setting the book aside, she set her lips in a firm line. She and Leigh *had* gotten off to a bad start, and Renelle knew—by Leigh's questions about how Jeff was doing in school and reminders that rent was coming up—that she still had doubts they could make it on their own. Renelle gave a resigned sigh. She didn't blame her mother-in-law. But Leigh didn't need to worry. Renelle would make her proud. Things were going to be different this time. They were a family now.

She and Jeff had lain in bed many nights talking about their future. He would finish school and start his new job as a computer tech. Then, she would start school. She was going to become an elementary school teacher. She'd already gone online to find out the requirements. And then they would adopt. They'd already opened a savings account for the baby with five dollars from each of their paychecks.

She rose and limped back into the living room. Things were going to be different this time.

"Anybody home?" Leigh shouted though her parents' front door as she pulled her key out of the lock.

Not hearing an answer, she crooked the KFC barrel in her arm, stepped into the entry, and shut the door behind her. As she shoved her keys in her pocket, she called out again. "Anybody home?"

The house was quiet.

When she'd finished at work early, she'd decided it would be fun to surprise them with dinner. Feeling the wall next to the front door, she flipped on the light switch, then made her way to the kitchen and set the chicken on the counter.

A glance into the family room confirmed her parents were gone. She probably should have called first, but she hadn't thought they'd be out on icy roads after dark. Suddenly, she caught her breath. Had something happened to her father?

She rushed to the door that led to the garage and opened it. Her father's car was gone, her mother's parked in its usual place. She released a sigh of relief. Her father was driving. He was between rounds of chemo and had been getting stronger. They'd probably run to the store.

Good. She smiled. That meant they hadn't eaten.

Returning to the entry, she turned on the outside lights and looked through the long narrow window next to the front door. It was beginning to snow in earnest. She hesitated a moment, then opened the door and dashed to the mailbox. By the time she returned, she was covered with snow.

She stepped onto the throw rug her mother kept in the hallway. Holding the mail in her mouth, she took off her boots and unzipped her fleece vest. Taking the letters in hand, she walked down the hall to her father's office.

She felt for the lamp on his desk and switched it on. As she started to toss the mail onto the desktop, she saw that her father had papers spread out on it. She moved closer, looking for a place to put the mail. An open letter was in full view. Without any thought, she took in the heading and the partially covered papers beneath it.

Pacific Northwestern Life Insurance Company.

Setting the mail down, she moved the open letter to the side, revealing a life insurance policy. Looking at the policy, she could see it was term insurance that had been taken out years before. The death benefit was $100,000.

And she was the beneficiary.

Tears sprang to her eyes. Death benefit. The typed letters seemed cold and hard. A tear slipped down her cheek. *Dear Lord, You can heal him.* If only the power of the Holy Spirit were hers, her father could be healed.

She returned the letter to its place as she sank into the chair next to the desk. For reasons she couldn't explain, she felt shocked to find her father had made such a generous provision for her. As the realization settled on her, a thought came from out of nowhere.

R.J.

She frowned, then slowly rose, scanning the desktop. To the right, partially covered by a large manila envelope, was what looked like another policy. A glance confirmed it was for R.J.

Filled with conflicting emotions, she peeled the envelope back and looked for the death benefit.

$100,000.

A guilty feeling winged across her back as she let go of the breath she'd been holding. An odd feeling of validation took its place.

She was an equal to her brother in her father's eyes. These policies made it so . . . for the first time in her life. She closed her eyes, savoring her father's approval.

She let the envelope fall back into place.

Picking up the open letter she'd set aside, she carefully put it back where she'd found it. Straightening, her eye passed over the face of it. Two words jumped out at her . . . *Leigh Scott.*

She hesitated. These were her father's personal papers. She probably shouldn't have been looking at them at all.

Still, they were on his desk, and since the cancer had returned he'd been more open about his business affairs with her, knowing she was the one her mother would turn to when he was gone.

Frowning, she allowed herself a few more words . . . *death benefit withdrawal . . .*

Her heart lurched. She picked up the letter.

Dear Bob,

This letter is to serve as confirmation of your request to make a partial death benefit withdrawal from policy #1873-0983L.

As indicated by your signed request (copy

enclosed), you will be receiving a check for $60,000, representing the requested portion of the total death benefit of $100,000. The balance of $40,000 will be paid to Leigh Scott, beneficiary, upon your death.

The remaining two policies of $100,000 each, with your wife and son as designated beneficiaries, will remain unchanged and will be paid in full to them upon your death.

Sincerely,

Don M. Lynn

Pacific Northwestern Life Insurance Company

Her father was cashing in over half of her policy! Why?

She read the letter again.

Why? Why was he doing this to her? Her lips trembled as she fought to hang on to the feeling she'd had just moments before as an equal to her brother.

R.J., perfect in her father's eyes. R.J., who didn't have a care in the world. No children to burden him. No financial pressure. The center of his own universe. He'd never lifted a finger to help during her father's illness. Her mind raced . . . And he was gay. What would her father think of that?

She choked on a sob as past memories and deep wounding put her in her place, far behind R.J. What if her father knew R.J. had stayed in a hotel with his boyfriend right under his nose?

A razor-edged voice shouted through her thoughts. *"Tell him."*

The sound of muffled voices drifted to her from the kitchen.

Her parents were home.

Her eyes cut to the letter, framed by the policy behind it.

Death benefit . . . he was dying. What difference did money make? Maybe he needed the money. His illness had been a drain on their finances.

It wasn't about the money.

Tell him.

Leigh moved blindly out of the office to the hall.

"Leigh, is that you?" Her father's voice.

She stepped into her boots, listening to the sound of footsteps in the kitchen. "Leigh?"

She rushed out the front door, then yanked it shut behind her.

Fumbling with her keys, she got in the car and started it, then pulled out of her parents' driveway onto the road, sliding on the icy streets as she headed out of the subdivision.

The thought of going home to an empty house only made her feel more isolated and angry. As she neared the main road, she heard her cell phone ringing. She pulled into the parking lot of a 7-Eleven and dug it out of her purse.

Her parents' home phone number filled the screen. As she stared at it through a lifetime of pain and rejection, angry tears pricked her eyes. "Why?"

Suddenly, a thought occurred to her.

She dropped the phone on the seat. *Johnny.* That had to be it. At the wedding rehearsal her father had gone out of his way to avoid Johnny, and at the wedding he'd hardly spoken to him. Johnny had tried to be friendly. It was her father who seemed aloof.

Everything was becoming clear. She'd obviously misread her father when they'd been at Two Forks River. She'd thought he'd softened toward Johnny. But he hadn't. She wiped her eyes with her sleeve. Her father still hated him. This was about her seeing Johnny again. She leaned back against the seat.

So this was how her father had decided to punish her for seeing John Higheagle? Even with death lingering nearby, he couldn't give up his prejudice and hatred of him. She slowly shook her head as she began to sort through the enormity of what she'd just discovered. Her father was to be pitied.

She pulled out of the parking lot. She wasn't going to go home. She was going to see John. For the last six months she'd asked him to take a backseat to her father's feelings. She'd kept him at a distance, hoping that eventually her father would accept him. And God bless Johnny, he'd patiently gone along with her.

The snow began to let up as she made her way north. By the time she reached Ridgeline, she found herself thinking about her prayer journal, and her book, and all she had learned recently about the Holy Spirit. She couldn't let herself get caught up in her father's hatred if she wanted the blessings of the Spirit. And she did. She wanted the gifting she'd read about in Acts and other books of the New Testament. The kind of gifting Johnny had. The kind of gifting she was writing about. Then she could make a difference in people's lives.

Her cell phone began to ring. Picking it up from the seat, she saw it was her parents' phone number on the screen. She thought for a moment.

"Hello?"

"Leigh, what happened? Your car was in the driveway, and then when we got into the house, you were gone."

"I'm sorry, Mom. I couldn't stay. Guess we just missed each other."

"Well, you were so sweet to bring us dinner. I wish you could have eaten with us."

"I'll be by to see you tomorrow, Mom. Maybe there'll be some leftovers."

"Okay, honey. See you then."

She turned onto the road that led to John's house, still deeply hurt, but determined to put it behind her. Just like Johnny had. He truly was a godly man.

He'd forgiven her father years ago.

❦

Sweetheart jumped up at the sound of the knocking on the front door.

"So you heard that too?" John grinned as Sweetheart, ears forward, ample hips swaying with purpose, beat him across the living room.

Stepping around Sweetheart, he pulled the door open. "Leigh!"

She stared at him with red-rimmed eyes. "I—" Her lower lip began to tremble. "I just—"

As he reached out to take her hand, Leigh stumbled

into his arms. Between sobs he caught fragments of jumbled sentences about her father and her brother.

As he guided Leigh to the couch, Sweetheart pushed rudely past them, making huffy little snorts as she returned to the kitchen.

John sat with Leigh in his arms, gently stroking her hair, waiting for her to cry herself out. Her raw emotion and stuttering about her father and R.J. stirred the past. He leaned his cheek against her head. Her father had hurt her all her life. And, apparently, he was still doing it.

The bitter anger John had felt when he'd seen her father at the mailbox rose in his chest. He closed his eyes and clenched his jaw. He'd done nothing but think about it since it happened. He had to get past it. Leigh's breathing quieted.

Opening his eyes, he let his gaze drift across the room to the bookcase where he kept his Bibles. It wasn't of his own volition that he was seeking peace with the man who had ruined his life. He knew in his heart he still hated Bob Williams.

It was because he wanted peace with God.

Leigh pushed against him. "Oh, Johnny." She straightened, facing him, eyes cast down. "I'm sorry. I'm a mess."

He put his forefinger under her chin and tilted her head up. "Do you want to talk about it?"

Nodding, she pushed her hair out of her face. "Do you have any tissues?"

John rose from the couch, retrieved a box of Kleenex from the bathroom, then sat down next to her.

Leigh pulled out a few tissues, and then set the box on the coffee table.

As John watched her dab her eyes and nose, he couldn't help but remember how many times he'd seen her like this when they were kids. He'd been in love with her then. He was even more in love with her now.

"Thank you." She gave him a weak smile. "Now I'm ready."

As Leigh told him all that had happened, he kept his thoughts to himself. If he told her what he thought about her father's actions, it would only feed his own root of bitterness.

She clenched her hand into a fist. "Johnny, it was all I could do not to walk in there and tell them about R.J."

It was all he could do to hold his tongue and not encourage her to tell her father about R.J. There wasn't a doubt in his mind that he could use this to draw Leigh closer to him, building a future on the foundation of their shared, painful past.

Icy claws of fear squeezed his chest as he recognized the prompting for what it was. He had to get past his anger. If he didn't, it would grow like a cancer until it destroyed him and his relationship with God. In some ways, it already had.

He brought his focus back to Leigh. "I'm glad you didn't. That wouldn't have accomplished anything."

Leigh's cell phone began ringing.

She glanced at him, then took it out of her pocket.

Surprise flashed across her face. "It's my agent." She flipped the phone open. "Hi, Riva."

Leigh's eyes widened as she listened. "That's so awesome. I can't believe it." She reached for his hand and squeezed it.

"Yes, I've really been working on it. Since I gave you the synopsis and three chapters, I've outlined the book, and I've been writing while I've been waiting. So I'm just missing a few scenes." She glanced at John. "And I should be able to get some information I need and write those over the next few weeks."

Leigh nodded her head. "Talk to you tomorrow."

Jumping from the couch, she clapped her hands together and stamped her feet. "Whoo hoo. Paramount wants to buy the book."

John felt his heartbeat quicken as the memory of the vision God had given him returned, and how clear it had been to him that night that somehow her books, and not their relationship, was the reason God had brought Leigh into his life. He shifted in his seat, knowing that he'd made only token efforts to follow what she was writing. He had never understood how he could be of any help to her, and she'd put him off every time he asked her about the book. Although he'd accepted her mild rebuffs, he'd seen the book as something that stood between them.

"I knew it." Animated and breathless, Leigh climbed onto the couch next to him. Pulling one leg underneath her, she faced him. "There's so much I haven't told you, Johnny."

"I've noticed." He couldn't help but smile at her. Her eyes, which moments before had glistened with tears, now sparkled with excitement.

She tilted her head, giving him a mischievous grin. "*You* gave me the idea for the book."

He drew back. "Me?"

"Yep, you." She gave a sharp half-nod. "Remember that night you told me about Tito?"

John nodded.

"Well, over a year ago Grace Bible Church had a whole study on the book of Acts and the Holy Spirit. The gifts of the Spirit are something I'd never understood, even though I'd been saved for years. I started to pray that the Holy Spirit would work in my life. Right after that, I got the interest from Paramount. I knew that had to be answered prayer. I felt so empowered. The idea that I could pray and He would answer so quickly." Her eyes became distant for a moment. "It was awesome."

She knotted her hands, leaning forward. "So I started praying that the Holy Spirit would show me the book of God's heart." Her eyes began to tear up again. "Johnny, I want so much to work for God. I mean, think of my dad. For all he has done to me, I still pray for his healing every day." She looked at her hands. "Even after what happened tonight, I'll still pray for him. It's within God's power. If He would just give me that gift of healing, I would use it." She raised her eyes. "That's what my book is about. The gifts of the Spirit." She grinned at him. "In a way, it's about you."

John tried not to look alarmed. "What are you talking about?"

"I'm talking about what you told me about Tito. You said that God calls to you and speaks to your spirit. The minute you told me, I knew that was the Holy Spirit show-ing me what my book was supposed to be about."

He searched her face. "And exactly what is that?"

"My book is about a woman of purpose, who's received and uses the gifts of the Spirit." She squared her shoul-ders. "I patterned her after a godly man I know. At least I thought he was." She lifted her chin. "She's used by the Lord in mighty ways. She has the gifts of healing, prophecy, and discernment. And she uses them to do God's will in this world. I didn't tell you anything about it because I was waiting to see if I got the book sold." She hesitated. "And then I was hoping that you'd tell me about some of the other things you've done."

He couldn't believe what he was hearing. "Leigh, that isn't how it works. You sound as if you're talking about channeling. The Holy Spirit is not *from* God, the Holy Spirit *is* God. We are not to use Him, He is to use us. You're talking like 'It' is some kind of weapon you use as you see fit."

She dropped her legs to the floor and pushed up. "I'm not saying that. I'm saying what Jesus said. He said we would do greater works than He did. That's exactly what it means."

John rose. "It's exactly the opposite of what you're saying. *We* can't do anything. It's when we realize we can do nothing, when we totally surrender to His will, that the impossible becomes possible."

Leigh turned to him, her voice rising. "Why do you feel like you have to argue with me? You, of all people, know the gifts of the Spirit are available to every believer. Don't you see? This is a way to spread Jesus's message

303

through the use of story. I prayed and asked God for months to show me the book of His heart. I'm positive this is it."

Dread filled John as he remembered the vision the Lord had given him at Leigh's house and how he had railed against it. How, even though he had told God that night that he would submit his will to Him, he hadn't done so in his heart. Now it was clear. This was what he had not been able to see. Because he had not wanted to. This was the unintended consequences of his disobedience.

Suddenly, what could have been was revealed to him. In a unit of compressed time he saw the beginning and the end, played out behind a misty veil. How God had planned to use him in Leigh's life as she wrote the book, how he could have helped her understand God's gifting in a different way, how that was to become the foundation of their relationship and future. God's plan was to prosper their love to the furthering of His kingdom.

He stood. "You can't write that."

Leigh's mouth dropped open. "Why would you say that?" She started for the door. "Do you think you're the only one who listens to God?"

She flung the door open. "I can't believe how wrong I was about you. I thought you'd be excited to share that part of your life with me. I even thought if I could get you and my father together, maybe you could pray and use the Holy Spirit to touch him and heal him. How stupid could I be? Apparently you don't believe in sharing the Good News." She slammed the door behind her.

John stood staring after her, the tension in the room

palpable even in her absence. Everything she'd said told him she was completely confused about his gifting—its power, its purpose, and its position in the eyes of God.

But she was right about one thing. It wouldn't have done any good to ask him to pray for her father. He hadn't felt the presence of the Spirit since the day he saw Bob Williams getting the mail.

Standing in the silence, it suddenly hit him. The thing he wanted most was being taken from him. Leigh. Not by divine intervention, but by his own. He'd embraced his anger toward her father and ignored the Spirit's leading to become involved with the writing of her book. Blind to God's plan, he'd gone his own way. And it was destroying his chance for the only thing he wanted in life. To make Leigh his wife.

He was losing her again . . . and this time it would be forever. He could feel it.

He raced to the door and flung it open. "Leigh."

Tearing across the porch, he screamed into the night. "Leigh! Come back!"

But she was already pulling away.

Her taillights, like two fiery red eyes, observed him, as her car disappeared down the drive.

21

Shivering, Jeff started the car and turned on the heat as the snow began falling again. He glanced down the street at the house, then angled his watch toward the light from the dashboard. Ten more minutes. At 4:00 a.m. it would be time for him to go in and check on the patients again at the house where Renelle was working.

Her neuropathy had been brought on by the diabetes. That's what the doctor had said. But they couldn't find the cause of Renelle's chronic pain, or what had sent her heart racing last week. That had ended up with her being admitted to the hospital and a battery of tests . . . and more bills.

It was a blessing that Betty had moved Renelle to a residence where she was not required to clean. All she had to do was check on the patients every hour during the night and be available to call other staff and 911 in case of an emergency. It had meant a pay cut to seven dollars an hour, but that was better than losing her job. They had to have her income to survive, but even more than that, they needed the health insurance. Her pain meds were taking most of their paychecks, and now this recent hospital visit.

He lowered his eyes, remembering their meeting with Betty. They'd both come in to talk to her because Renelle had gotten an unsatisfactory review, and she had been scared to death she was going to get fired. He'd gone along only to give her moral support. But as she and Betty talked, he began to realize how poor Renelle's job performance had become. He also realized that Renelle had tried to hide it from him, telling him that by sleeping a lot at home and staying off her feet, she was saving her energy to do her job. He quirked his mouth. The truth of the matter was something he hadn't allowed himself to dwell on. As her health had worsened, she'd begun to withdraw from him and was insistent that they not tell his mom anything about it.

He released a sigh. Even the small amount of work required at this new house was becoming difficult now. Her feet were numb, and she had trouble balancing because she couldn't feel the bottoms of her feet. It had also meant she couldn't drive anymore. She couldn't feel the gas and brake pedals. She couldn't feel anything through the pain. Glancing at the gas gauge, he turned off the engine, then pulled the blanket he had in his lap up around his shoulders.

The doctor had asked her to keep a daily pain journal and color code her levels of pain throughout the day. Green was to be used for low pain, red for the worst. They'd stopped on the way home from the doctor's appointment, and she'd bought a big spiral notebook and a box of pens. They both hoped this would point to something that might help with a diagnosis.

He checked his watch again. Then bracing himself

against the wet snow, he opened the car door and made his way through icy slush to the house.

Opening the front door quietly, hoping she was still asleep, Jeff stepped into the living room and pulled the door shut behind him. The glow from the television revealed Renelle lying on the couch asleep, her sweet face peaceful. Her dreams the only place she was really free of the pain. He let his gaze rest on her, thankful that it had worked out so he could help her, and she could rest. He bent down and took off his wet shoes.

Moving quietly, he crossed the room to the couch. He squatted beside her and kissed her lightly on the forehead. Then, sitting back on his heels, he studied her face.

"I love you," he whispered. She was such a special person. She'd overcome every obstacle life had thrown at her. And even though everyone she had loved either abused or abandoned her, she had dared to love again. Deep in his heart he believed that was why God had brought her into his life. *Thank You, Jesus.*

"Jeff?" she mumbled, starting to wake.

He rose, then bent over her. "It's me. Don't be afraid, I'm here with you. Go back to sleep."

She blinked as though trying to focus her eyes on him.

With a tender sweep of his hand, he brushed her hair from her face. "I'm going to check on everybody. You go back to sleep."

Her eyes fluttered closed.

Jeff made the rounds and found all the clients sound asleep. Returning to the living room, he went to the couch. He wished desperately he could sit with her and hold her until the next shift came. But his being there would be frowned on by management, and only raise unwanted questions about Renelle's health. He tiptoed to the door and put on his shoes.

Trudging back to the car, he suddenly remembered they were supposed to go to his mom's for dinner. He grimaced. Renelle so seldom felt good enough to go out, and they'd already put his mother off twice. And she'd said his grandparents were coming.

Jeff climbed back into the car and started the engine. It was the only thing they ever argued about. Renelle didn't want his mother to know anything about her health problems. She was convinced that his mom wouldn't understand. Renelle had made him swear on the Bible that he wouldn't say anything to anybody.

"I'm not going to burden my family," she'd told him firmly. "I've waited all my life to have one." Then she'd looked away.

It was the looking away . . . looking away from the burden she was becoming to him. His teeth chattering, he removed his wet shoes and put them under the heat vent.

He understood her feelings. And it only made him love her more deeply. She'd fought all her life to survive, hoping to find what others were born to. And now that it was within her reach, she was fighting again. Renelle was terrified her "mom" would find her unworthy.

Jeff pulled the blanket up around his shoulders. He loved his mother. But the truth was, though she would deny it, accepting Renelle was based on credit counseling, on him keeping his grades up, and on their living their lives the way she expected them to.

He laid his head against the back of the seat and closed his eyes. At the wedding someone had asked his mother why Renelle called her Mom. His mother had answered saying she thought of Renelle like a daughter.

What would his mother think about Renelle if she could see him now . . .

It would tear everyone apart.

❦

"Smells good, doesn't it, Max?" Leigh smiled as she closed the oven door on the baking chicken. It had been a long time since she'd had the family over for dinner. It had been awhile since she'd had anybody over for dinner.

Two weeks had passed since she'd walked out of Johnny's house. He'd tried calling her several times and had left messages. But after a lot of soul searching and prayer, she'd decided that this was not the time for them. That had been her gut feeling when she'd found out her father's cancer had returned, and now with Johnny's opposition to her book, it seemed like God was confirming it. She was positive that *The Gift* was the book she was supposed to write. She didn't need anyone's counsel about that. It was no coincidence how all the doors had opened for her.

She scooped Max up in her arms and headed for the back hall. "You've got to go outside, buddy. You're not invited tonight." Opening the back door, she set the big cat on the garage steps.

Riva had negotiated a nice advance from Paramount,

and unexpectedly a slot had opened up on their fall list. Now, instead of having to wait until next year to get her book on the shelf, it would be out in October, which also meant she'd be getting the other half of her advance sooner than she'd originally thought. The doorbell ringing cut into her thoughts.

She hurried to the front door.

"Oh, Mom and Dad. I thought the kids would be here first." She pulled the door open, then took her father's arm and helped him in.

"The only reason we're always late is because it takes your mother forever to get dressed."

The two women exchanged a glance as her mother stepped through the door behind him and closed it.

Leigh quickly changed the subject. "Can I get you anything? How about some hot tea?"

As her parents took off their coats and got situated in the family room, Leigh made them each a cup of chamomile, all the while keeping her eye on the clock. Before Jeff was married, he was never late.

"Here you go." Leigh set the tray on the coffee table and served her parents.

"Smells wonderful." Her mother blew on the hot beverage. "Anything new with the book?"

"Riva called me today and she had more good news. Since the book is coming out in the fall, they're going to include it in a huge promotion they're doing to launch the Life Journeys imprint."

"You deserve it, honey. You've worked so hard." Her mother took a sip of the tea. "It looks like things are finally breaking for you."

"It seems like it." Leigh glanced at her watch. "And the first half of the advance won't come a minute too soon. I've got so many bills to catch up on with the wedding and everything."

"Things really seem to be breaking for R.J. too." A broad smile lit her father's face. "He says that some big wheel that he met in that movie he was in is giving him more work." He set his cup on the table. "I'm sure proud of that boy."

It was all Leigh could do to ignore the comment. "I think I'll check on the chicken."

Once in the kitchen, and out of their sight, she let her anger surface, and with it came a replay of that evening in her father's office when she'd found the letter from the life insurance company. She walked to the stove and set the oven on warm. This wasn't the time to bring any of that up. It was beyond her power to control anything her father did, and she wasn't going to waste whatever time they had left trying to sort though a lifetime of pain. All she could do was continue to pray for him and hope God would change him.

Returning to the family room, she took her seat on the couch.

"How do the kids like the little place you got them?"

"Okay, I guess. They had me over there once when they first moved in, and that was it." She didn't add that every time the first of the month rolled around she held her breath. Afraid she would get a call from Raley Richmond, the agent in the office who had taken a chance and rented to them. Jeff's recent behavior had only added to that concern. But so far no news was good news.

Her mother lifted an eyebrow. "Well, now that you mention it, they've *never* had us over to see their new home and only stopped to see us a few times since they got married." She took a sip of her tea. "Now that I think about it, Renelle came only once."

"You women." Her father set his cup down. "They've got their own lives. It's none of your business."

With Jeff and Renelle due to arrive any minute, there was no point in reminding her father that Jeff's business *had* become her business when he showed up in her bedroom in the middle of the night with no place to go. And if that happened again, this time he wouldn't be alone. "Well, let's hope they've learned from their past mistakes. They both have jobs and no expenses really, other than the payment they make on that consolidated debt the credit counseling people set up for them," she said, with more confidence than she felt.

Her mother turned toward the kitchen. "Isn't that the phone ringing?"

Leigh jumped up and ran to the kitchen.

"Hello?"

"Hi, Mom."

Leigh's grip tightened on the receiver. "What happened?"

"We won't be able to make it tonight. I'm sorry."

"Why did you wait till now to call and tell me? Your grandparents are here waiting too."

"I have to go into work."

"I thought today was your day off."

"Someone didn't show up."

"Well, can't Renelle come anyway? We'd love to see her." Leigh leaned against the counter.

"I don't have time to drive her over."

"Can't she drive herself?"

"She can't drive her car right now."

Leigh reached over and turned the oven off. "Why? What's wrong with it?"

"Uh . . ." Silence. "Mom, I've got to go. We'll talk more later."

"Wait a sec. How about we pack up the food and bring it over to your place? We could eat there, and then you'd have a nice meal waiting for you when you get off work."

"Uh. No, never mind. Don't worry about us. See you later." He hung up.

Apprehension rose in Leigh's chest.

A stab of fear jolted her. Was the marriage in trouble? Were they fighting again over Renelle running up credit card debt . . . or worse? It suddenly occurred to her that they hadn't been in church the past few weeks either.

She set the phone in the cradle. Something was going on, and she was going to find out what it was.

∞

Renelle watched from the kitchen window as Jeff drove away.

When Betty had called to see if either one of them could cover for Helga, it had been a godsend. Renelle quirked her mouth. At least something good had happened. Not only had it given them a perfect excuse to bow out of dinner at Leigh's house, it meant a little extra money on Jeff's next check.

Renelle picked up the purple spiral notebook and box of colored pens from the kitchen counter, then limped to the rocking chair in the living room. She'd avoided writing in the journal all day because her hands hurt. But the doctor had said it was important to track the levels of her pain, so she was determined to do it no matter how much it hurt.

Dropping into the chair, she stretched her legs out in front of her. It had been a bad day. She'd looked forward all week to going to Mom's for dinner, and seeing Grandma and Grandpa Scott. When they arrived home from work, Jeff had given her her meds and they'd both lain down and slept a couple of hours. When they'd awakened, Jeff had helped her bathe and wash her hair. He'd patiently combed out the tangled mess, then blown it dry.

She'd watched him in the mirror, knowing he was exhausted after doing her job all night, knowing this wasn't what he'd signed up for. But he was smiling as he worked. And when he'd caught her watching him, he'd winked at her as if they shared a wonderful secret, and then he'd mouthed, Love you, Babe.

Please don't leave me.

She worked the pen box open and looked at the colored markers she'd bought to write about her pain. The doctor had said to use green for low pain, blue for moderate pain, and red for high pain. She took out the blue pen . . . baby blue. She slowly began to rock. Blue gingham lining a bassinet . . . a teddy bear with a blue bow . . . fairies dancing on blue wallpaper.

Her eyes teared up. Someday they would have a baby. When she was well, she would go back to school and get a good job, and she and Jeff would adopt. She turned her attention to the blank page in front of her. She was going to get her diabetes and pain under control. It was important for Jeff and for the baby who would be waiting for them.

She tapped the marker on the paper, trying to get ahold of the recent thought about washing her hair. Lately she'd noticed thoughts that seemed familiar came and went. Unfinished, unconnected.

Frowning, she pressed the pen to the paper and wrote, *Feel confused.*

Forming the letters somehow connected her to the task, and she moved on to the next line: *Morning—woke up with a bad headache and joints aching. Sharp pain in my toes and fingers. Lay in bed for—*

Tilting her head back, she closed her eyes, trying to put the pieces of the morning together. Jeff had gone to the laundromat . . . she'd wanted to wear her pink pants to Mom's dinner, and they were dirty. When he'd come back he'd helped her get up.

—an hour.

Her lower lip began to tremble and she blinked rapidly. Mom's dinner. It had all been ruined. She'd worked hard to be ready early so she could rest. And at five she'd lain down again, hoping that she could get her strength back, knowing she'd have to keep it together while she was at Leigh's house. If Leigh found out how sick she was, she'd find out everything. She'd find out her daughter-in-law was nothing but a burden to her son and that she was the reason he was failing in school. She'd find out that everything she'd told Jeff in the beginning was true and that he shouldn't have married her.

She clenched her jaw. It wasn't true. This was just a temporary setback. It was going to work out . . . it had to work out.

When Jeff had called Leigh to tell her they couldn't come, Renelle had wanted desperately to get on the phone and explain everything. But how could she? How could she explain that she was sick and fat and useless? Most of the time she couldn't walk without holding onto something, and tonight she hadn't even been able to open the container her medicine was in by herself. Jeff had had to do it. There was no way she could have hidden how bad she hurt and how bad she felt from Leigh and Grandma and Grandpa.

I'm sorry.

She stared at the marker in her hand, her thoughts drifting again. She longed to talk to her "mom." But phone calls had proven to create more problems than they solved. Leigh would want to take her out to lunch, or come to visit, or a hundred other things moms do with their daughters. And that would leave Renelle making excuses, which would only lead to more questions. She turned the page of the journal. Besides, it made her uncomfortable to share her feelings. It wasn't safe.

After smoothing the clean sheet, she began to write.
Leigh,
She paused, then crossed it out.
Drawing a deep breath, she began again:

> Mom, I love you so much. I'm sorry I couldn't
> come to dinner. I really wanted to, and worked
> all day at getting ready. But I was hurting

terribly. Don't worry. I'm going to get better. I promise. I'm going to be everything you want in a daughter-in-law. And a good wife to Jeff too. And we're going to give you those grandbabies you've always wanted.

She set the pen down and stretched her aching fingers.

Picking up the pen again, she began to smile.

We'll take the kids to the park then. All four of us. The whole family.

She reread the sentence, then tilted her head to the side and wrote the words again. *The whole family.*

Closing her eyes, she shut out the reality of her circumstances. And there, at the nexus of what she so desperately wanted and what she so desperately feared, she dared to let herself feel.

She had a family now. A husband who loved her. A mother-in-law who considered her a daughter. Grandparents who she considered her own.

Clenching her fingers into a fist she tried to grasp it, tried to hang on. But the moment was slipping away into the desperate certainty that was her life.

Icy fingers of fear gripped her. Stilettos weaving the past into the future, ripping away the moment, punishing her for daring to believe. A smoky voice whispering what she already knew.

One day they would abandon her.

22

Leigh tapped her pen on her prayer journal, then sighed and leaned back against the headboard of her bed. What was the Lord trying to show her? Why wasn't He answering her prayers?

For months she'd prayed faithfully, asking Him to prosper Jeff's life and marriage, to touch and heal her father, and most of all to let her feel the presence of the indwelling Holy Spirit in her life.

She frowned. It was His will to do all of those things. There were dozens of Scriptures confirming that. She'd looked them up, and even prayed the Scriptures as part of her prayer time. But nothing seemed to be happening.

Her eyes drifted to the computer. Well, at least God had given her book favor. The contract from Paramount would be coming any day, and shortly after that the first half of the advance. Her eyes moved to the stack of envelopes on the corner of the desk. One of them was a letter from the landlord saying the rent was going up. She closed her eyes. *Lord, You know my needs. I'm trusting You to provide for me.*

Worries crowded into her mind. What if Paramount

didn't like the manuscript? Johnny hadn't helped her like she thought he would. She set her mouth in a firm line. Hadn't helped her . . . that was an understatement. He'd told her not to write the book. And even though he'd tried to call her over the past month, she'd stood her ground. There was nothing he could say that would change what he'd said that night. Things were tough enough without that kind of opposition to what she was trying to do.

She opened her eyes and glanced at the picture of him next to the computer. As he held her gaze, she felt a familiar yearning. She immediately turned her attention back to her prayer journal.

She'd spent most of her prayer time talking to the Lord about Jeff and Renelle. After cancelling out on dinner two weeks ago, they'd continued to avoid her. They seemed to have an excuse for everything. Oh, Renelle was sweet as she could be on the phone, but she kept the conversation away from anything of substance. Leigh never got a straight answer about Jeff's grades, or their jobs. "Everything is okay," was as far as it went.

Tears stung her eyes. The truth was, it seemed like they didn't want her to be part of their lives. Maybe she had been too nosy and asked too many questions. She lifted her chin. It was just that it had all gotten off to such a bad start. And deep down, she still didn't trust Renelle. This recent behavior had only strengthened that feeling. She had to admit that praying for the girl was more from a sense of duty than anything else. *You can love the sinner, but hate the sin*. And that was what she was doing.

Leigh slowly shook her head. There was so much at stake that Renelle didn't seem concerned about. Like the loan on Leigh's parents' house. Those payments would start in June, and if Jeff failed to make them, her parents could lose their home. A wave of nausea churned in her stomach. That was unthinkable.

An email alert sounded from her computer.

Swinging her feet off the bed, she rose and crossed the room. As she moved the cursor to the little envelope icon, she sat in the desk chair.

The message popped up. It was from Raley. The agent who had rented to Jeff and Renelle.

> Hi Leigh,
>
> I really debated about telling you this, but your son didn't pay the rent on the first. You know I rented to them only against my better judgment and only because you thought that they would pay on time. You more or less said you'd make it good if they didn't.
>
> They're supposed to pay me next weekend. I'll let you know if they don't.
>
> Raley

Her jaw dropped open.

"No." Her voice came out a whisper as weeks of suspicion coalesced into anger. "I knew it. I knew they were hiding something."

She looked at the clock. If she hurried she could stop at their apartment on the way to work. If she was lucky, Jeff would be there and Renelle wouldn't be home yet.

Maybe then she'd have a chance at getting at the truth. She cursed the day the girl had come into their lives. And that story she'd given about how she'd changed. She hadn't changed one bit. It was starting all over again. Calling herself Renelle didn't change one thing. Jessica was destroying Jeff's life.

As Leigh dressed, she thought about how she could get some money together to pay Raley if they didn't. She couldn't think of anything, other than borrowing from a credit card.

Johnny.

She dismissed the thought. This was her problem, not his. She ran a comb through her hair, grabbed her coat and purse, and headed to Jeff and Jessica's house.

On her way to the apartment she couldn't stop herself from going over and over all the warning signs. How deep down she knew this would happen. How she should have stopped it for Jeff's sake. He was her responsibility. Not Jessica's.

She pulled to the curb in front of the mailboxes. Jessica's car was parked in the driveway. Jeff's car was gone. Fine. If Jessica was the only one home, then she'd talk to her. She parked, then strode to the front door and rang the doorbell. Standing with her arms folded across her chest, she waited for Jessica to answer.

Minutes passed. She knocked on the window. No answer.

As she waited, she noticed there were several newspapers lying in the flowerbed next to the front door. Had they gone somewhere?

"Can I help you?"

She turned to the voice. A man was looking out his door from the duplex next door.

"Oh. Hi. I'm Leigh Scott. Jeff's mother."

The man's eyes narrowed slightly.

"They didn't answer the door and I thought they'd be home by now."

The man's face began to relax. "Oh yes, I remember seeing you when they moved in."

"Have you seen them?"

He shook his head. "Not in the last few days. But they're pretty quiet. I really don't see them that often anyway. I think they sleep in the day."

At least they were good neighbors. "Well, thanks. If you see them, tell Jeff to call his mother right away. It's important."

Curiosity sparked in the man's eyes. "I'll be sure to tell them."

"Thanks." She turned and left as he shut the door. Was it possible they had gone somewhere?

As she approached the car, her gaze lingered on the mailboxes.

Walking to the passenger side of the car, she opened the box with the name Scott on it. It had several letters in it. The one on top had a return address of an attorney in Florida. She'd seen that address before, when Jeff had come home the first time. It was a collection agency.

She slammed the box shut and walked around the car to the driver's side. Opening the door, she reached inside and got her purse. After finding a scrap of paper and a pen, she scribbled a note: *Call me. If I haven't heard from you by tonight, I'll be back.*

"What was that piece of paper stuck in the door?"

Jeff helped Renelle onto the couch, then pulled the paper out of his back pocket. "It's from my mom."

Renelle looked at him silently.

"I guess she was over here while we were gone. She wants me to call her. It says if she doesn't hear from me, she'll come back by."

Renelle's eyes widened. "No. She can't come here. The place is a mess." Her voice rose. "I'm a mess too. My legs hurt so much and those sores are back in my mouth." Her eyes filled with tears. "I don't want to see anyone right now. Turn off the lights."

Jeff watched his wife as her brow creased with concern. They had just come back from the hospital because she had been running a fever off and on for the past week, and her pain kept breaking through the Durgesic patches she wore on her back. When they'd first gone to the hospital the morning before, the doctor had asked her to try to get through the pain by sticking with her regular dosage of pain medicine. But she'd cried most of the afternoon because the pain was so intense, and last night he'd finally taken her to the hospital again and begged them to do something for her. He'd used the rent money to pay for the prescription.

It wasn't the first time he'd had to come up with money for her medications. Several times he'd stretched his Strattera by skipping some doses, or taking only half a dose. What it had saved in money it had cost him in grade points. He was flunking out of college.

Her speech became deliberate as the shot they'd given her at the hospital took effect. "Please. Turn off the lights."

He stared at her. High color in her fevered face, dull eyes fearful, breathing labored. His jaw set, he walked into the kitchen and turned off the overhead lights, leaving a single dim lamp on in the living room. Then he sat beside her, and pulled her into his lap. "Renelle, we need to talk." He felt her tense up.

"About what?"

"We can't do this anymore."

Ever since he'd called his mother and cancelled out on the dinner with his grandparents, he'd thought about what he would tell his mom. That night he knew it was only a matter of time until she found out the truth. Now, sitting in the dark, the rent unpaid and an ad in the paper to sell Renelle's car in one more desperate attempt to keep their heads above water, he knew the time had come. He had to reach out for help.

"Do what? Live our lives?"

"We can't keep hiding from my mother. She'll understand if we tell her what's happened."

"And what is that, Jeff? What are you going to say happened?" She struggled to get out of his arms. "You're going to make it all my fault. You're going to blame everything on me."

He knew she didn't mean what she was saying, but her words still cut him. Tightening his grip on her, he kissed the top of her head. "I love you. It's *not* your fault. I know you can't help being sick. She'll understand too."

"She won't. That afternoon at your house. She made it

clear. We were on a trial basis." She paused, the uneven, drugged speech slowly making its way from her lips through a vanishing portal of clarity. "And I'm trying. I'm trying hard."

He closed his eyes and rested his head against the back of the couch. They'd had this conversation in some form a hundred times.

He startled at the sound of the doorbell.

A tear splashed on his arm as Renelle turned her head toward the door. It had to be his mother.

He desperately wanted to answer the door. She would understand. She'd immediately see that he and Renelle needed her. And she could comfort Renelle, stay with her while he went to cover for her at work. He'd called Betty earlier to let her know Renelle was sick again and that he couldn't make his shift, but he would cover graveyard.

"Jeff?" His mother's voice came through the door.

He shifted on the couch.

"No. Please, no." Renelle moaned through a desperate whisper.

"Jeff?"

He sat still, staring through the darkness at the front door until he heard his mother's footsteps fade as she left.

Renelle moaned again.

Putting his lips next to Renelle's ear, he whispered, "I'm here. I love you."

He held her, staying with her as long as he dared. With school and jobs and caring for her, there was seldom time for the two of them to just be alone and enjoy each other. There were some days she couldn't bear to have him touch her because of the pain. He kissed her hair.

Realizing she was asleep, he eased himself off the couch. She moaned as he gently laid her head on the cushion.

He took a quick shower and headed for work.

As he drove, his thoughts returned to his wife and the way she courageously lived every day knowing the suffering that awaited her, the way she dared to dream dreams of a future in the face of the present, and how, for all she had been through, she still wanted to love and be loved. It humbled him. Despite the relentless pain that tortured her day after day, she had never given up. She continued her fight because of him and the children they wanted, and the family she'd prayed for all her life. He pulled in front of the residence at Haven House.

Turning off the car, he sat for a moment. For the first time since they had married he allowed himself to consider the truth. The doctors couldn't help Renelle. He lowered his chin to his chest and prayed.

Jesus, it is so hard to watch her suffer. And tonight she seemed so full of fear. In Your Word You say perfect love casts out fear. He drew a deep breath, then released it. *Where I am not perfect, You are. Please take care of her while I'm gone.*

He pulled the keys from the ignition, grabbed his book bag, and headed into the house.

Karri, one of the supervisors, was watching television on the couch when he arrived.

Jeff took off his coat and hung it up. "Hi."

"Hi, Jeff."

He walked into the living room. "Everything okay here tonight?"

Rising, Karri nodded. "Everyone's asleep. Betty came by earlier. Juanita is going to relieve you in the morning, but she's going to a training session at eight o'clock, so Betty wanted you to cover for her until she can get here at nine."

Jeff nodded absently as he dropped his book bag next to the table.

"Jeff." Karri took an envelope off the coffee table and handed it to him. "When Betty stopped by, she left something for Jessica."

He could see the yellow paper in the envelope's window. It was a check.

Karri's eyes filled with compassion and she gave him a quick hug. Then she turned and left.

He dropped onto the couch. Tapping the envelope on his knee, he gazed out the front window. It was a check. A yellow check. Everyone at Haven House knew all checks were printed on green stock. Except the yellow ones. The ones that came with your two-week notice.

He threw the envelope back onto the table and leaned against the couch. Right now he was too exhausted to think about what this would mean. But one thing he did know—as much as he hated to upset Renelle, he would have to tell his mother. They needed her help. He would tell her tomorrow, after work. He'd check on Renelle, and then he'd go see his mom.

He pulled his book bag onto the table and for the next several hours tried to study. Finally, after making the rounds at 4:00 a.m., he lay down on the couch.

He could rest an hour before he had to make rounds again.

The moment he closed his eyes, benevolent and obliging, sleep overtook him.

He could hear the sound of the ocean in the distance, and he found himself walking in a silvery mist. Then, as the sound of the waves grew louder, he felt sand beneath his feet and before him was an expanse of blue water.

Still and smooth, and the most beautiful blue. Strangely familiar, it filled him with wonder.

Smiling, he raised his hand, and though he did not move, he touched the water.

Beneath his touch it vanished. In its place was a woman.

"Renelle." His voice came out a whisper.

She turned to him. Her beautiful azure blue eyes before him, clear, lucid, joyful.

And in that one exquisite moment, he was allowed to glimpse his love for her . . . made perfect.

❧

Renelle tried to open her eyes but she couldn't.

She'd taken her last dose of medicine like she was supposed to. She was sure she had. And just in time. Someone had been stealing the pain pills the doctor had given her. The bottle was almost empty.

She lay on the couch, a prisoner of her pain. Afraid that anything could send the wretched shards of glass moving through her calves again. And she was thirsty, so thirsty.

She felt herself drifting, unfettered by time, but all

the while listening for the sound of Jeff coming home. She needed him so much. When he was near, she wasn't afraid. He loved her. Life with him was worth fighting for. Soon she would be better, and things would be different. She was going to get well.

A stabbing razor of pain slashed through her leg, punishing her for the thought, jerking her back to the present.

Disoriented, fear rose in her chest and her heart began to pound.

Immediately she felt the sweet, familiar presence of love. As had happened many times before, she felt him before she actually saw him. He loved her so much.

"Jeff?"

"Don't be afraid. I love you. I'm here."

She felt his presence. "Thirsty. Water."

The touch of an unseen hand brought the sensation of cool water to her lips. Life-giving water.

The touch wasn't Jeff's, but the love was his love. Or so it seemed, though she couldn't say why.

Each sip of water brought a vision, vignettes of her time with him . . . smiling at her across the front seat of the car when they first met . . . gently brushing her hair when she couldn't . . . holding her as she sweat with fever and pain.

In that moment, she knew the truth. And she spoke it. "Jesus."

Life giving, the water seeped over her tongue. Every surface it touched made new. From the inside out, it permeated her skin, moving up to her hairline, down

330

through her parched throat, into her stomach, and out through her body.

Living water. Transforming her. Setting her free.

The chains that bound her slipped from her, taking the natural world of pain and sorrow and hopelessness with them as they fell away.

The love became light. And she followed it. Up and up, she soared, borne toward heaven on an angel's wing. Until she found herself over an ocean. And to one side was a lone figure on its shore.

Jeff.

As she looked at him, he raised his hand. As if to touch her.

The unfailing and unselfish love that had been her life with him rose from the fingertips of his upraised hand and became one with the light. Releasing her to that place where there is no suffering and pain. To her inheritance, incorruptible and undefiled, reserved for her by the power of God, before the foundations of the earth were laid.

23

John Higheagle stood in the clearing atop the ridge, facing the rising sun. He hadn't been to this hallowed spot since the day he'd driven to Bob Williams's house. But this morning, when he'd awakened from a restless sleep, he knew he couldn't face another day estranged from God.

He'd tried to repent of his anger toward Leigh's father. He'd spent time in the Word and prayed for forgiveness. But it hadn't been more than lip service, done in the flesh. He had been unable to abandon himself to God. To surrender to God's will and allow the Holy Spirit to work within him at God's direction. And he knew why.

Lifting his eyes toward heaven, he sank to his knees in the icy snow. God wanted all of him. He couldn't withhold any part of his heart if he wanted God to use him to further His kingdom.

He not only had to forgive Bob Williams, he had to be willing to love him, to allow God to love through him. Divine, unconditional love was the catalyst that brought the power of heaven to earth. He couldn't truly forgive with hate in his heart.

Shivering in the cold, he began to pray the fifty-first Psalm. "Create in me a clean heart, O God. Renew a right spirit within me." The conviction in his heart poured from his lips. "Cast me not away from thy presence, and take not thy Holy Spirit from me. Restore unto me the joy of thy salvation; and uphold me with thy free spirit." A warm wind began to swirl around him. "Then will I teach transgressors thy ways; and sinners shall be converted unto thee."

As his last word rose, the wind that encircled him passed through him. Filling his heart with joy.

He raised his hands. The frigid winter morning faded from around him, transfigured by the Shekinah glory of God. And for as long as the Spirit touched him, he worshiped.

Finally, he rose to his feet. God was calling him.

By the time he made his way down the icy mountain roads to Cedar Ridge, it was after nine o'clock. He drove as fast as he dared to the Williams's home. He was not only willing but anxious to make peace with Bob Williams. He parked in their driveway and bounded out of the car.

He knocked, then clasped his hands behind his back as he waited for someone to answer.

Bob Williams opened the door.

John met the man's eyes and smiled. "Good morning. I hope I'm not interrupting anything."

For a moment Leigh's father didn't move. Then he extended his hand. "Good morning. Come in."

John shook his hand and stepped into the entry. Suddenly, the thing that had seemed impossible to do only the day before, the thing he'd allowed to hold him prisoner for months, the thing that had robbed him of fellowship with God, was as simple as speaking the truth.

"I want to apologize. I've harbored some hard feelings from the past. That was wrong of me. I'd like to ask you to forgive me."

Leigh's father's eyes teared up, but he held John's gaze.

John felt goose bumps rise on his arms as the power of God touched the man's heart.

Bob Williams slowly nodded. "I forgive you." He drew a deep breath. "Can you forgive me?"

⊂⊃

Throwing the curling iron down on the bathroom counter, Leigh ran to answer the phone by her bed. It had to be Jeff. He'd never called after she left the note on his door, and no one had answered when she'd gone back last night. She was positive they'd been home. She'd decided, even if she had to spend her whole Saturday parked in front of their house to talk to them, she would. There was no excuse for this kind of behavior and she would tell them so.

She picked up the receiver. "Hello."

"Mom—"

"Jeff, what's the matter with you? I know you were home when I came by last night. I also know your rent is late. This is the very thing I was afraid of." She stopped to draw a breath.

"Mom, Renelle died last night."

She heard the words, but she couldn't grasp the meaning. "What?"

"Renelle died. I came home and she was gone. I called 911. They're here now."

"I'm . . . I'm so sorry." Slowly, a weight settled on her shoulders. "What happened?"

He didn't speak.

"I'll be right there."

"No." His voice sounded distant. "There's nothing you can do."

"I can be there for you." She tightened her grip on the phone. "I'm coming over."

"Mom, I'll come there as soon as everything is taken care of."

"Jeff. I want to come over. You shouldn't be there alone."

"Really, I wish you wouldn't."

Apprehension rose in her chest. "Why?" Thoughts of how they'd avoided her over the past months flashed through her mind. Had Renelle's sordid past caught up with her?

"Renelle wouldn't want you to see the place like this." He paused. "Or her."

Leigh dropped her gaze to the floor. Even in death, Renelle was keeping her at bay. "Are you sure it wouldn't help to have me there?"

"There's nothing you can do. I'm going to call Grandma and Grandpa now. I'll see you soon."

She heard him hang up.

Leigh stood with the phone still pressed to her ear, trying to pull her thoughts together. Renelle was gone.

It didn't seem possible. She'd been thinking about her only moments before, while she was curling her hair.

She turned and set the phone back in the cradle, choosing not to revisit the thoughts she'd had about Renelle before the phone rang.

Dropping to the edge of the bed, she sat in stunned disbelief. Renelle had health issues, but nothing life threatening. At least Renelle had never talked about anything serious. She was being treated for diabetes, but other than that, nothing had ever been mentioned . . . and Leigh had never asked.

Her gaze came to rest on her nightstand, her prayer journal opened to the entry she'd been writing that morning. She picked it up.

Renelle's name jumped out at her, peppered through the even strokes of her handwriting. She turned a few pages back. More entries . . . detailing Renelle's shortcomings for the Lord.

Leigh took the edge of the journal and let weeks fan by, stopping at an entry dated November. The kids had been living with her then.

She read: *Renelle is the wrong girl for Jeff. She's so secretive.*

Leigh remembered how Renelle would get phone calls and drop her voice. Leigh felt heat in her cheeks. She'd actually thought the caller was probably someone from Renelle's past that Renelle had no business talking to.

She continued thumbing back through the pages, finally spotting entries about "Jessica."

This is my only son. Don't let him throw his life away. Lead him to the ministry You planned for him.

She read on: *Send Your Holy Spirit to work in Jeff's life, to show him that this is not the girl You have for him. Please, take Jessica out of his life.*

Her heart lurched. The words she'd written when she was blind to the future now seemed cold and unloving. But she hadn't known Renelle was so close to the end of her life. No one knew.

God knew.

The weight on her shoulders became a heaviness in her heart. She had only wanted what was best for Jeff. It wasn't that she didn't love Renelle. She'd taken her in, given her furniture, and even more than that, she'd prayed faithfully for the girl.

Asking God to change Renelle.

Suddenly feeling uneasy, Leigh closed the journal and set it back on the bed stand. She'd done her best, and Renelle hadn't made it easy. The truth was, Renelle had ruined Jeff's life. Leigh pushed up, folded her arms across her chest, and strode to the window. And in spite of that, Leigh had forgiven her and taken her in.

She clenched her jaw. She'd done the Christian thing. And still, once the kids had married, Renelle had slowly cut her off. The last few times she'd seen the young woman, Renelle had been unkempt, unfriendly . . . unlovely.

Leigh spun on her heel, tears stinging her eyes. What had happened in the past couldn't be changed. She'd done her best for Renelle. Maybe she should have tried harder, maybe she had been a little too quick to judge, but right now the important thing was to give Jeff the support he needed.

As she was buttoning her blouse, she heard the email alert sound from her computer. Stepping to her desk, she clicked on the alert icon.

The message popped up. She scanned the text. *Still haven't heard from your son.* Raley Richmond.

She battled a wave of conflicting emotions. She had to stay strong. There was a burial to be paid for now, and who knew what other financial problems Jeff was in.

The loan due on her parents' house surfaced at the fringes of her thoughts.

She clicked Reply and typed: *I'm sorry I haven't gotten back to you but Renelle died unexpectedly last night. I will be in touch with you soon. Right now, I'm going to be spending time with my son.* She'd deal with this later. No matter what Jeff said, he needed her now.

Hurrying, she finished dressing, then got in the car and sped to Jeff's apartment.

Pulling to the curb across from the mailboxes, she turned off the engine. It had been only the night before that she'd parked in exactly the same place, then pounded on their door in anger. The memory overwhelmed her with feelings of sorrow, anguish . . . and guilt.

Suddenly she felt desperately alone.

Johnny.

She hadn't seen him for weeks, even though he'd tried numerous times to contact her. She'd avoided him because he'd been against her writing *The Gift*. He'd basically told her she didn't understand anything about the power and working of the Holy Spirit. And that her book's message was somehow wrong.

She straightened in her seat, remembering how sure

of herself she'd been. Righteous anger, that's what she'd called it driving home that night. He thought he was giving her godly counsel, but she was certain it wasn't God's counsel.

Somehow, today she wasn't so sure. Her eyes drifted to Jeff's front door. What had seemed like righteous anger now seemed like self-righteous pride. She lowered her eyes.

Taking her cell phone out of her purse, she punched in John's phone number. "Please answer."

As the phone continued to ring, she realized she wanted to hear what he had to say. When voice mail picked up, she realized she wanted to talk to him. She needed to talk to him. "Johnny, it's Leigh. Please call as soon as you can. Something's happened."

She picked up her purse, dropped the phone in it, and climbed out of the car.

Jeff opened the door just as she reached it. He looked exhausted, but his eyes were peaceful.

"Jeff, I'm so sorry this has happened." They embraced.

"Come in, Mom." He led her toward the kitchen. "I was trying to clean up a little. I called work and told them about Renelle. I'm pretty sure some of her co-workers will come by."

Leigh glanced around the room. There were dirty plates and fast-food containers everywhere. The garbage was overflowing and the floor was filthy. "What happened?"

Jeff shrugged. "She was in too much pain to do anything." He stuck his hands in the sink full of dishes he was washing. "I tried to help, but with my job and school and caring for her full-time, I just didn't seem to be able to get much else done. And these last few weeks I've been doing her job at Haven House too." He paused. "I didn't even get to school these past few days."

Leigh could hardly process what he was saying. A myriad of emotions fought for her attention. The tragedy of the situation, the truth of what her son was facing, and the impact of it all on her own life. "Why didn't you ask me to help you?"

The moment the words were out of her mouth, Leigh knew the answer to her own question. Asking her for help would have been asking for her judgment.

Jeff cut his eyes to her, then simply said, "We didn't want to burden you with our problems."

Slipping out of her jacket, she threw it on one of the dining room chairs. "Where do you keep the dish towels?"

As she worked beside her son, drying the dishes, scrubbing the counters and floor, and wiping down the cabinets, the story of his married life began to unfold. He told it with a compassion that moved her. The story was not about how hard his life had been. The story was about how courageously Renelle had fought her illness.

"Where's the vacuum?" Leigh dried her hands on a dish towel, then hung it over the oven handle.

"It's in our bedroom."

On her way through the living room, Leigh saw the pillows from the bed were on the couch. The pillowcases were stained and dirty.

A wave of deep sadness passed over her. Her daughter-in-law had died here. In a filthy apartment, alone. And Leigh hadn't been more than a phone call away.

She clenched her jaw as tears stung her eyes. She'd had no idea how bad things were. They should have told her.

But they hadn't . . .

She shied away from the thought. Renelle hadn't wanted her in their lives. Whatever Renelle's real reasons were had died with her.

Picking up the pillows, she saw that the couch cushions were also stained. She turned them over, then continued to the bedroom. There was nothing in it but a bed and one bed stand.

"Jeff, where's the chest of drawers I gave you?"

Jeff appeared at the bedroom door. "We took them to the pawn shop a couple of weeks ago. We needed the co-pay for her meds." His face filled with concern. "We really thought we'd be able to buy them back." He hesitated. "We hoped you'd never find out."

Leigh dropped the pillows on the bed, then turned to her son. "Why? Why was it so important that I not find out anything? There was no reason for you to live like this. You could have come back home and lived in the basement. There was plenty of room for the two of you there. I could have helped care for Renelle."

"I know what you're saying, Mom. But all Renelle's life her foster families let her know that she wasn't wanted. She was a nuisance they tolerated for the money." Jeff's gentle eyes studied her face. "She didn't want to be a burden to anyone."

The sound of knocking interrupted them.

Leigh stared after her son, gasping for breath. How could Renelle have thought Leigh would treat her like her foster families had? From the little she'd said about those years, those people had rejected her, favoring their own children over her, always letting her know she wasn't wanted.

Leigh startled at the sound of her parents' voices as Jeff opened the front door.

Emerging from the bedroom, she saw her parents hugging Jeff.

"Johnny!"

John stepped from behind them and walked over to her. Taking her in his arms, he whispered, "I'm sorry. We're all going to miss her."

Somehow his words, so heartfelt and genuine, dwarfed Leigh's feelings of sadness. "Yes, we will."

John released her. Reluctantly, she stepped out of his arms. "Who told you?"

"I was at your parents' house when Jeff called. I drove them over."

Leigh blinked. "What?"

"I went there to have a chat with your dad."

Her father's voice cut in as he appeared next to John. "And I'm glad he did." He put his hand on John's shoulder. "He's a good man."

As the morning wore on, people came in and out. Apparently Raley Richmond had paged the information to the agents in the office after receiving Leigh's email. Her boss, Jan Jenks, and the broker had come by.

Their concern for her and her son and the young woman they had never met touched her. But listening to Jeff talk about Renelle changed her.

342

"She was tall," he would say, and then his face would soften, "and she had the prettiest blue eyes you've ever seen. She was a wonderful person." Those that he spoke to left feeling like they had met the tall, beautiful, auburn-haired woman that he'd had the privilege to be married to.

"Last night, before I went to work, I got to hold her. Sometimes her pain was so bad I couldn't touch her. She couldn't even stand her clothes to touch her, but last night I got to hold her," she'd heard him tell one visitor. The pearl of great price, in his hands.

"Every moment with her was special." And he meant it.

He loved her.

The truth of what that meant hit her. Hard. Jeff had loved Renelle.

She'd often heard pastors quote the Bible verse, "Husbands, love your wives, just as Christ also loved the church and gave Himself for her." This is what it meant. This was Christ's love.

By the time everyone had left, and her parents and Johnny were gathering their things together, she realized, not only had she not known Renelle, she hadn't known her son either.

As her parents walked out the door, John walked over to her, put his forefinger under her chin, and tilted her face to his. "It's going to be okay. Tonight you're going to want to talk to me. And I'll be there." He kissed her lightly, then turned and left, giving no further explanation of his cryptic words.

Closing the door behind them, Jeff turned and faced her. He looked exhausted.

"You need to get some rest." Leigh glanced toward the bedroom. "Why don't you let me change your bed, and you take a nap. I'll shut the door and I can continue cleaning up in here while you sleep."

Jeff gave her a weak smile. "Mom, you don't need to clean. I'll be okay. Thank you for all you've done already."

"Go on." She moved past him to the bedroom.

He took a shower while she changed the bedsheets. His head was on the pillow and his eyes closed before she pulled the door shut behind her.

She stood in the living room, wondering where to start. When people had begun arriving, she'd hurriedly picked up things, but the room was still a mess. Seeing something thrown under the rocking chair, she walked over to it and picked it up.

It was a spiral notebook. Written across the face of it in bold letters were the words, *My Pain Journal*.

24

Leigh sat down in the rocker in Jeff's living room, staring at the bold red letters, *My Pain Journal*. Would it be wrong to read what Renelle had written?

Leigh felt like this was the only link she had to Renelle now. And after everything that had happened and everything she had heard, she realized she hadn't known her daughter-in-law at all. And she desperately wanted to.

She turned back the cover.

There were pages of writing in different colored pens. She glanced at the entries: *Extreme pain. Very bad headache. Sores like small paper cuts all over the roof and sides of my mouth, can't sleep.*

She turned a few pages. The entries here were written in red pen: *Joints stiff, stabbing pain in my legs. Medication isn't working. If I could have just one hour without pain.* Suddenly short of breath, she looked away from the bright red words.

How could this have been going on and she not know it, not even suspect something was wrong? Renelle had sounded fine on the phone whenever they'd talked. She'd never mentioned anything. If Leigh had known, she could have brought the people from the church that had the Gift to pray for Renelle. That was an opportunity missed that could have made a huge difference in Renelle's life.

She slowly turned to the next page. *Leigh.* The word had been crossed out.

Mom, I love you so much. I'm sorry I couldn't come to dinner.

As she read on, a swell of guilt rose in her stomach.

I really wanted to, and worked all day at getting ready. But I was hurting terribly.

Everything she'd thought about the kids that night they hadn't shown up at her house for dinner with her parents returned to her. She bit her lower lip until it throbbed with her pulse.

Don't worry. I'm going to get better. I promise. I'm going to be everything you want in a daughter-in-law.

The words became a window through which Leigh saw herself as Renelle saw her. A woman who Renelle felt wouldn't accept her unless she worked all day at getting ready. A woman whose love had to be earned. A woman from which *hurting terribly* had to be hidden. Leigh dropped the book to the floor.

That woman sickened her.

Deeply shaken, she rose.

Finding her jacket, she put it on and gathered her things. Mindlessly, she walked to her car and drove home.

As she walked through the door to the back hall, she heard the doorbell ringing. Hurrying to the entry, she opened the front door.

The man on the step smiled at her. "FedEx."

She signed the screen of the handheld tracker and then took the envelope from him.

"Thank you." She stepped back into the house and closed the door.

The return address was Paramount Publishers.

The envelope she'd waited months for, the fulfillment of a dream and a quest, clearing the way for a book of God's heart to reach many. But the moment was empty. The events of the day too unsettling. The woman in the window too repugnant . . . too real.

Though she couldn't say why, suddenly the book's bold message of the mighty power of the Holy Spirit, available to all believers just for the asking, rang hollow to her. A sounding brass, a tinkling cymbal.

She carried the envelope to the kitchen and threw it on the table.

The pain journal. Renelle's book. That was a bold message. The raw truth of Renelle's life revealing the painful, raw truth of her own life.

She'd never loved Renelle. She had judged her and found her unworthy.

And Renelle had known it.

Reaching for the counter, she steadied herself.

While she had been absorbed with writing the book of God's heart, she had been blind to the heart of God. *Love one another, as I have loved you.*

She gasped for breath through the suffocating conviction of the truth.

She needed to talk to someone.

Johnny.

The last thing Johnny had said to her was, "Tonight you're going to want to talk to me. And I'll be there."

Is this what he had meant? Her heart lurched. Had he said that because God had shown him something? The way He had shown him things about Tito? The thought strengthened her. Johnny would have the answers.

She hurried to her car. He would be waiting for her. He'd said so.

As she drove, she began to try to right her world. Recalling dozens of instances where she'd done the right thing by Renelle. But no amount of revisiting the months before Renelle's death could change what Leigh knew in her heart. Everything she'd done, she'd done out of a sense of duty, while carefully protecting her resentment and anger.

She was a hypocrite.

Tightening her grip on the steering wheel, she stepped on the accelerator, winding through the mountain roads until she reached John's property. Finally turning into the driveway, her headlights flashed on the house.

His car was gone and the house was dark.

After bringing the car to a stop, she climbed out of it, crossed the porch, and pounded on the door.

Why? Why wasn't he here? He'd told her he'd wait for her and she'd trusted him, believed in him.

There was no answer.

She hurried back to the car and got her cell phone. The log showed she hadn't missed any calls. Sitting in the driver's seat, she keyed in John's number. No answer.

Suddenly, all the events of the day came crashing down on her. Her world was no longer secure. Nothing made sense. The son and daughter-in-law she thought she knew had been living a secret life. The dream to write the book of God's heart had been rendered hollow and meaningless. And the one person she was sure she could count on had let her down. Tears began streaming down her face as her world disintegrated around her.

Disoriented and despondent, she headed back to Cedar Ridge.

As she neared the town, it suddenly hit her. This wasn't about Renelle or Johnny or her dreams. This was about her own relationship with God . . . and God's relationship with her.

The revelation stunned her.

She needed to talk to someone . . . she needed to talk to God.

"Jesus." She heard the cry in her voice. "Jesus, can you hear me?" Her eyes were dry. She had no more tears. "Jesus, help me."

The church. She wanted to go to the church. The church Jeff had grown up in. The church he and Renelle had been married in. The church where she'd first sought the gifting of the Holy Spirit, so she could work for God—healing, prophesying, and praying with the tongues of men and of angels.

Skirting the edges of town, she drove to Grace Bible Church, drawn there in a way she could not explain. As she pulled into the parking lot, she scanned the building. There was no sign of anyone.

She continued across the lot until she reached the spot closest to the sanctuary. She parked, then jogged to the front doors. They were locked.

She'd never been to the church when it wasn't open. She turned around and leaned against the building. Closing her eyes, she tried to get in touch with the certainty she'd felt only moments before.

Instead, doubt crept into her mind. She'd called out to Jesus, and it seemed like he'd answered. She dropped her chin to her chest. But she wasn't sure. She wasn't sure about anything anymore.

She raised her eyes toward heaven, staring into the winter sky canopied above her. The Bible said God had placed it there. Could he draw her to Grace Bible Church if that was where He wanted her?

She chose to believe.

If He had called her here and the front door was locked, then He must have opened another door for her somewhere. She walked around to the back of the church and jogged up the steps with confidence. The door was locked.

Maybe she'd been wrong. Maybe she'd only imagined she'd actually felt a connection to God.

She turned to start down the steps. In the moonlight she could see the open field where she'd attended so many gatherings with Jeff, Easter egg hunts, summer picnics, and friendly football games.

Something Renelle had never enjoyed.

Somehow the sweet memories of time with her own son triggered thoughts of the empty, hellish childhood of the young woman who had asked to call her "Mom."

As though scales were being lifted from her eyes, Leigh suddenly understood what Renelle had really been asking for. A mother's love.

After a lifetime of rejection, wounding, and pain, Renelle had dared to risk it all . . . again. In the face of everything she'd endured, a spark of hope had still remained. Hope that maybe this time her "mom" would love her.

Tears began to pour down Leigh's face as she sank to her heels under the crushing weight of guilt. If only Renelle were alive so she could beg her forgiveness . . . so she could love her.

Under the convicting glare of Truth, Leigh realized that her prayers, asking for the gifting of the Holy Spirit so she could do wonderful things for God, were shallow and prideful. She had not only desired spiritual gifts, she had pursued them. But she had never pursued love. What she wouldn't do for Renelle and what all her other "moms" would not do, Jesus had done . . . through Jeff.

"Oh, God. Oh, God, forgive me."

A wind blew around her, catching her words, carrying them through the night.

She had chastised her son for loving Renelle. And how many other times had she discouraged him from loving the unlovely. Maybe Renelle was the wrong girl for him, but he was the right boy for her. He had accepted her just as she was, and Renelle had come to know Christ's love by knowing Jeff. How many others had there been?

And how many others had there been for Leigh . . . her father . . . R.J.?

The enormity of her sin crushed her. How could God forgive her?

The wind strengthened and the trees began to sway. Leigh rose at the sound. A movement caught her eye.

A buck.

Beneath the light of the moon, she could see a buck emerging from the trees across the field. Her lips parted.

The wind began to die down as the huge animal raised its magnificent head, looking at her. Serene and peaceful.

Snow began to fall like a silvery mist. She lifted her hands and her face toward the sky. As the flakes touched her, they melted. Gentle and cool, they bathed her face. Washed away her tears.

And she felt the love of Christ. Truth revealed.

The Gift.

She could hardly grasp what was happening. But the deep despair that had burdened her moments before was gone. And her heart was filled with love, renewed . . . reborn.

"Leigh."

She spun around at the sound of her name. The back door of the church was open and a man stood in its shadow.

"Johnny!" She stared at him in disbelief. "What are you doing here?"

"I told you, 'Tonight you're going to want to talk to me. And I'll be there.'"

She paused. "How'd you get in? The door was locked."

"I found an unlocked door on the side of the church." His voice was gentle. "The Lord showed it to me."

His gaze held hers, his eyes full of understanding, as if he knew all that had just happened.

She walked across the landing and into his arms.

He kissed her. "Come on, let's go sit down."

They walked to the sanctuary hand in hand. He guided her to the pew in front of the altar, then sat down. She sat beside him.

Turning to her, he took her hands in his. "I really messed things up. The Lord showed me why he brought me into your life a long time ago." He lowered his eyes. "And even though I didn't understand at first, I knew I was supposed to help you with your book."

Her heartbeat quickened.

"But I was angry. That wasn't what I had in mind for us." He raised his eyes to hers. "And my heart wasn't in it. When you didn't talk about the book, I didn't bring it up. But that night, when you told me what you were writing, I knew it was completely out of the will of God. His Holy Spirit is not something you call down from heaven to use like a weapon."

She dropped her gaze. "I know." She hadn't been seeking God, she had been seeking God's power.

His hands tightened on hers. "His Spirit is something you surrender to. You can't know the mind of God. You can't look at things and decide what He should do. You can only be a vessel for His will."

The seriousness of her self-centered journey, and the consequences of her blindness, continued to convict her. This was her nature apart from His grace.

She raised her eyes to John. "I prayed for God to show me the book of His heart. I meant it too. And then you told me about Tito and it just seemed like that fit. I'd been fascinated by the gifts of the Spirit for years—" She felt a check in her spirit. As clearly as if words had been spoken, she knew she had always prayed with a certain result in mind. She had never gone to God as an empty vessel. "It all made sense at the time." Her voice trailed away.

"You can't discover God's truth by analyzing things. Truth is never discovered, it's only revealed." He studied her face. "He's called you to write, Leigh. He has a story for you to tell."

The moment he spoke the words, she knew. God had given her a story. One she knew intimately.

It was the story of Christ's love for humankind. Not played out in the grand scale of His life and death and time on earth. But played out in the simple life of one man. A man who had the Gift. The ability to love while expecting nothing in return, to forgive unconditionally, and to truly lay down his life for another. Living a life that brought glory to God.

The story of Jeff and Renelle.

25

Leigh laid the list she'd made during the night on top of her desk.

The list of her sins against God. The list she'd written with the help of the Spirit. God's power, in God's hands, used to accomplish His purposes. *Let me be an empty vessel for You, Jesus.*

At the altar of the church, she'd asked God to send the power of the Holy Spirit upon her. Not so she could use it to do work for God, but so God could use it to search her heart.

As the thick veneer of pride, ego, and hubris as stripped away, she'd asked God's forgiveness. And received it.

The sun was rising when she'd driven to Jeff's house. Sitting in the car, she'd waited for some sign that he'd awakened. When he passed by the front window, she went to the front door. He invited her in, and Leigh told him how wrong she'd been. How badly she'd treated Renelle and him.

Though she tried to keep it together, she hadn't been able to swallow the deep remorse that rose in her throat. And when she broke under the terrible guilt she felt, he took her in his arms. Her big, burly son, who had gone through so much, held her as she cried, gently reassuring her that she was a good person, a good mother, and he loved her very much.

Leigh blinked rapidly. Jeff was an amazing young man. Knowing he forgave her gave her hope that someday she could forgive herself. But right now she had other things she wanted to make right.

She began rummaging in her desk drawer. She hadn't seen R.J.'s phone number since the night her father had given it to her. Straightening, she put her hands on her hips. She'd looked everywhere.

The phone ringing interrupted her thoughts. She ran to answer it.

"Hello."

"Hi, honey. It's Mom. Are you okay? I called last night and you didn't answer."

"I'm okay. Jeff and I went to church this morning, and I just got home."

"We were going to drive over and see him later, but I'm not sure we'll be able to. How's he doing?"

Leigh had no doubt that the visit to Jeff's house the day before had drained her father. He'd been fading steadily in recent weeks. "Jeff's very much at peace with things. I heard him tell someone after the service, 'Today's Renelle's second day without pain.'" She felt herself tearing up. "It was as though he were comforting them."

"Well, I hope we can get by to see him. He's going to need our support for quite a while. Do you know when the burial will be?"

"After church we talked about funeral arrangements.

356

I'm going to meet him at the funeral home Monday. It's going to be rough on all of us for the next few days." As she talked to her mother, she couldn't help but think that they could be having this same conversation about her father before the end of the year. *Oh, Lord, I'm trusting You for my strength.* "Mom, I've lost R.J.'s phone number. Could you give it to me?"

Her mother recited the number from memory, then asked, "Will we see you later?"

Leigh blinked hard, her time at the altar still fresh. "I planned to stop by a little later."

"I'll tell Dad. It'll give him something to look forward to."

They said their goodbyes, then Leigh hung up the phone.

Taking a deep breath, she sat on the edge of her bed and dialed R.J.'s number. She knew what she had to do . . . and she wanted to do it.

He answered on the second ring.

"Hi, R.J. It's Leigh."

"Hi, Leigh." His voice sounded tentative. "Jeff called yesterday and told me what happened. I'm sorry. I know he loved her. We'll all miss her."

They reminisced a few moments about the last time he'd seen Renelle, at the wedding.

Leigh took another deep breath. "Speaking of the wedding, I wanted to tell you that I'm sorry for the way I acted at the hotel."

He didn't respond.

"R.J., we've never been close, and these past few years we've seemed to drift even further apart." She reached

357

over to the bed stand and picked up her Bible, folding it into her chest. "I'd like to change that. Can you forgive me?"

"There's nothing to forgive, Leigh."

She heard his voice catch.

Struggling to control her own emotions, she continued, "I don't know how much more time Dad has left. And I want you to know that I'd like it very much if you'd come up and visit often. You can stay with me. I'd love to have you."

"I'd like that too." His voice broke.

Her heart went out to him. This had to be hard for him . . . for so many reasons. "Let's talk again next Sunday. I'll call you."

"I'd like that," he said, sounding steadier. "Give Dad a hug for me, will you?"

"You bet I will. But you get up here and hug him yourself." She set the Bible down on the bed next to her. "Talk to you soon." She started to hang up. "R.J.?"

"Yes?"

"I love you." And for the first time in a long time, she meant it.

She hung up and flopped back on the bed.

Max made a soft landing next to her.

"Hey, Max." His purr became louder. "That wasn't really that hard to do." She sat up and ruffled the big cat's fur.

But now it was time to call Riva . . . as much as she dreaded it. She reached for the phone.

Riva's voice immediately registered concern. "What's wrong? Didn't the contract come?"

"It came yesterday. But I need to talk to you about it."

"I'm listening."

Last night at the altar, Johnny had said God wanted all of her. Her heart, her creativity, her dreams.

She winced. "I can't write the book." The words rushed out. "I should say, I can't write the book as planned."

"What are you talking about?" Riva's voice was rising. "We negotiated in good faith with Paramount. They even got you on the fall list. You told me the first draft was almost finished."

"It was, Riva, but something happened. Renelle died early yesterday morning."

Riva caught her breath. "What?"

Leigh spent the next few minutes explaining to her agent all that had transpired. But, in reference to her spiritual journey and the book, she said only that she had come to a new understanding of how God works in the world.

"It isn't that I don't want to write the book. I want to write it more than ever. It's just that I realize I gave the story the wrong emphasis. It wasn't supposed to be about what the heroine teaches the other characters as she pursues the gifts of the Spirit, it's about what the other characters teach her as they pursue the gift of love. I can't sign the contract because I can't follow the synopsis I sent them."

She heard Riva release a deep sigh. "I fully support your desire to be true to what God is calling you to. But it kind of leaves us in a mess." She paused. "How long will it take you to do the rewrite?"

"I think I can do it in four months, so I *can* meet the

contract deadline. It's just that the story will be different."

"Let me see what I can work out."

"I'm sorry, Riva. It would be a lot easier just to go ahead with the book I proposed. But God has made it clear to me that the greatest of the gifts is love. *His* love."

Riva's voice softened. "You go, girl. But even if I work this out, it's going to delay the first half of your advance."

Last night, at the altar of Grace Bible Church, with Johnny by her side, she'd surrendered all. "I know."

With a promise to get back to her next week, Riva hung up.

Leigh rose and put the phone back on the nightstand.

It was time to go see her father.

As she drove, her thoughts returned to the phone call with her mother. There had been no point in telling her that the conversation with Jeff about the funeral had also been a conversation about paying for it. And that's when Jeff had told her he would be going back to work full-time at Sears right away, giving him two full-time jobs. His last semester in school wasn't salvageable. He was too far behind, and he was failing two of his classes.

Leigh's grip tightened on the steering wheel. She hadn't mentioned it to him, but clearly he wouldn't be able to make the payments on the loan against her parents' house that were scheduled to start in June. And with the book advance now in question, she couldn't help him.

She glanced toward heaven.

Twenty minutes later she pulled into her parents' driveway and parked. She climbed out of the car and hurried up the walkway.

When she got to the front door, she stopped. Closing her eyes, she whispered, "Let me be an empty vessel for You, Jesus." Then she opened the door.

"It's me," she called out as she made her way to the family room.

Her mother rose from the couch and hugged her.

"You stay right there, Dad."

"I was up and around this morning. I'm just taking a little rest." The rules were in place.

Leigh pulled a stool over to her father's chair. "I came over to talk to you."

"Go ahead. I'm not going anywhere." He gave her a weak smile.

"Dad, I want you to know that ever since that night I said those awful things to you, I've regretted it. I know you thought keeping Johnny and me apart was what was best for me." As she spoke the words, she realized she knew even better than her father how wrong a parent could be. "I hope you'll forgive me." Leigh put her hand on his arm.

She could hear her mother weeping quietly behind her.

He squirmed in his chair. Then he turned his eyes to hers. "I've got something I've been wanting to talk to *you* about."

Leigh straightened.

"We never said too much. But for quite some time we've been concerned about the loan on the house."

Leigh lowered her gaze and pulled her hand into her

lap. There was nothing to say. He was right. And there was no solution to the problem. It was one of the things she'd specifically turned over to God last night. Johnny had reminded her that God knew her needs, and that He promised in His Word, if one would seek first His kingdom and His righteousness, He would take care of the rest.

She raised her eyes. "I'm concerned too."

"I have a life insurance policy that I took out for you."

Leigh stiffened at the memory of finding out he'd taken over half of her policy and left R.J.'s untouched. She rejected the feelings that began to rise in her. Old things had passed away, all things had become new.

"I cashed part of it in and paid off the loan on the house." He took her hand. "Your debt's been paid."

Leigh's lips formed a silent O and tears began to stream down her cheeks.

Her father blinked rapidly. Clinging to the rules. "The house is free and clear now. It'll belong to you and R.J. some day."

Leigh jumped up and hugged him. "I can't believe it. I can't believe it." She turned toward her mother. "Thank you both, so much." She turned back to her father. "Thank you, Daddy. Thank you."

She felt as if a huge weight had been lifted off her shoulders. She closed her eyes a moment. *Thank You*.

God's Word was truth.

She walked to the couch and sat next to her mother, taking her hand. "I talked to R.J. this morning."

Her father's wan face brightened.

"He's going to try and get up here soon to visit."

A smile spread across her father's face. "When he was here for the wedding, we agreed that next summer we'd go camping. We're going to haul a boat up there to that Two Forks River."

She felt her mother's grip tighten in her hand. It was likely that her father would never see next summer.

"Did he mention that when he talked to you?"

A still, small voice brought R.J.'s words to her mind. *Give Dad a hug for me, will you?* She rose.

"He just said that he wanted me to give you a hug. He loves you so much."

As she stepped toward her father, she felt a sensation that started at the bottom of her feet and moved up her body until it reached the top of her head. An empty vessel filled. The love that consumed her was so powerful that she felt she was but an observer of her own actions.

Her father began to fade from her sight behind a silvery mist.

"And I love you too." Closing her eyes, she reached out to him.

She was aware of a light shining above her. Creating a portal in space and time, allowing the light of heaven to fall upon her and her father. Making the floor beneath her holy ground and, through her, releasing the love of Jesus Christ. The Great Physician. Who wants to heal not only the heart but the body of man.

Leigh squeezed her eyes shut. Embracing her father, holding him, loving him. Knowing he would be with her long after he fished at Two Forks River with R.J.

Epilogue

Six Months Later

It was a breathtakingly beautiful fall afternoon. The azure blue sky arched lovingly over the Idaho mountains surrounding Two Forks River, and the stream bubbled happily over pebbles and rocks. The perfect wedding gift for a perfect wedding day.

Leigh raised her eyes toward heaven. *Thank You, Jesus.* Then she took her father's arm.

"Umm." Her father smiled at her shyly. "I'd like to say a few words before we start."

Leigh quietly closed her eyes and bowed her head.

He cleared his throat. "Lord, bless my daughter and John as they make their life together. Please continue to prosper Leigh's book and John's ministry with the Indians. I love You. Amen."

Her eyes misted as she turned her gaze to her father. "Ready?"

He nodded.

They walked together, arm in arm, from the edge of

the forest toward the stream. Pastor Jim on the bank facing her, Johnny and Tito standing to his left.

To her right, her mother smiled at her through happy tears, and Jeff beamed.

They stopped in front of Pastor Jim.

"Who gives this woman to be married to this man?"

Her father straightened. "Her mother and I." He dropped his arm and stepped back.

Leigh turned to face Johnny.

Pastor Jim nodded toward Johnny and then toward her. "We are assembled today in the presence of God and the face of these witnesses to celebrate the joining . . ."

Leigh felt goose bumps rise on her arms. Just over John's shoulder, in the distance, a magnificent buck stepped out of the trees. Head raised, he gazed at the visitors, observing them.

"Leigh, do you take John to be your lawfully wedded husband?"

For a moment, time stood still. The bubbling water seemed to become music, as a gentle wind encircled her. *Oh, Lord God, truly the greatest of Your gifts is love.*

"I do."

Acknowledgments

This book was very much a personal journey for me. The people and places in this book are fictitious, but as with most of my novels, the events were inspired by my own life experiences. For that reason I want to give a special thanks to my family, especially my son Esteban, for encouraging me to write this story.

Jennifer Leep at Revell, I want to thank you for the freedom you give me as I write the books I believe God has put on my heart. This is our fourth book together, and each time I have felt supported and encouraged every step of the way.

To Carol Craig, friend and editor, your patient, kind, and caring guidance are a treasure to me. You tirelessly motivate me as I strive for excellence in my writing, and for that I am forever grateful.

Mom and Dad, you have been on my journey with me since my first breath in Tokyo, Japan. Thank you.

I also want to acknowledge Susan Lohrer, The Write

Words Editing, and Brita Darany, president of Friends of Autistic People, for your contributions to this book.

My dear friends, Sue Callen and Barbara Rostad, you always seem to appear just when I need you. I sometimes disappear into my books for weeks at a time. Thank you for keeping me connected to the real world.

Tex, Donna, Glenn, and Renae, thank you for your constant, fervent prayers. This book is the fruit of your labor.

Natasha Kern, who I love like a sister, grace to you and peace from God our Father and the Lord Jesus Christ. I thank my God upon every remembrance of you, always in every prayer of mine making request for you with joy. Your unfailing faith in my books and my dreams is truly a blessing from the Lord.

And my Lord and Savior, Jesus Christ, You know the plans You have for me. I pray You will continue to light the path of my writing journey and give me the courage to walk on it. Stir in me a passion for Your truth that translates to the written word as You express Your creativity through me. *Baruch atah, Adonai.*

Real life. Real books.
Novel ideas.